Wildflower Wednesday

Dorothy Willman Cummins

Wildflower Wednesday

Copyright 2021 by Dorothy Willman Cummins
All rights reserved. No part of this publication may be reproduced or transmitted in any form or by any means, electronic or mechanical, including photocopy, recording or any information storage and retrieval system, without permission in writing from the author and publisher.

Printed in the United State of America.
Also available in Kindle eBook version

Written from the Heart Publishing
Inola ,Oklahoma

Copyright 2021 Dorothy Willman Cummins
All rights reserved

ISBN: 9798599373674

ACKNOWLEDGMENTS

Wildflower Wednesday, the third novel in my Days of Flowers series, is complete due to inspiring help from special people:

Sandy Logan and "The Suzannes" - Suzanne Ware and Suzanne Tomasko proved to be manuscript readers with valuable suggestions.

Stacey Butler – book cover designer who manages to read my mind every time.

Jim Elliott – retired banker and dear friend who kept my story lined up with financial realism.

Gordon Kessler – writing coach, author, editor and friend who has again helped me "make a good story better."

-Thank you.

Prologue

A Sunny August Morning

Sixteen-year-old Brian Wilson wore a proud grin and waved the new driver's license at his mom and brother, who had waited as he completed his driving test. "I aced the test—so, can I drive home?"

"Certainly, absolutely!" Lyndsey Wilson answered her oldest son as she opened the passenger door and slipped into their Lexus. "*Yes*, you can drive us home."

Brian's fourteen-year-old brother moved into the back seat directly behind her and teased him, "Drive on, *chauffeur*."

Brian started the car, carefully backed out of the parking spot and headed home. He laughed as he told his brother that he would be happy to act as his chauffeur. "I'll need the driving practice," he added.

"Nonsense," chimed in their mom. "Your father taught you well, and you've had Driver's Ed, too. You're already a good driver."

Brian smiled his thanks as he braked to a stop at the first red light. When it changed to green, he started across the intersection.

His mother screamed, "*Brian!*"

Brian never saw the loaded dump truck until it slammed into them. Their car flipped onto its top as the big truck pushed it along the street. The *last thing* he saw was red—so much of it—as pain sliced through his body and everything went black.

When he tried to open his eyes, he had to squint, then close them again because the bright light hurt. He sensed, rather than saw, his father's nearness.

"*Dad?*" he whispered, his throat dry and raw.

"Brian—oh my God, son! I was afraid you'd never wake up."

*****

Douglas Wilson tried but failed to keep the tears from cascading down his face as he called for a doctor.

Within a minute, two physicians and an RN were at Brian's side, checking his vital signs, peering into his eyes, asking him if he could move his fingers, his toes.

At the conclusion of their bedside exam, the doctors stepped into the corridor with Douglas, leaving the nurse behind with Brian.

The older doctor with bushy grey eyebrows, peered over his wire-frame glasses. "Sir, the fact that your son is conscious and able to move a bit is a very good sign. We'll need to do more tests, but it looks like he should fully recover."

"*Thank you*," were the only words Douglas could utter, his eyes welling up with tears.

The second physician, a younger, dark-haired man nodded. But then he cleared his throat and said in a cautioning tone, "You must realize that this young man is in for a long and painful recovery and rehab period. We don't even know the full extent of his injuries just yet."

"I understand that. Whatever he needs—special nursing care, physical therapy, *anything* that I can do to help him recover. Somehow, I'll make it happen. Brian is all the family I have left." He turned to walk back into his son's ICU room. "He's *all* I have."

Chapter 1

Mary Miranda Johnson reached from the back of a skittish horse to sign for the registered letter. "Whoa, boy. Easy—settle down, now," she said, patting the big horse's rump, while handing the clipboard back to the driver. With another horse to ride yet this morning, and a feed delivery truck coming up the drive, she had no time to read the seemingly urgent mail. At lunchtime, she had brought it to the house, tossed the envelope atop the big stack of mail on her dusty desk and forgotten about it. Until now.

Well past her usual bedtime, she sank into her office chair, turned on the reading light and tore open the envelope. She quickly skimmed over the short message, and her eyes filled with tears that trickled down her cheeks.

She felt like she was drowning and her final lifeline was being severed. Her last credit card was almost maxed out. And now this—a banker was insisting on meeting to discuss the status of her mortgage.

Mary Miranda, M&M to her friends, was no cry baby. She was no quitter, either. She had survived losing the love of her life, hung on to their dream farm to breed and train top horses and riders. She was also the single parent to their only child.

She lifted her chin, reached for a bandana in the back pocket of her jeans and blew her nose. After a pause while staring at the remaining stack, she straightened in her chair and pulled another envelope from the pile of neglected mail.

The next message almost brought another flood of tears. It

was a warning notice that her electric service would be cut off unless she paid her bill within ten days.

Scowling, she sorted the neglected mail into two piles. A stack of advertisements and sale catalogs went directly into the trash can. The other more ominous pile looked like an assortment of finance-related notices and statements. She chose to open her bank statement first and breathed a tiny sigh of relief.

"At least I'm not overdrawn," she whispered to herself, then added an honest, "*Yet*."

Taking out her little calculator and armed with a pencil and tablet, she continued to open, read and carefully list every balance-due number.

List complete, she fearfully added them up and started crying again. She couldn't seem to stop sobbing and she was soon gasping for breath.

That's when Jerry burst into the room.

"Mom! What's wrong?" Her hurried to her side and hugged her as fiercely as a gawky 16-year-old can.

She was still struggling to breathe normally and didn't answer as he continued, "Mom, really! What is it? It's almost one in the morning and you are never up so late—I heard you crying."

Obviously worried, Jerry's questions kept coming, "Are you in pain? Do you need a doctor, or should I call an ambulance?"

She shook her head, but he reached for the phone. "Then I'm calling Uncle John,"

"*No!* Don't do that. *Please* don't."

With a worried frown, he put the phone down, but kept asking, "What's wrong? Mom, *what's* wrong"?

"Sit down, son, and I'll try to explain. There are some things I hoped never to have to say to you."

He flopped down on the little leather loveseat near the desk and waited.

She looked out the big picture window to the barn and paddocks she and her late husband had dreamed of and so carefully designed those many years ago. She choked up at the thought that she might not continue to enjoy the view. Then she turned and faced her frightened son.

"You're scaring me, Mom. You *never* cry. Are you sure you're okay?"

She nodded, swiped at her wet eyes and blew her nose again before answering. "Jerry, I just opened enough mail to remind me of what I already knew, deep down. Pine Park is in debt, *serious* debt. I'm in real financial trouble, and I don't know what to do."

"But Mom, I know you pay the bills—for utilities, horse feed and care and all that. And we haven't gone hungry, or without clothes to wear, even though I keep outgrowing mine."

"Well, I've got to be honest with you, now. I've kept paying *on* the bills, but not paying them off completely. I've used credit cards, only making partial payments, and I thought about taking a second mortgage on this place. That's like making two house payments, for just our one house. I'm pretty sure the bank will turn me down on that."

"But you have horses in training, and boarding, and you teach lessons."

"I do, and I work as hard as I can, but it's just not bringing in enough money to keep us going here.

"When your father and I planned this business, we also factored in a small breeding operation, plus counting on both of us working at training and showing the horses and offering lessons at several levels. With just me, there aren't enough hours in a day to teach enough and train enough to make it work."

"What about the breeding farm part?"

She nodded. "We did manage to buy a few really classy broodmares, but after your dad was killed, I couldn't afford to breed them to the kind of studs that would produce top foals, so I ended up selling the mares, one by one, to make ends meet."

"I thought I could teach and train enough to keep Pine Park going, make a home for us, but...." She started crying again. "Jerry, honey, I am *so* sorry. We may have to give up Pine Park."

"And then what?"

"That's the *really* scary part. I don't know." Shakily, she stood, embraced her son and said, "We can't do anything more now. Let's try to get some sleep."

"Okay, but I still think we should call Uncle John." Hesitantly, he added, "And I'm going to ask Ross about praying for us."

Jerry headed to his room, but M&M paused at the window and looked once more at the barn spotlighted in the security light. Her favorite school horse was hanging her head over the bottom stall door, looking toward the house.

She didn't know how she would find the strength to move away from Pine Park, the only home Jerry had ever known, and all she had ever wanted. Just the thought of leaving brought on more tears.

She didn't want John Hunter or anybody else to know what a mess she had made of her horse business. She hoped Jerry wouldn't call the dear friend he called Uncle John, or this Ross person. *Who's Ross,* she wondered.

And then Mary Miranda Johnson went to bed and cried herself to sleep for the first time since the night Gerald Johnson died.

Chapter 2

Chaos reigned in the Wilson Real Estate Office.

Founder and owner Douglas Wilson paced around the building barking orders.

His distraught employees were scrambling to keep out of his way. Some were on phones conferring with clients. Two were frantically pounding the keyboards in front of their computers. His personal secretary, resigned to dealing with him when no one else could, or would, stepped into his path and said, "Sir, could I speak with you, privately, in your office?"

Icy blue eyes flashing, he stopped and scowled, then nodded and followed her into his office.

"Well! What is it?" he demanded.

"Mr. Wilson, I know ... we *all* know, what a difficult time this is. We want to do whatever we can to make things better for you—and for Brian."

"Good! Then tell me who has found a place I can take my son for some kind of therapy or treatment. Something that will make him want to live."

"We're all looking, sir."

"Stop '*sir-ing*' me!"

"Yes sir ... I mean, *Mr. Wilson*."

With a snort, he turned and stormed out of his office and into the secretarial pool. The women were all at their desks, on their phones or their computers, avoiding eye contact with each other or their boss.

As he was about to question them on their progress, Grace Jones, his human resources manager approached.

Attempting to soothe her boss, she encouraged him to join the office manager in the conference room.

"What now?"

"The job applicant I interviewed this morning told me about this unique therapy group in a nearby town, and I thought maybe, just maybe, it would be something that could help Brian."

Douglas Wilson straightened to his full six-foot height, his eyes softened, and a hint of a smile touched his face for just a moment before he said, "Let's go."

Sam Cunningham, his office manager, was waiting. "Doug," he said, "I don't want us to give you false hope here, but this young woman told us such an uplifting story."

"Well, where is she?"

"She left a few minutes ago after her interview. We didn't know when you would be in, or whether you'd even be receptive to taking with her."

"What young woman? *I need* to talk to her."

Grace said, "Good. We felt she was a good candidate for the job, so we asked her to come back this afternoon for a second interview. You can talk with her then. We will likely go ahead and start her in the secretarial pool."

"Meanwhile," Sam added, "Let me fill you in on the basics."

"I'm listening."

"She was the victim of domestic abuse, severely beaten, both physically and emotionally. Looking at her today, it's hard to believe, but she says she felt worthless. She credits a program she joined in Marshall with turning her life around. It's a non-profit run by a former New York model, helps abuse victims get a new start."

Doug Wilson yelled, "Sam, how in this world is some

program for abused women run by some prissy model going to help my son get over losing his mom and his brother and blaming himself?"

He was starting for the door when Sam shouted back, "Just wait a minute! I was getting to the part that might be useful to you—might help Brian."

Doug Wilson paused, "Keep talking."

"A part of the program included equine therapy. The women were recovering both emotionally and physically, and found riding horses to be healing, uplifting."

"Well, I've heard a little about equine therapy. I just never thought of it as something to help Brian. But he liked horses when he was a little boy. Maybe, just maybe it would be worth a try." He sighed and continued, "I'm desperate. He's distant, depressed. I'll do anything on this earth to help him." He glanced at both his employees and then nodded. "Thank you. I'll be in my office. Call me in here when that woman comes back."

He went immediately to his desktop computer and spent the rest of the morning searching the Internet for more information about equine therapy. Encouraged to read that such programs had proven beneficial not only to people with developmental disorders, but also those physically challenged due to injury, and even some with emotional imbalances, he hoped he might be onto something.

His big fingers flew over the keys as he searched for equine therapy programs in Texas. There were two in neighboring towns, and he was reaching for his phone to call for more information when Grace Jones rapped lightly, then stuck her head in the door.

"She's here, waiting with Sam in the conference room."

Doug Wilson was on his feet and hurrying down the corridor before she could finish telling him that Ms. Jameson was already nervous about meeting the big boss.

He fairly charged into the room and said, "Hello."

He noted that Violet Jameson's hand trembled slightly as she reached to shake hands, but she lifted her chin and looked directly into Douglas Wilson's icy blue eyes and said, "I'm glad to meet you, sir."

"Ms. Jameson, relax. I'm not in here to do another interview. I trust my staff to do the hiring and if Grace Jones says you're hired, you are."

Violet took a calming breath and managed a smile as he continued, "I want to find out more about your experience with equine therapy. I'm hopeful that it can help my son."

She sat at the table and explained her experience with the *Speak Up, Step Up, Sign Up* program and its founder, then added, "The part about riding horses was the director's idea to give us, the battered women in the shelter, confidence—and even have some fun."

He started firing questions. "Okay, where did you ride? Did you have a teacher? Physical therapist? What?"

"We went to Pine Park. It's this really nice stable, and the owner was our instructor. Her name is Mary Miranda Johnson. I don't know if she does therapy classes for other people or not. She trains horses and gives lessons to competitive riders, too."

"Thanks, Ms. Jameson," he said as he stood, turned and headed back to his office.

Back at his own desk, Doug summoned his secretary, and told her, "I need information, lots of it, about a stable or horse farm owned by a Ms. Johnson. The place is called Pine Park, located in or near Marshall. Get somebody out of the secretarial pool to help you. The sooner the better."

She nodded and went to get help with her unusual assignment.

An hour later, she was back in his office with a list of facts relating to the stable and its owner. He thanked her and waved her out before making the first of what would be many calls to Mary Miranda Johnson.

Chapter 3

M&M was already in the middle of her first training ride when her cell phone chimed. She had left it in the tack room and had no intention of hurrying back into the barn and dismounting to answer it.

"Whoever it is will call back, or leave a message," she told the horse she was schooling in the ring. She could almost laugh at herself for hoping it was a robo call or a wrong number. "Better than a bill collector or my banker," she told herself.

It rang a few minutes later, and again as she was finishing her ride. When she decided to take a quick lunch break, she picked up the phone and carried it to the house.

Checking recent calls, she saw there were four from a name she didn't know, some real estate company. Then she saw a name she knew well, John Hunter.

Both he and the real estate guy had left voice mails and she punched in to hear John say, "Hey, M&M, I don't know what's up with you, but Jerry called, sounded worried. Not like him. He just asked for me or Susanna to check on you. Are you sick or something? Sure hope one of those unruly horses you're training hasn't dumped you. Check in with us as soon as you can."

She sighed. She had her son so worried that he'd called on their friends for help even when she'd asked him to refrain. That meant she was going to have to tell them how much financial trouble she was in.

Wildflower Wednesday

"Darnation," she muttered.

She listened to the other message. "Hello, Ms. Johnson. My name is Douglas Wilson from Wilson Realty, over in Longview. I am most anxious to talk with you about your equine therapy program. Please call me back at your earliest convenience."

She didn't bother to save his contact information. "Nothing to talk about," she mumbled, again to herself.

M&M went back to the barn and saddled another horse for training. When she completed her session on him, she got the pony saddled for a little girl coming to her first riding lesson.

Jerry got home from school just as that lesson started, waved to his mom and went to the kitchen for a snack.

As he rummaged in the refrigerator, he heard her cell phone chime. Surprised, he turned to the sound, saw the phone had been left on the kitchen table and answered the call.

A gruff voice requested to speak with "*Ms. Johnson.*"

"I'm sorry," He politely responded, "My mom is teaching right now and cannot come to the phone. May I take a message?"

The man almost screamed. "I've been calling her all day. Left several messages. She hasn't returned my calls."

He repeated his contact information and Jerry, thinking this must be somebody trying to harass her about a bill, simply said, "I'll tell her you called," and disconnected.

Jerry finished his sandwich and washed it down with a glass of milk before heading to the barn to start his chores. He had a horse to exercise, another to groom. Then, he could start cleaning stalls and filling the hay nets and water buckets. If he hurried, he could get it all done and his mom would only have to dispense grain before going to the house.

*****

M&M immediately liked little Patty. A shy, chubby child,

she announced that she loved horses and wanted one of her own. Her mother nervously watched as M&M told Patty how to climb into the saddle.

"Have you ridden before?" she asked, and Patty shook her head. "My mommy said I wasn't old enough 'til now. I'm five and this lesson is my birthday present."

"Then, let's make this a happy birthday ride," M&M encouraged, and Patty listened carefully and seemed to try very hard to do exactly what M&M directed. The lazy pony walked around in circles and trotted slowly only when insistent little heels tap, tap, tapped at his round sides. He stopped at her "Whoa," and Patty caressed his neck and whispered, "You're a *good* pony."

When M&M helped her dismount, she ran to her mother saying, "It was fun. *Please*, Mommy, can I come again?"

Her mother shrugged, threw up her hands and laughed as she told M&M, "We are not a horsey family. Honestly, I don't know where she got this thing about horses. But clearly, she loves this. I'll be calling you about more lessons."

M&M thanked her, told Patty goodbye, and led the pony back to the barn, hoping she would get that call.

Jerry had the hay nets filled and was taking care of water buckets when she put the pony into a paddock. When she walked into the feed room he called out, "Hey, Mom, this guy called while I was in the house. I was so surprised to find your cell phone on the table that I answered it. He sounded kinda mad that you hadn't called him back."

"Thanks. He's called more than once, I really have no reason to call him back, since he has clearly been misinformed about me running an equine therapy program."

"What about that class for Tiffany's friends?"

"Well, it *is* a kind of therapy, but I don't think it's the type he's calling about. Anyway, I just did that one class."

Jerry shrugged. "Maybe you should consider it, if there's a demand."

"Wise words, my son. I will at least think about it. Probably need a special license, a permit, more liability insurance and likely take tons of money plus months to work through the red tape."

Jerry and his mom were just finishing supper when John and Susanna arrived.

"Surprise!" Susanna called as she came in, followed by John.

"What's up?" M&M asked, although she was pretty sure she already knew the reason for their visit.

"We brought dessert," John announced, handing a grocery bag filled with brownies and ice cream to Jerry.

Susanna wore a worried frown and asked M&M, "Are you okay?"

"Why do you ask?" was the evasive response.

"I'm asking because both your son and my husband are worried about you. That means I'm worried too. John said he left a message for you to call us. You didn't."

Then John asked. "So, what's up?"

M&M threw up her hands, shot Jerry a warning look, and insisted she was fine.

"*Mom!* If you don't tell them, I will."

"Okay, *okay*. I didn't intend to drag you into my troubles, but it seems I'm outnumbered here."

At John's suggestion, Susanna dished up brownies, topped them with ice cream and handed the plates around the kitchen table.

He took a bite, looked at M&M and demanded, "Start talking."

Drawing a deep breath, she began, fighting back tears as she admitted her fear of losing Pine Park.

Her best friends listened carefully, and Susanna got up and hugged her when she began to sob.

"We can help," John insisted.

"John, you *have* helped, in so many ways and so many times, but I just can't teach and train enough to keep this place going, and I can't see any way to turn this around. And before you even say it, I will *not* accept money from you. It would be a loan I couldn't hope to repay."

He opened his mouth to argue, then thought better of it. "Then let's put our heads together and try to think of something," he suggested.

"Mom, what about that horse therapy thing?"

Susanna asked, "What therapy *thing*?" and Jerry related the phone calls from Longview.

M&M told them, "He is misinformed and thinks I have an equine therapy program for disabled or disturbed clients, or something."

"Have you ever thought about doing that?" Susanna asked her.

"No."

"Maybe you should," suggested John, just as her cell phone chimed.

Glancing at the caller ID, she shook her head and ignored the call, followed by another ding to let her know a message was waiting.

"Is it that guy from Longview again?" Jerry asked.

M&M nodded. "I *will* call him back, tomorrow."

Susanna hugged her again as they stood up to leave.

"We need to go relieve our babysitters," she explained, and John laughed.

"They wouldn't care if we stayed out all night."

"So, why didn't you bring the twins?" Jerry wondered.

"It's our 'night out' and my parents love coming to stay with

Wildflower Wednesday

Lee and Laura so we can go somewhere, just the two of us. Tonight, we went to the ole drive-in for burgers, then picked up dessert and came to see two of our favorite people."

"And, we'll be back soon," John said as they went out the door.

M&M turned to her son. "I really wish you hadn't done that."

"I know. I'm sorry, Mom, but I didn't know what else to do. They're the closest thing you have to family, except for me, and I don't know how to help you."

"It's okay, Jerry. It's okay." She paused then added, "We'll survive ... somehow."

Jerry headed to his bedroom, and she was turning off the kitchen light when her cell phone chimed again.

Resigned to having a conversation with a man she didn't know, she took the call.

"Doug Wilson here," he began, "I've been trying to reach you all day."

"Sorry, I've spent most of my day riding and training and couldn't answer my phone. Honestly, from your messages, I don't think we have anything to talk about, I don't operate a therapy program."

He interrupted, "But I've talked to a woman who was in one of your classes. From everything she told me, I think you can help my boy."

"*Who* are you talking about?"

"Violet Jameson."

"Oh. She rode in a class that I taught for a few battered women, something to give them confidence. I actually did that class as a favor to a good friend. I'm really *not* qualified to do equine therapy."

"But—"

"Listen, I'm sorry, but I can't help you. Check out some

certified equine therapy programs. I think there's a good one in Shreveport," she said and disconnected the call.

He called right back but M&M didn't pick up.

Chapter 4

Wilson Realty employees were put to work on a single project the next morning, and it had nothing to do with buying or selling real estate.

Their boss went first to the secretarial pool and told them he wanted to know *everything* about certified equine therapy programs. "How do they get certified? Where are they located? Get me the names of the ones within 100 miles. I want reports on my desk before noon."

Then he went to his secretary and asked, "Don't you know a private detective?"

"Yes."

"Can you get him in here to see me today? Wait, better yet, if you can tell him what I want to know, he could just start gathering information."

Seeming puzzled at the request, she said, "I'll try."

"I want to know everything there is to know about Pine Park Stables near Marshall, and the owner, Ms. Johnson. And I mean *everything* he can find out—personal info, financials, professional qualifications."

She nodded and picked up her office phone.

By noon, Doug Wilson had a pile of papers on his desk. Planning to skip driving home for lunch, he called home and spoke to Jean, his longtime housekeeper who doubled as the cook, and then to the male nurse he had hired to take care of Brian every day until he got home. Both assured him that nothing had changed. Brian was still eating little, speaking less and generally lethargic, as he had been for weeks.

With a sad sigh, he got up, stomped out to his pickup and headed to his favorite downtown diner. As he slid into a booth, the waitress greeted him with, "Want your usual, Doug?"

He nodded, waiting for her to put a tall glass of iced tea and a club sandwich in front of him.

Then she softly asked, "How's Brian?"

He just shook his head.

When she checked to see if he wanted dessert, a random thought caused him to ask, "Dolly, do you believe it's harder to say 'no' to somebody asking for a favor if they are face-to-face with you, instead of on the phone?"

The waitress nodded, "Sure is harder for me."

"Thanks!" he boomed as he got up, tossed a twenty-dollar bill onto the table and rushed out the door.

He fought for the self-control to drive within the speed limit as he headed toward Marshall.

It seemed like hours instead of minutes before he saw a sign identifying the entrance to Pine Park Stables and turned into the drive. He saw a modest brick and frame house at the back edge of the drive, but he opted to park near the big barn.

When he stepped out of his truck and looked around, he was somewhat surprised by the sights before him. After reading financial reports about the place, he expected a run-down old farm, not a large barn with adjoining riding ring and spacious paddocks. The facilities and the horses appeared well-kept.

"Hello! Anybody home?" He hollered.

When a curly brown head popped up above a stall door and the hand that followed it waved, he hurried in that direction.

"I'm looking for Ms. Johnson, Mary Miranda Johnson," he said.

"Well, you've found her," replied the woman behind the

stall door. Her tattered dusty jeans almost matched her round cheeks as she warily watched her visitor's approach.

"If you're a bill collector, I'm scrambling to catch up. If you're a salesman, I'm sure not buying."

Douglas Wilson was shaking his head, trying to get a handle on this confrontation. "I'm not here to buy or sell anything except an idea. I'm Doug Wilson."

"Mr. Wilson, I'm sorry, but you've wasted your time driving over here. I've already told you I am *not* the person you are looking for. I don't have a therapy program. I am not a therapist. I thought I told you on the phone to call around, find the kind of program you need."

"You did. And I did. The two facilities in this part of Texas, aren't able to help. One has no client openings for at least six months. The other only works with small children because they use ponies or miniature horses, or whatever you call those little critters that can't carry a big kid."

M&M almost smiled at that. Shaking her head again, she told him, "I do have full-size horses, but—"

He interrupted, "And you have a nice facility here. If you can help battered women, you can help my son."

"It's not that I don't want to," she began.

"Look, maybe we can help each other. I know you're in a financial bind, and I'm willing and able to pay—"

"My finances are none of your business!" she snapped and turned away as tears formed. "Just go home, Mr. Wilson."

He backed off. "Okay, okay, I'm going. But I'll be back, tomorrow and every day until I can get you to work with me. I've *got* to believe we can help each other. Ms. Johnson, my son was critically injured physically, and he is still a mess emotionally. I am desperate – grasping at any and every little thing that just might work for him. Ms. Jameson's story gave me a glimmer of hope, something I haven't had in weeks. So, I'll be back," he promised as he went to his truck.

When M&M went into the house, Jerry was at the kitchen table, finishing up his homework.

"Are you starving?" she asked.

He grinned. "No more than usual. You know I'm *always* hungry," he admitted.

"Well, I can have spaghetti ready pretty soon," she told him as she washed and dried her hands and started reaching for ingredients from the pantry.

"Can we talk while you cook?" he asked.

"Sure thing."

She winced when he added, "Mom, about the idea of having some kind of therapy program at Pine Park, why not consider it? It just *might* be something we can do."

"Well, I consider myself kind of an old dog to be learning new tricks, but considering our circumstances, I'll at least try to find out more about equine therapy."

When he nodded approval, she continued, "I'll call Tiffany and see what info she has to share."

"When?"

"When what?"

"*When* will you call her?"

"Right after we eat supper and do the dishes," she promised.

While they ate, Jerry said, "People are praying for us, Mom."

Surprised, she asked, "Who? How'd that happen?"

"Remember? I told you I was gonna ask Ross about it?"

"Who's Ross?"

"He's the youth pastor at that church I sometimes visit. He's always encouraging us kids to talk to God. He says we just have to ask for what we need because God always listens and answers prayers." After a thoughtful pause, he continued. "So, I called

Ross and talked to him, and he helped me pray, and he said he would ask others to pray, too."

She held back tears.

"Mom, why are you looking like that?"

She shook her head. "Guilt, I guess."

"About what?"

"Your conversation with that youth leader, it reminded me how I've neglected the faith lessons of your upbringing."

"*Really.* You're the best mom ever. I don't feel neglected."

"Well, I should have taken you to Sunday school or church or read *Bible* stories to you."

He waited for her to say more, but she didn't.

"But you let me go to Vacation Bible School with friends and encouraged me to read my *Bible.*"

"That probably wasn't enough. I'm sorry, Jerry. Truth is, I guess I was mad at God because of your dad being taken away from us. I'm over that now, but I haven't done anything about it."

Jerry seemed puzzled. "What do you mean, haven't done anything? Like what?"

"Haven't been back to church, for one thing."

"Okay, so we can go sometime," he said. "But right now, you are *supposed* to be calling Tiffany about horse therapy."

"Right."

Jerry stayed in the kitchen to listen in when she made good her promise.

Thirty minutes later when M&M ended the call with a "Thanks so much," he was still waiting.

"Wow!" You talked long enough. Does that mean you got some good stuff?"

M&M nodded. "I think so. She gave me the name of the doctor that got her started with her program, made suggestions for getting a grant. She even told me someone who might help with that. Now what I really need to do is get a lot of information about PATH."

"What's PATH?"

"It stands for Professional Association of Therapeutic Horsemanship, and it's an international agency—sort of the umbrella over all kinds of horse therapy programs."

"That sounds pretty impressive," Jerry said as he let out a little sigh of relief.

"At least we have plenty to think about."

Both went to their beds and fell asleep doing just that.

*****

M&M found herself still thinking about equine therapy when she awoke.

She had just finished washing the breakfast dishes and started for the barn when her cell phone rang.

Checking her caller ID, she answered with, "You are nothing if not persistent, Mr. Wilson."

"You ain't seen anything yet," he half-joked. "Want me to come over this morning to plead my case, or should I wait until after lunch?"

She almost laughed. "Neither. But before you start yelling at me, please know that I would like nothing better than to help your son, and you already know I am looking for any additional source of income. The problem is I am *not* qualified to do equine therapy."

"But I know you helped those women."

"That was different. They are adults, and they had already recovered from physical injuries when they started riding sessions. However, I have made some inquiries and I'm trying to pull together enough information and skilled people to create some kind of activity just for your son. "

"Ms. Johnson, I can't thank you enough,"

"Don't thank me yet. I'm not at all sure about this."

"How soon can we come for a session?"

"I think it will be weeks before I can get something organized enough to feel comfortable with it."

"*That* long? Then could I just bring Brian over to your place and let you show him around, maybe build up some enthusiasm?"

She wanted to say *no* but there was so much hope in Doug Wilson's voice that she uttered reluctantly, "Okay, next Tuesday, but let's wait until afternoon so I can get my training time in for the day and prepare for your visit."

After relaying the information to Jerry as he was leaving for school, she decided this was a good opportunity to reward him by keeping him involved.

"Help me," she said. "Which horse will be the best choice for this introduction?"

Jerry paused in thought before answering, "Goldilocks, if she's big enough to carry him."

"He won't be riding at first," M&M said.

"I know, but if you're counting on a horse to make friends with him and one that is totally trustworthy, that will be the one he'll start on. Right?"

"Right. So, why did you pick Goldilocks?"

"She's very sweet. She's pretty. She loves being petted. And she certainly won't hurt him."

"You're right. Goldilocks it is!" she told him with a smile and a loving pat on the shoulder, and without saying it was the same horse she would have picked. She watched her son's departure and sighed. He was growing up to look just like his lean but muscular handsome dad.

*****

M&M didn't feel anywhere near ready on Tuesday, but she was determined to get off to a good start with Doug Wilson's boy.

Before Jerry left for school, she told him she was going to count on Goldilocks to do her part, "I think I'll give her a bath and really get her shined up for the introduction."

Hours later, with six horses ridden, cooled, and returned to their stalls, M&M took Goldilocks to the heated area of the wash rack for a bath, giving special attention to her white socks and snowy mane and tail. She walked her in the sun to dry and then brushed her until her golden coat was shiny.

Realizing she probably didn't have the time to do much for her own appearance, M&M hurried into the house, managed to eat a half sandwich after she washed her face and hands, and slipped into clean jeans. She had just brushed the tangles from her curly hair and was applying lip gloss when she heard a vehicle in the drive.

Pulling on her jacket, she hurried out and started toward the big barn, waving for her visitors to follow.

After Doug Wilson went around to assist his son into a wheelchair, she saw the reason for his concern and determination to help Brian.

M&M couldn't remember seeing such a frail teenager. He was gaunt, his skin was the color of paste and his eyes didn't quite seem to focus. M&M approached him slowly and offered a welcoming smile.

"Hello, Brian. I'm Mary Miranda Johnson. My friends call me M&M and you may do so if you wish. This horse farm is home to me, and to my son, Jerry. I imagine he's about your age."

She scanned the barn, paddocks, and fields, as a touch of pride in this place she loved so much made a grin form, temporarily pushing back the fear of losing what she and her husband had worked so hard to build. Then she continued. "Since we're considering setting up a special program for you here, I'd like to show you around and introduce you to some horses."

Brian remained silent until his father started pushing the wheelchair in the direction of the barn. Then, he sucked in his breath and muttered, "I can do it myself," as he began to maneuver the chair.

M&M now wondered what she had gotten herself into, agreeing to help this fragile boy who clearly had deep underlying issues.

Once inside the barn, she turned to him and said, "Jerry and I chose a horse that we think will be suitable for you. Let's go meet her."

Brian didn't speak or show any interest in the stalled horses they passed as they moved down the center aisle. Goldilocks did her part, hanging her elegant head over the bottom stall door and neighing a soft greeting as they approached her.

Brian hesitated then, muttering something about the chair.

"It's okay," M&M assured him. "She's seen wheelchairs before; she won't be scared."

When Douglas nudged the boy forward, he frowned and uttered a few words as he parked right up by the stall door.

"She *is* pretty," Brian said. "What's her name?"

"Goldilocks."

The dainty mare's nose reached out to Brian and he froze, then looked to M&M for a clue to what he should do.

She grinned. "Goldilocks is a little beggar. She wants a treat."

Reaching into her pocket, she pulled out a small alfalfa cube and showed Brian how to offer the treat. "Hold it flat in the palm of your hand, not in your fingers. She might accidentally get your fingers in her teeth and both you *and* Goldilocks would be sorry." She placed it in his outstretched hand.

Hesitantly, he extended his hand toward the horse, and she nuzzled it carefully before gently taking the cube.

Brian squirmed, half-giggled then grinned as he said, "That tickled."

M&M seized the opportunity to tell Brian, "You've made friends already. Come back and see her anytime. And she will be your mount when you're ready to ride."

Doug Wilson remained silent, his eyes glistening with emotion.

The three turned away from the stall and headed back to the driveway. Doug helped Brian from the chair into their vehicle and closed the door.

Then he turned to M&M.

"That's the first time I've seen even the hint of a smile in months. *Please*, do whatever you have to do so Brian can come and ride. I'll foot the bills, whatever it takes."

M&M nodded, then waved to Brian as they left.

*****

When Jerry got home, his first words were, "How'd it go with Mr. Wilson and his son?"

M&M flashed a smile and tossed a compliment to her son. "It was all good. Thanks to you."

"Mom, I wasn't even *here*."

"But you picked the perfect horse to get him hooked. Goldilocks turned on the charm and he actually chuckled when she took a treat from his hand. It was a great beginning. Mr. Wilson was almost crying when they left—told me to set up the sessions and he'd pay whatever necessary. He said it's the first time he's seen a happy face on his son in a long time."

"Wow!" was all Jerry could say.

"So, I've got to talk to lots of people to get sessions set up so I can actually *help* Brian."

Jerry frowned. "What's wrong with him?"

"I only know he was seriously injured in some kind of automobile accident. He is mostly in a wheelchair. He looks very frail and he seems *so* sad." She gazed at her son's sympathetic face and continued, "I guess I'll need to find out the particulars of his injuries to be able to do the right things in his sessions. And I've got to learn more *about* and *from* PATH." M&M sighed. "I feel like I'm going back to school."

"Don't worry, Mom "I'll help you study. You've always helped me with my homework."

*****

Mother and son worked together to complete the barn chores and went to the house for supper. Both *did* have homework, and M&M's began with a series of phone calls.

She called Tiffany first. "Hey, Girlfriend, it's payback time."

A puzzled voice responded, "Okay, what do I owe you?"

M&M chuckled, then explained, "You said I was doing you a favor when I started that riding class for your SSS women."

"And?"

"So now, because one of them, Violet told somebody else how it helped her, and I've been asked to do another session."

"That's great—you have an opportunity to help others, but—"

M&M interrupted before she could finish the sentence, "Well, this is different. It's to help a teenage boy who has been seriously injured. He's got a long road to recovery, and I don't know anything about *that* kind of equine therapy."

She then listened carefully as her friend told her the little she knew about equine therapy programs, concluding with the encouraging words, "You *do* know about how horse and rider bonds make for happier people."

Before the call ended, Tiffany suggested talking with Dr. Clay and getting names of local physical therapists who might be able to help.

Too late to make calls to business offices, M&M sighed and started scribbling notes, listing calls for the next day. She then went to her computer to find contact information for PATH and for area physical therapists. When she finally went to bed, she fell asleep thinking of other calls to make.

*****

M&M put off those calls until after her training rides the next day, but before she finished with the rides, her cell phone began to chime.

After cooling off the young filly and putting her in a turnout paddock, she pulled the phone out and smiled at the caller ID. Susanna had called and left a simple voice mail message to call her back.

Suzanna answered on the first ring. "I thought I was gonna have to come out there to get your attention," her friend half-scolded her.

"I was atop a horse—just got off. So, what's up?"

"News to share. Tiffany and I have put our heads together and are doing some fact gathering for you. We will have even more info by tomorrow, so plan on a late lunch, with us. We'll bring it out to you, and we can tell you what all we've found out while we share our meal."

"It's a deal," M&M responded. "And thanks."
Although she couldn't quite figure out what her two best friends were doing, she knew their intentions were good, and she looked forward to seeing them and enjoying a meal she didn't have to prepare.

Chapter 5

M&M followed her usual routine the next morning, dispensing hay and grain and filling water buckets at daybreak. Then she went back to the house to have a quick breakfast with Jerry before he left for school. She waved him off as she headed back to the barn to pick out stalls and start riding.

She always started with the most unruly horse while she was still fresh. He was a headstrong young gelding, spoiled by his amateur owner. M&M hoped she could fix his bad habits then tactfully show his owner how to keep him going in the right direction.

"Okay, *Hard Head*, let's do this," she told the horse as she asked him for the third time to pick up the correct lead on cue. He chose to buck instead. M&M pulled his head up, kept a shorter rein and cued him again. He balked. She whacked him with her crop and then let him stand and think about his next move.

"Listen, *Hard Head*, I have better things to do than fight with you. Here goes." She again asked him to start on the correct lead and this time he did.

"Good boy. Third time's a charm," she told the horse and rewarded him with a pat on the neck. She finished their session without further difficulty and when she unsaddled the gelding, she promised herself to stop calling him Hard Head, especially around his doting owner.

The other horses were less troublesome, and M&M had all five ridden, cooled and put in stalls or paddocks by noon.

Wondering what Susanna had meant by "late lunch" she went to the house to wash up and make iced tea.

She had just poured herself a glass and sank into her chair when she heard a car in the drive. Within a minute, Susanna came in, followed by Tiffany, both carrying bulging bags.

"Hey, this is such a treat! Do I need to get out bowls, plates, forks and spoons, or what?

"Not a thing," Tiffany told her. "We've got it all, including plates, forks, napkins, but we do need drinks, and I see you already took care of that."

The three were soon seated around the little table enjoying huge chef salads accompanied by chunks of French bread.

"This is *so* yummy," M&M told them.

"Healthy, too," Tiffany added, and Susanna chuckled. "Except for the double chocolate fudge brownies I made."

As they ate, Susanna started explaining what they'd been doing. "I called Dad and told him about your new client ... and you know Dad, he always has suggestions."

M&M nodded. "So, what did he say?"

"He said if you do equine therapy, you probably should get a physical therapist involved.

He also wondered if the boy is seeing a counselor, and thought that would be a good idea."

Tiffany spoke up, "If you're going to get a counselor involved, I recommend Dr. Clay, He's the best. He's been incredibly helpful with my SSS program."

Susanna added, "I also did some checking about PATH, and guess what! There is a PATH certified program in Texarkana. I called and talked to the director and got tons of information from him."

"Wow! You two *have* been busy."

Susanna raised her eyebrows. "Well, we want to help, and we can't train horses or teach lessons, so—"

Wildflower Wednesday

Tiffany interrupted, "But, speaking of lessons, have you thought about doing some special classes for kids during the summer? Or maybe day camp? I hear parents of horse-crazy kids pay big bucks for that sort of summer activity,"

M&M replied, "I wish I could, but I don't have enough suitable horses for classes of any size, plus it takes more than just me to corral a bunch of kids."

"Let's think some more on this," Susanna suggested. "I bet you could enlist volunteer helpers from a couple of advanced students and Jerry is a great helper."

"We could help, too," Tiffany added.

"That's sweet of you—both of you, but you have plenty to do already. Susanna has twins to take care of, and you, Tiffany, have SSS."

Tiffany opened her mouth to protest and Susanna interrupted before M&M could refuse their offer.

"Like I said," let's be thinking about this."

With a lot to consider about ways to get Pine Park out of the red, they ate their brownies in thoughtful silence.

By the time Jerry got home from school, his mom was exhausted both physically and mentally. She had done all the riding and training on schedule, plus again picked out stalls and refilled water buckets, all the while considering the ideas tossed to her by her best friends.

"How's it goin' Mom?"

She sighed and sat down at the kitchen table to enjoy the rest of the tea she'd made.

"Get yourself a snack and I'll tell you the latest."

Delighted to find brownies on the counter, he grabbed them and poured a glass of milk before joining her.

"You had time to bake today?" he asked.

"No way, Susanna and Tiffany were here. They brought lunch and the brownies, plus a whole bunch of information and ideas."

Jerry grinned. "I hope the ideas were as good as these brownies."

"Maybe. Not sure. Susanna had talked to her dad about how to help Brian and also checked out PATH certified equine therapy centers. There's one in Texarkana."

"So what?"

"Well, she called and talked to the director, found him to be helpful, so maybe I'll need to do that too, sometime. But, in the immediate future, I need to talk to a professional counselor and a physical therapist about working with me to do sessions for Brian."

"Do you think you might want to develop a PATH certified program here?"

"Maybe. Tiffany also made some suggestions about having summer day camping sessions with riding lessons included. She says parents of horse-crazy kids pay big bucks for that kind of thing."

"Let's do it, Mom! I can help, be sorta like a camp counselor for the kids, and show them stuff about grooming, cleaning tack and taking care of horses."

"I'm not sure we have enough horses to make that work."

"Couldn't we borrow some?"

"Tiffany, or maybe it was Susanna, mentioned that possibility. But I'm not sure how to go about borrowing horses, or if I even want to." She smiled at him. "Tell you what, since you seem pretty enthusiastic about this, why don't we both think about it some more, and write down the pros and cons, ideas for set up, that kind of thing. In a day or two, we can compare our notes and talk about it some more."

He tossed her a pouty look, but he couldn't help but chuckle. "Great, Mom. You just gave me another homework assignment."

Wildflower Wednesday

*****

Tiffany and Susanna had gone home with their own ideas about making money for Pine Park.

When they parted at Susanna's house, Tiffany said, "I'm going to talk to Dr. Clay and kinda pave the way for M&M."

Susanna told her, "I know several of M&M's clients, plus other horse owners that have gentle retired show horses turned out to pasture. I'll feel them out about sending them to Pine Park for summer camp."

Another thought popped out, "And John and I might send Gwen. She's going to be sad at weaning time and might be better off away from her filly. Plus, she could use the conditioning."

She turned and hurried inside to get John's opinion.

"John," she called out as she went through the door.

"*Sh-h-h-h!* I just got the twins to sleep. If you wake them, it's your turn to get them down for a nap."

Susanna chuckled softly. "Did they give you a hard time?"

He grinned and admitted, "It took a while to get them settled in, but I had fun with them. What have you been up to?"

"Tiffany and I went out to see M&M, shared some ideas about how to boost her bank balance, and I wanted to get your opinion about one of them."

"Shoot."

"She's thinking about doing a horsey summer day camp but says she doesn't have enough horses. I think I can ask around, get them lined up among her clients, but what about sending Gwen over on loan."

"Gwen's busy being a momma to that still unnamed filly."

"I know, but weaning time isn't too far off, and I thought it might be easier for both mare and foal if they are where they can't see or hear each other."

"Okay."

"Okay! That's it? No discussion?"

- 35 -

"Honey, I know you love those horses and will make good decisions about them. I'm fine letting you do that. I just wish I had some good ideas about how to help M&M, since she made it clear that a loan from us is out of the question. You know we could just give her...."

"John, you *know* M&M won't accept money from us, not as a gift or a loan. I wish she would."

She told John she planned to call some Pine Park clients and feel them out about loaning horses for camp, and he encouraged her to start calling while Lee and Laura slept.

Susanna had time to make several phone calls, and even she was surprised at the positive responses.

By the time the twins awoke, and she had to put aside her calling list, she thought she probably had enough horses lined up to make summer riding camp and class lessons doable. Even better, she had offers for volunteer helpers.

Chapter 6

The next morning, M&M again rushed through her feeding and training tasks, saving the easy mounts to squeeze in between two scheduled lessons in late afternoon.

She figured she and Jerry would be eating a late supper, but there was no way she could skip out on her visit to the bank. She had put off the requested meeting there as long as possible.

After a quick lunch, she showered and changed into one of her few "go to town" outfits, a beige pantsuit, brushed her hair into submission and smoothed on a bit of lipstick.

Glancing in the mirror, she stuck out her tongue and told her reflection, "You'll have to do."

She gathered up her neatly typed notes outlining plans she and her friends had made to expand Pine Park's income potential. She was so nervous that she was afraid she wouldn't remember half of what she wanted to say. She tried to rehearse her little speech as she drove into town, finally giving up as she pulled into the bank parking lot.

Stretching to her full height and pulling her shoulders back, she marched into the building, approached the reception desk and asked to see Elliott James.

She was directed to his office and told to make herself comfortable. Before she even took the offered seat, the bank vice president strode into the room and extended his hand.

Struggling to appear confident, or at least calm, M&M lifted her chin and looked into his eyes as they shook hands.

"Well, Ms. Johnson, it's good to finally have this opportunity to talk with you."

She tried to smile—couldn't quite manage it. "Mr. James, I know I'm behind on my mortgage payments, and I hope you know I am not deliberately—"

He interrupted then, "Ms. Johnson, I *know* you must be struggling. Please understand the bank's position here. We expect to collect on mortgage payments, just as we do on other types of loans. But the last thing we want to do is foreclose on your property. I assure you, the bank doesn't want to own your horse farm."

As that message sank in, M&M drew in a deep breath of relief, then spoke up.

"That's good news, and I'd like to outline some plans I have to expand my business and boost my income. Problem is, it will take a few months to get the new program or programs going."

Elliott James listened attentively as she explained the goals of hosting summer camps and increasing her lesson schedule. She even touched on the possibility of starting an equine therapy program.

"It sounds like you've put a great deal of thought into these plans," he said.

"Yes, sir. I have, and I've had help and suggestions from several good friends."

"That's all well and good. Now, do you think you can manage to pay the past accrued interest, just the interest, on the mortgage?"

She shook her head. "I'm not sure. How much would that be?"

When the banker handed over a paper highlighting the amount, $2,344, she felt somewhat hopeful. "Maybe. I'll have to go home and break into the piggy bank," she half-joked.

"See what you can do," he encouraged her. "If you can pay

that past due interest, we can defer your mortgage payments for six months and give you time to build up a cash flow."

"Thank you!" she said as she rose to leave. "I'll let you know in a few days."

She exited as quickly as she could, hoping not to fall apart before reaching her vehicle.

She cried all the way home, but they were tears of relief. She just *might* be able to keep Pine Park. She started thinking of what she could sell quickly to raise the money and some of her most treasured tack came to mind—two or three saddles well worth the money, if she could find a buyer right away. Or maybe she would try to sell one of the school horses.

*****

The next night, her friends gathered around M&M's table and took their seats as she passed around plates laden with steaming spaghetti and meatballs.

"This smells delicious," Tiffany said as she took her plate.

Jerry grinned. "Yeah! Glad you all could come eat with us." As he loaded his plate he added, "Mom doesn't cook this much good stuff just for us."

He caught a stern look from M&M before she turned to John. "Please bless this food so we can eat before it gets cold."

After a simple grace, they all began to eat.

"Okay, this *is* yummy. So, are we celebrating a special occasion?" asked Susanna.

M&M answered, "Yes and no. I planned it to be a thank you dinner, since you all have gone above and beyond anything I could ever expect to help me pull Pine Park out of debt. Then, I guess it's a celebration, too. With your help I'll be starting some new programs here."

Susanna raised her tea glass in a toast. "Then here's to new beginnings."

They all began to talk at once, with Jerry letting the adults know that he, too, was involved in the summer plans. "I'm going to be a camp counselor," he told them, "And if I'm lucky, I might even get to do lessons for some of the beginning riders."

Susanna spoke up, "I hope to be doing some lessons, too."

Tiffany raised her hand to get into the conversation. "I want to help too, but I don't know enough to teach riding. Find me something to do during camp." She paused, then told M&M, "I did talk to Dr. Clay and got some tips for you regarding therapy."

"Let's hear them," M&M encouraged her.

Tiffany reached into her purse and pulled out several sheets of neatly folded paper. "I typed up the notes, so I wouldn't forget anything," she said as she handed over the paperwork.

M&M glanced at the notes and nodded, "You've done me a big favor with these ideas." After a moment, she continued, "Now, I need to have another conversation with Mr. Wilson and get the particulars about his son's injuries. I want to move forward right away on setting up a therapy program for him. I think the PATH certified program is too complicated for me right now, and I've got to focus on getting a summer camp and more lessons scheduled while kids are out of school—see if I can generate enough income to actually have a sufficient cash flow." She scanned the faces around the table, "So, you are the first to know, I have been granted a grace period before making my mortgage payments. Thank you all for helping me put plans together for the bank to consider."

"That's awesome," Susanna said.

"Now, Jerry and I have a chance, at least, of staying here. I'm so grateful for that chance."

Susanna nodded, "Well, there are a lot of people who *really* want you to stay here. I took the liberty of talking to a few of your clients and former riding students and several want to either give you a retired horse to use in camp and for lessons, or loan you one for the summer."

M&M's jaw dropped in surprise, "I don't know what to say."

"You'd better say *yes*," John told her. "When they offer something that will fit your needs, you've got to accept! Besides, it makes folks feel good when they're able to help a worthy cause."

M&M nodded with a smile.

"Then we'd better clear out of here and let you get started on making schedules and all that stuff we can't do for you," Susanna said. "Almost forgot, Gwen can come over to be a lesson or camp horse for the summer months if you think she'll fit."

That said, she, John and Tiffany said their goodbyes and left, with Jerry clearing the table and talking about how fun it would be to have summer camp.

*****

The next morning, M&M left the breakfast dishes, waved Jerry off to school and hurried to feed and water the horses Then she went back inside, gathered her notebook and pencil before calling Doug Wilson.

He answered on the first ring.

"Good morning, Mr. Wilson. I hope this isn't a bad time for a phone conversation. I have put serious thought into planning a riding program for your son, and I have input from knowledgeable medical people. As I've told you, more than once, I am not really qualified to operate as an equine therapy center, although I admit that I am now considering trying to develop that in the future. But for now, I want to help your son."

"Once again, thank you."

"As you mentioned, we all can benefit. But the thing is, I need a lot more information about Brian's injuries and prognosis for recovery."

"Of course. It's not a pretty story, Ms. Johnson, and I think

I'd prefer not to do this on the phone. Give me an hour or so of your time for a face-to-face meeting, and I'll come over."

M&M felt she had to say yes, and suggested that early afternoon would be best, as she expected no one to be there for lessons until after three.

"I'll see you about 1 p.m., okay?"

They found the time mutually agreeable and M&M dashed back to the barn to start the training sessions. She finished by noon, turned horses into their paddocks and went in to have lunch. She had just finished when Doug Wilson drove up.

"I know I'm a little early."

"It's okay," she assured him and offered him a glass of lemonade as they sat down at her kitchen table. She took a pencil in her hand, slid the notebook closer and waited for him to speak.

Doug Wilson swallowed hard, struggled and began, "I don't know where to start. As I told you, it's not a pretty story."

M&M sensed how painful this conversation must be and told him she'd like to know something about Brian—what he was like before he was injured.

He brightened a bit as he replied, "Brian was lean, athletic, physically fit. He was a star on the soccer team, played center forward. He was also a straight *A* student, with teachers and coaches alike telling him he had chances for scholarships due to grades as well as his soccer skills. He was a confident, happy teenager, excited to be getting his driver's license." Doug Wilson paused, and he frowned. "Then his world—our world, came apart."

"What happened?"

"His mother and his fourteen-year-old brother went with him to take his driving test, which of course he passed with flying colors. I'm sure he was excited when his mom told him he could drive home. On the way, they were hit broadside by a loaded dump truck. The impaired driver ran a light, and he destroyed my family."

He choked up, paused to regain his composure.

"I'm *so* sorry," M&M said. "And I'm sorry I asked."

"No!" he assured her. "You need to know. It might help you understand and be better able to help Brian." After a deep breath, he finished with, "My wife, Lyndsey, and younger son, Thomas, died at the scene. I'm told they died instantly. Brian was critically injured. He was unconscious for two days and nights, and doctors at first feared brain damage. He had a severe concussion, compound fracture of his left leg, and a number of less critical injuries. He was in ICU for ten days, and those were the longest days of my life."

"Oh my, no wonder he looks frail."

"He *is* frail, Ms. Johnson, and it's not just his physical health that worries me. He doesn't seem to care about getting better. He's been an uncooperative patient with his physical therapist, hates counseling and exerts minimum effort with his studies."

Doug's voice quavered as he continued to talk. "We got him home in time for Thanksgiving dinner, for which I was grateful. It was, however, the most grim holiday I've ever spent, and Christmas was no better."

M&M interjected, "I remember. The first of any special day without someone you love is the hardest. It does get better. Honestly, it does."

"Oh, how I hope so. Meanwhile, I've hired a male nurse who stays with him all day, every day, plus tutors for three of his school subjects. Then there's Jean and Jessie. They spend lots of time with him."

"Are they family members?"

He smiled a bit, "No, but they are like family. They live on our property, she is our housekeeper and cook, and he's the landscaper for our place, plus properties that I show and sell."

"You have a live-in cook and housekeeper and a landscape guy?"

Surprise showed at M&M's response. He played it down. "As I said, they are more like part of the family. They've worked for us for years and Brian has known them most of his life. And, back to Brian, he probably responds and reacts with them more positively than with anyone else, even me."

He sighed and continued, "So, I've driven my office staff crazy helping me look for something, *anything* that might help him. That's how I came to hear Violet Jameson talk about you and Pine Park."

M&M felt overwhelmed and remained quiet.

After a rather uncomfortable silence, Doug Wilson said, "Sorry to just dump it all out like that. Guess I needed somebody to talk to."

M&M nodded, "I'll want your permission on this. I'll need to share some information with a counselor, primary care doctor, and physical therapist that will be available here for Brian. I want to help him as much as possible, and I certainly want to be sure we don't *hurt* him or set him back in any way."

"Thank you. And *certainly,* you may pass along information as needed. I'll also send over names of his medical team in case these doctors and therapists want to compare notes, so to speak."

"Good. Then I'll get started right away, and let you know when we can have Brian back here for his first session."

"I'm hoping for soon," Doug said as he rose to leave. "One other thing," he said as he reached for his wallet. "I know none of this is without cost, so here's a first payment," He handed her a folded check.

"No, Mr. Wilson, I think you or your insurance company should be paying directly to the doctors and therapists."

"I agree," but I don't expect you, or your horse, to work for free. This deposit is for you."

M&M opened her mouth to protest, but he spoke first, "Ms. Johnson, the deal is we are in this to help each other. I know you have financial needs. Money is one thing I have. No arguments, *please*."

She was too moved to say more, just nodded as he went out the door.

Then she sat down and unfolded the check. It was for $2,000, far more generous than she'd expected. She said a little prayer of thanks for Doug Wilson's generosity before she called Elliott James to say, "Yes, I can pay that past due interest."

M&M was so relieved that she was actually humming a happy tune when Jerry got home and found her shoveling out stalls.

"Hey, Mom! What's up?"

"Let's just say we are on probation with the bank, but now we have a real chance to get back in the saddle and put Pine Park back to making us a living. I'll fill you in at supper."

Chapter 7

Two hours later, as they were finishing ice cream sundaes, Jerry said, "Gosh, Mom, it sounds great. Mr. Wilson and his son sure came along at the right time. Are you still thinking about starting a therapy program?"

"Maybe. Probably. But not just yet. First, I am going to get a program set up just for Brian Wilson. Then line up those summer camp and lesson programs we've talked about. I'm counting on your help, big time."

He beamed. "I'm excited to think I'll be sort of a camp counselor. How can I help with Brian Wilson?"

"I don't know. Maybe just get to know him, be a friend. It seems like he could use one."

Jerry nodded, He didn't know enough about Brian Wilson to know what they had in common except age, and maybe a fondness for a cute little palomino named Goldilocks.

*****

M&M had to rush through her morning barn chores and training sessions again. Tiffany had called first thing and said, "I set up an appointment for you to meet with Dr. Clay. He said I could come too. We're to see him at 2:00 P.M."

Then Susanna had called and said her dad wanted to chat with them about the plans for Brian.

"Dad's free late this afternoon and I told him to come over to the house. We'll have a really informal meeting out on the porch with lemonade."

"Sounds good," M&M said, not yet thinking about how she

would get all the horse sessions fitted into her day.

Just past noon, she put horses in paddocks and ate a bite of lunch so she could shower off the sweaty horse smell and dress appropriately. Tiffany came and picked her up for the drive to Dr. Clay's office.

"What's he like?" she asked her friend as they approached town.

"Oh, you'll like him a lot. If you're thinking he talks that professional jargon that nobody but other shrinks understand, he's just not like that. He's really, well, he's just nice. He'll be helpful, I promise."

M&M hoped Tiffany was right. She was nervous about the whole therapy thing.

An hour later, she was relieved. Dr. Clay, as Tiffany had promised, had proven both nice and helpful. After hearing her brief report relating how Brian was injured and the progress since the accident, Dr. Clay stressed that Brian would benefit from professional counseling as well as having a physician and a physical therapist involved in the special program being designed for him.

When he learned that M&M would soon be talking with Dr. Lyons, he said, "If you're thinking of forming a team on this boy's behalf, I am willing to be on that team, if you wish."

"Thank you so much," M&M said as she shook his hand in farewell. "I'll get back to you on that as soon as I've talked to the others."

Tiffany dropped her off back at Pine Park in time to welcome Jerry home from school, hand him a hearty snack and ask him to get on his homework so he could help her later at the barn.

"I have to go over to John and Susanna's now, to meet with her dad. We're putting our heads together to plan the therapy sessions for Brian."

Jerry scowled. "I wish I could go too and maybe see the twins."

"I know, and I'm sorry, but not this time. Okay? I really need you to get that homework done because I have to have help at the barn later, and you, my man, *are* the help."

"Okay, Mom."

She grabbed up her notepad and hurried off before she weakened and let him come.

*****

M&M and Susanna were sitting on the porch with glasses of cold lemonade when Dr. Lyons arrived.

"Where are the kids?" he asked as he bounded up the steps.

Susanna grinned. "Now we know why you *really* wanted to have this meeting at our house."

He grinned back. "Never miss an opportunity to play with those twins," he admitted. "But, I do want to help with this project you girls have been talking about."

"Thank you for that, Dr. Lyons," M&M said.

"Well, from what little I've been told, this boy has had a really bad experience, both physically and emotionally. It'll be a privilege to help him if I can."

Susanna handed her dad a glass of cold lemonade and said, "M&M can now give you more information about his injuries and his emotional state. She got the whole story from Mr. Wilson, with permission to share it."

Within minutes, Dr. Lyons was shaking his head in wonder. "In one way, this boy is lucky—he survived. In another, his life is painful in every way, right now. I've already asked a colleague who specializes in orthopedics to join in creating a good program."

"Great! I talked to Dr. Clay earlier today, and he thinks counseling needs to be included, and he offered to be part of the team."

Wildflower Wednesday

"Good, then I will ask my colleague who else needs to be involved. Of course, you 'horse people' will be in charge of the riding sessions. What or who will that include?"

M&M said she wasn't sure. "I know there will be someone leading the horse. That could be me, or someone else who is comfortable handling a horse. There will also be what is called a 'side walker,' somebody who stays right beside Brian to help him balance and remain upright in the saddle as needed."

"Okay, here's what I think," Susanna interjected. "Why not get the main participants together to get it all lined up as it needs to proceed."

"Good idea, Daughter. My orthopedic doctor friend is Dr. Jason Hood. Why don't you take charge of setting up a meeting with him and Dr. Clay and M&M here, plus whoever else needs to be involved."

"Okay, Grandpa, you can go play with Lee and Laura now. I think John is with them in the family room."

M&M thanked Susanna and got up to leave. "I have horses and barn chores waiting. Just give me enough notice that I can shower and change before attending this planning meeting."

Susanna nodded. "Any preferences as to day or time?"

M&M shook her head. "The sooner the better. Mr. Wilson will probably call me every day to ask how soon Brian can come for a session."

*****

Two weeks later, M&M still wasn't sure she was ready to start the program, but Doug was literally pleading with her, and the assembled team expressed confidence in their plans, so when she got the second call of the day from Doug, she said, "Okay, we're ready for him to start this week."

She told him Wednesday or Thursday mid-day were the times that all the team members could be there.

"Team?" he wondered aloud. "How many people are we

talking about? And why not just you and another horse person and Brian?"

M&M patiently explained that she had conferred with several people more qualified to determine how to best help Brian, and they had agreed that this uniquely designed program needed to include a counselor, a physician, and a physical therapist, as well as "horse people."

"Okay," she began to outline the first session. "All of us will meet briefly to go over our goals, and Brian needs to be part of the discussion. Then, within a few minutes, we'll have him mounted and hopefully, enjoying his ride."

"He's not gonna like this meeting part," Brian's dad said.

"Mr. Wilson, he may not *like* it, but he *has* to do it this way. With any luck at all, he'll soon realize that we're all on his side."

"You're right. We'll be over Wednesday at whatever time you say."

M&M contacted Dr. Clay, Dr. Hood and the physical therapist. Susanna had insisted on being the horse handler, so she called her too. They all agreed on Wednesday at 2 p.m. and she called the real estate office and left a message for Doug Wilson.

*****

Wednesday was warm and sunny at Pine Park, so M&M set up a round folding table and chairs under a tree near the arena gate.

After completing her morning rides, she put a cooler filled with ice and cold drinks by the table, then hurried to the house to grab a sandwich and clean up before others arrived.

Susanna came an hour early. "Thought I'd help you get the horse saddled, or whatever you need."

"Thanks, Susanna. I'm *so* nervous."

"*Why?*"

"Because I don't know what I'm doing."

Wildflower Wednesday

Susanna laughed at her. "None of us know, exactly, but we're all in this to help a hurt kid. That's all that matters."

Nodding, M&M glanced outside and saw that other vehicles were approaching. It was 1:30. She waved to them, motioning for them to park and come to the little table she had set up.

"Make yourselves comfortable," she said, "while Susanna and I go get the horse ready for today's session."

M&M and Susanna hurried to the barn, leaving the doctors and physical therapist to share their thoughts. They had just finished saddling Goldilocks and taken her to the tie rack when they saw Doug Wilson turn into the drive. M&M waved and motioned for him to join the small group gathered around the table.

He got out and approached them. "I have to tell you, Brian is *not* happy about so many people being here. I guess he feels like he's got a spotlight on him or something. I hope I can get him to get out and give this a try. He's been looking forward to it 'til now."

"Can I talk with him?" M&M asked.

When his father nodded, she slowly approached the vehicle and motioned to Brian to roll down the window.

"Hey, Brian. I kinda understand that you didn't expect an audience for your riding session. To tell you the truth, I didn't either. The thing is, I don't know enough about equine therapy to be confident and your dad would never forgive me if I got you hurt. So, I asked these people that know more than I do, I trust them to help us—you and me—do this right."

Brian said nothing. He didn't move.

M&M continued, "*Please*, Brian. Let's give this a chance to work. I know you like Goldilocks, and she's all saddled up and waiting for you. I hope these riding sessions will be fun for you, as well as help you get your strength back."

The boy still said nothing. But he nodded slightly and

opened the door. His father was immediately there, getting out the portable wheelchair and helping him settle into it.

M&M led the way to the group at the table and quickly introduced Brian to the others. Each briefly explained their roles in the sessions and wished Brian well on his first ride. Susanna went ahead and led Goldilocks to the mounting block at the center of the arena. Doug tried to propel the wheelchair in that direction, but Brian protested, insisting, "I can do it myself."

M&M and Stanley, the young physical therapist, stayed by him until he reached the mounting block. Susanna positioned the mare just right for Brian to go up the three steps and swing his leg over the saddle. He had to cling to the rail and pull himself to get up the steps, and he sucked in a deep breath as he swung his leg over the saddle.

With a sigh of relief, Susanna and M&M positioned his feet in the stirrups, and Stanley took up his position next to Brian's right foot. M&M then stepped away and told Brian, "Today, your horse handler will guide the horse. In later sessions, you will hold the reins and do it yourself."

"Now, when you tell Goldilocks *walk on*, Susanna will lead her in a circle around me, while I call out directions, with Stanley hanging close in case you need help. Your job is to stay upright in that saddle.

"Goldilocks doesn't know the *walk on* command yet, but she will learn quickly and soon respond to your voice, and she already knows the command for stop. It's *whoa*. And when you say it, she'll stop." M&M smiled and asked him, "Are you ready?"

Brian nodded slightly and tried to smile. "I think so."

"Then tell your horse *walk on* and let's go."

At the verbal command, Susanna led the mare forward and began to guide her in a circle. Brian slouched slightly to one side and Stanley helped him shift to sit up straight.

"Try to put your heels down, with balls of your feet on those stirrups," M&M told him. "It helps you stay balanced."

Brian dropped his heels and straightened his back.

"Good job," encouraged Stanley.

"Let's practice the stop," M&M instructed. "Say the word, Brian."

Brian said, "Whoa," and Goldilocks didn't take another step.

"See, she's letting you tell her what you want, already," M&M said. "Now, let's make some more circles."

When Brian said *walk on* again, the mare began to move before Susanna took a step or pulled at her head, and everybody praised Goldilocks.

The horse continued to carry her rider until he grew tired and started to slump sideways and M&M said, "Let's take a break—tell her to stop."

When she heard *'Whoa'* Goldilocks planted her feet, and Brian let out a relieved sigh.

"Are you tired?" M&M asked him, already knowing that he was.

"Yes, but I'm not ready to stop."

"Okay, then let's turn around and circle the other way, then head to the gate. I'm going to let you dismount there."

At the gate, M&M told him to swing his right leg over the back of the saddle and try to lay across the seat to free his left foot from the stirrup. "Try to just lay across the horse on your belly before you slide down." To Susanna and Stanley, she said, "Give him a hand."

Susanna saw the terror in the boy's eyes and assured him, "We're here for you. Your knees may buckle when your feet hit the ground, but the worst thing that can happen is you'll just sit down. It's okay."

He struggled to dismount then. Stanley and Susanna moved in to keep him upright until he caught his breath, and his dad brought the chair to him.

"Now, sit down," M&M suggested. "That was a good first ride," she told the pale, sweating teen.

"Thanks. At least Goldilocks did everything right."

"Yes, she did. And every time you come to ride, both of you will learn new movements and commands."

"Really?" he asked. "Do you think I can *really* learn to ride, I mean like a cowboy?"

M&M grinned at him, "I *know* you can, if you want to enough to work at it,"

Doug took his exhausted son to the car and then came back to thank M&M and the others.

"I'm encouraged that he actually expressed an interest in doing something ... anything. When can he come back and how often?"

"On the way home, ask Brian how often he wants to come. Meanwhile the rest of us will discuss how we can schedule times for him. We can compare notes later and see how to set up the sessions."

With another "Thanks" he left, and M&M sat down to talk over the introductory ride with the others. They felt that Brian would benefit by riding three times a week, with plans to lengthen his sessions as he grew stronger. Dr. Clay said he would like to have a counseling session with him within the next week or so. "Have his dad call my office and set up an appointment. After our initial session, I can better determine when we need another appointment."

Stanley said he would be available three times a week during the rest of the spring. "Just let me know what days and times to set aside."

Dr. Hood was encouraged to see how protective and

encouraging the team had been, and he told them so. "I don't think I need to be here to watch every session. Just keep me informed, and if it's okay, I'll stop in occasionally."

Susanna said, "As the mother of twins, I am not sure I can always commit to a certain time three days a week."

"That's okay, Susanna." M&M said. "If we schedule the sessions in the afternoon, then Jerry can be the horse handler when you can't. I'd like for him to get to know Brian anyway."

Comfortable that they had a plan in place, they were leaving when Jerry got home from school. "Hey, how'd it go with Brian's first ride?" he asked.

M&M answered honestly, "It was very short, very slow, but a good beginning."

"Did he like to ride?"

She grinned. "I think so. He asked me if he could learn to ride like a cowboy?"

Jerry grinned too.

Susanna spoke up, "And you will have a job being on his team, because I'll need somebody else to be the horse handler part of the time."

"What does a horse handler do?" he asked.

"You just have to lead Goldilocks around, follow my directions of where to go," M&M assured him. "And we've already decided to schedule sessions in the afternoons, so you'll be home from school."

"Okay."

Susanna left for home with M&M and Jerry starting the next round of their usual exercise and training sessions before feeding time.

Chapter 8

The next session lasted longer and concluded with Brian smiling and his dad holding his breath.

M&M had noticed that the boy looked stronger and sat straighter. After halting at what everybody else thought was the end of the ride, she said, "Okay, now we're going to finish this session with something new. Brian, concentrate on keeping those heels down to absorb the bounce when Goldilocks trots with you."

With Susanna clucking to the horse, both of them trotted along, with Brian bouncing a bit but managing to remain upright. M&M only let them take a few strides before telling Brian to stop his horse.

"Always good to stop with an accomplishment," she said.

"You were awesome," Stanley told the proud rider, and Susanna praised him too.

When Doug Wilson found his voice, he echoed their comments. "Good job, son, I would have bounced right off that horse, but you didn't."

Brian just kept grinning while he managed to dismount with little assistance.

"I wanted to try and walk back to the truck today, but I think my knees will fold up," he told his dad as he sank into the wheelchair.

"That's okay," M&M told him, "You showed real improvement since your first ride. You *will* be riding like a

Wildflower Wednesday

cowboy one of these days."

The group briefly compared scheduling plans and agreed that they could set up sessions on Monday, Wednesday, and Friday afternoons for several weeks, then take another look at how they wanted to proceed.

As they started to leave, Susanna said, "Brian, I won't always be able to come because of my little twins, but we've already got it planned out. When I can't come, Jerry will lead the horse for you. Just know that I'll miss you when I can't be here, and I can hardly wait to see you ride like a cowboy."

Doug nodded his thanks to the people who had formed a team for his son, and then stepped into his truck to head home.

"Well, what do ya'll *really* think about how it's going?" M&M asked.

Stanley and Susanna agreed that they were off to a great start, already seeing Brian looking stronger, happier, and best of all, determined to improve.

Doug Wilson called M&M that night and reinforced that opinion. "I guess I just need to say 'thank you' *again*. Two times on that cute horse of yours, and he came home with an appetite. He even chatted during supper—told Jean and Jessie all about his ride. He said he wished he could ride *every* day, and that gave me some leverage to insist he do his schoolwork and rehab sessions. Maybe he'll even want to do better in those areas too."

M&M appreciated the report, and said so, ending the call with, "Thanks so much for calling."

"Who was that?" Jerry wanted to know.

"Brian's dad. He just called to say 'thanks' again. He's very pleased that Brian is showing an interest in coming to ride, or anything, for that matter."

"Gee, Mom, I don't know whether to look forward to meeting him or dreading it. I don't know what to say to him or anything."

"I understand that. I wasn't sure how to talk to him either, at first. Just be yourself. Try to talk to him like you would anybody else. Just be sensitive about how fragile he is and why."

Jerry nodded, but M&M doubted her son felt any more confident about meeting Brian.

*****

Two days later, Jerry got to practice what his mom had suggested.

Susanna called and said, "Sorry, this is last minute, but Laura and Lee are both teething, crying and feverish. We can't get them down for their naps, and I hate to leave John to keep consoling both of them."

"Not to worry," M&M told her friend, "Jerry can lead a horse as well as anybody, and I think it's time he and Brian got acquainted."

He was already at the barn to groom and saddle Goldilocks when M&M went to tell him, "You're horse handler of the day."

Stanley arrived next, soon followed by Brian and his dad.

Jerry put Goldilocks in crossties and went out to the truck.

"Hi, I'm Jerry. Sorry I'm not pretty like Mom's friend Susanna, but you're stuck with me as your horse handler today."

"Thanks for helping out," Doug Wilson said, nudging Brian to say the same.

"Yeah, thanks. I just hate having an audience. Wish it could just be me and your mom for these sessions."

"Well, I have good news for you. Keep getting stronger and improving your riding ability and you can ride with just my mom watching, *and* barking orders at you like a drill sergeant."

"She hasn't seemed like that at all," Brian protested.

"Just you wait and see. She will."

Brian's apprehensive look got Jerry's attention.

"She's not *mean*, I don't want you to even think that. She's just a really good teacher and she expects her riding students to be *the* best."

"I guess that means you're a really good rider," Brian said.

"I'm good enough, I guess, but I was practically born on a horse *and* I have a good teacher."

Doug interrupted their exchange by suggesting, "Let's get started."

He already had the chair in position and Brian slid down into it, then insisted on propelling it himself.

M&M met everybody at the arena gate and sent Jerry to bring Goldilocks to the mounting block.

"I guess you've met Jerry," she said to Brian. "He's been looking forward to getting to know you, so I didn't have to twist his arm about being the horse handler for today."

Brian nodded and glanced around to see Jerry approaching with Goldilocks. He brightened, and reached out to let the mare nuzzle his hand.

"We'll get a treat for her after you ride," M&M told him.

Brian managed to haul himself up the three steps, paused to catch his breath and then lifted his leg over the horse's back and settled into place.

"Good job," M&M and Stanley said in unison, and then the mare took her cue and walked along beside Jerry.

After a couple of circles, M&M said, "Let's see if we can pick up the pace a little. Jerry, I don't want her to trot, but I do want to her walk as fast as she can. She and Brian both look like they're falling asleep on me."

Jerry nodded and took bigger strides, forcing the horse to keep up. Brian slouched slightly sideways and then back and Stanley gripped his upper leg, thinking he needed support to remain in the saddle.

"No, Stanley, it's okay," Jerry said, "Mom, didn't you *see* it. Brian's moving his hips just a little, but he's in rhythm with the horse."

"Good eye, son."

Then she gave a thumbs up to Brian.

"Keep going," she told both boys.

They again ended the ride with a trotting session, this time for a full big circle around M&M.

Brian was tired, but stronger than on his previous ride. When he dismounted, without assistance, he managed to hold onto the saddle to keep his knees from folding up, then sank into his chair.

"Hey, I bet you're tired. Me too," Jerry told him. "Mom made cookies and lemonade. Let's have some."

Stanley had to leave for other appointments, but Brian and his dad joined Jerry and M&M at the little table to enjoy refreshments.

Brian asked Jerry, "What did you mean about me being in rhythm? Stanley thought I was sliding off the horse, but I didn't feel like I was."

Jerry looked to his mom and she nodded permission. "What I meant was, your seat was feeling the horse move and you were moving the same way. You weren't just a passenger, you were a rider."

"Is that good?"

"It's your first step towards riding like a cowboy," M&M told him.

The Wilsons soon departed with both saying they looked forward to the next session.

Two days later, they were back. The sessions continued for several weeks, with Brian continuing to show improvement in balance and strength. M&M thought he looked healthier too, like he'd put on a few pounds. He talked more, especially to Jerry. She was glad the two boys seemed to get along.

Chapter 9

Brian dozed off for a few minutes, then awoke with questions he could only ask his dad.

Doug glanced over when Brian stirred and sat up straighter. "I expected you to sleep all the way home."

"Not as tired as I thought I'd be," Brian admitted, then continued, "Dad, do you think Jerry likes me?"

"Sure. Why wouldn't he?"

"Well, you know, he could be just being extra nice to me because his mom has set up this program for me to ride."

He paused, then continued, "Well, I've overheard enough of your conversations to know that she's strapped for money, and you are paying her for these sessions. Maybe Jerry just thinks he *has* to be nice to me."

Brian paused again, then asked, "So what do you think? Does he like me, or does he think he has to act like he does?"

Doug Wilson sighed and spoke the truth as he'd always promised his sons, "I don't know for sure, son, but I'm guessing it could be some of both. Now, tell me why you'd even ask such a question?"

"Because, I guess I want him for a friend."

Doug smiled, recalling what his own father had told him, "You can never have too many friends."

He repeated those words to Brian, then added, "It seems to me, though, that you have lots of friends from school and the soccer team."

"Yeah, maybe. But it's not the same now. Some of the soccer

kids act mad at me because I can't play anymore, like I'm letting them down."

Tears began to fall then, both Brian's and his father's.

Doug recovered first, reaching out and touching Brian's shoulder. "I know, son. These are tough times. But we'll get through them." Almost as an afterthought, he added, "And I think it's good that we have Ms. Johnson and her son on our side, whatever their reasons."

*****

Back at Pine Park, Jerry and his mom were having a similar conversation.

"I'm glad to see you getting on so well with Brian," M&M said.

"Me too. I wasn't sure about it, at first. You know, I do feel sorry for him, losing his mom and brother plus being hurt so badly, but when I look past that, I really *do* like him. I don't know how much we'll have in common, but right now we both have the same goal—get him strong."

"Don't forget, he wants to ride like a cowboy. You can show him how it's done," M&M reminded him.

"Is he just sayin' that?"

"Not sure, but I *think* he means it."

Jerry thought about that for a while, then spoke up. "Mom, if he's gonna be a real rider, you know, after he's strong and well, we've gotta get him off Goldilocks."

"I know. But first things first. He's not too heavy for her right now, and he's got a long way to go before we worry about matching him to a horse that fits."

"How long do you think it'll take to get him going, you know, like a cowboy?"

M&M shook her head. "I don't know."

*****

Two days later, Brian and Doug Wilson were back for

another session.

M&M met them in the drive and noticed Brian's smile as he stepped out of the truck without assistance.

He took the walker his father unloaded for him and pushed it along to the barn.

Doug was shaking his head and frowning as he told M&M, "He's insisted on walking to and from the barn today, *without* help from me. He's gonna be tired before he gets on the horse."

"I heard that," Brian snapped.

"It's okay," M&M assured them. "The wonderful thing about riding a horse is letting it be your legs when you need to."

Just then, Jerry came out of the barn leading the palomino mare.

Stanley was waiting for them at the arena gate. M&M motioned for them all to go to the mounting block.

Jerry put Goldilocks in the perfect position for Brian to mount. He struggled but managed to get up the steps and onto the horse without assistance.

"Well done," said M&M, and Jerry nodded.

Brian's shoulders slumped as he relaxed and let out a breath, then slid his feet into the stirrups, straightened himself and looked right between the horse's ears.

"*Walk on,*" he said firmly, and Goldilocks responded. The group moved around and around the arena while Doug watched from the gate. M&M asked Brian if he wanted to try the trot again and he grinned. "I thought you'd never ask."

The little mare again took her cue and went round again, with Brian managing not to bounce sideways. When M&M thought her student was tiring, she called for a halt and Goldilocks didn't take another step after Brian called out, "Whoa."

"You're doing great!" she told him and meant it.

Brian managed to dismount without mishap, clinging to the

saddle when his feet touched the ground.

By then, his dad was at his side with the walker and he balanced himself with the handles, then leaned in and hugged Goldilocks before walking away.

M&M suggested they all go to the picnic table, sit down to talk about the session, and plan for the next one.

"What about the lemonade and cookies?" Jerry asked.

She smiled at her son. "That too, as soon as you unsaddle Goldilocks and turn her out in the paddock."

Stanley had to leave but the others took their seats around the table and thanked M&M for the cold lemonade.

She had already gotten Stanley's opinion on Brian's progress and started the discussion.

"I think we're ready to give Brian more responsibility with his horse.".

"What do you mean?" Doug asked.

"I checked with Stanley as he was leaving. He agrees with me that Brian is making such good progress that he doesn't need to hang onto him like he's been doing."

Jerry spoke up then, "He's not hanging onto the saddle horn, maybe he can handle the reins too."

Brian brightened at that. "You mean you won't have to lead me around like a baby?"

"Wait a minute," M&M cautioned. "One thing at a time."

She carefully explained that Brian would advance slowly, making just one change in the process for each session until he could be "on his own" astride the horse.

Brian grinned at that, thanked both M&M and Jerry and said he was ready to go home.

*****

On the way home, Brian dozed briefly, then awoke and started talking. " You know, Dad, it's neat that I can start riding by myself, sort of. I won't feel like such a baby."

Wildflower Wednesday

"You're no baby, Brian, but you've been critically injured. We don't want any accidents, on or off a horse, to set you back."

"I get that, but now that I'm gaining strength and weight, I'm really trying to do the things to be *normal* again—whatever that is."

"You'll get there. It's just gonna take some time."

"I know, but don't you think we can skip the nurse staying with me?"

Doug Wilson drew in a sharp breath and shook his head. "Brian, I have to go to the office at least part of every day. I haven't felt like it was safe to leave you alone. What if you fall and re-injure your leg? Or bang your head?"

"But, Dad, I'm never by myself. Jean is always in the house, and Jessie is nearby. And I'm not gonna fall. I *promise*, I'll use the walker or cane and I'll be really careful."

When his dad didn't quickly agree, Brian continued, "I'll do physical therapy *every* day and I'll work harder on my studies, if you'll get rid of my nurse."

Doug was still thinking when Brian begged, *"Please."*

"What's the deal? Don't you like him?"

"It's not that, exactly. He's okay. He just treats me like I'm about a year old. Maybe it's his job, but I hate feeling like I'm as helpless as an infant."

"Okay, Brian. Let's get on home and talk with Jean and Jessie to be sure they can be close when I'm working. I'll want to speak with your doctors and the physical therapist too. Let's be sure your new plea for independence is safe."

"Fair enough," Brian agreed and closed his eyes for another nap.

He was still tired when the truck stopped at the house, but he insisted that Doug hand him the walker and let him go inside without assistance.

"See, Dad, I can do this."

Chapter 10

M&M was shaking her head in disbelief when she ended the third call of the morning.

Three different people had called to offer use of their horses for her yet-to-be scheduled summer camp. Two were horses she had trained for their amateur owners to show, and she knew them to be gentle and even-tempered. The third was unknown to her, but the owner was a senior citizen M&M had coached several years ago. She deemed herself too old to continue in the show ring and wanted her fourteen-year-old gelding to have a good home.

Then Tiffany called. She was laughing. "Remember my highway patrolman friend? Well, I ran into him in the grocery store parking lot. He had heard about the SSS riding class and said one of the mounted patrol deputies was looking for someplace to send his mounted patrol horse for retirement. He's tried turning him out to pasture, but apparently the poor ol' fellow hates being by himself and paces the fence. You'll be getting a call. The guy's name is Bill Blackman, and his horse is Sarge."

Susanna walked in as M&M was tucking the cell phone into her jacket pocket.

"I've talked to John, and we want you to use Gwen this summer, for camp or therapy classes, or both, if she fits your needs."

M&M opened her mouth to argue, then thought better of it.

"Listen, *Girlfriend*," Susanna told her, "This is a win-win situation. It'll get Gwen away from her baby and back into condition, plus she'll love the attention."

"And I get another horse for my camp and therapy sessions."

"That's right."

"I can hardly believe this. Gwen is the fourth or fifth horse I've been offered *this* morning."

"How many more do you need?" Susanna asked.

"I'm not sure. I've been thinking that a total of 12 horses will be about all I can manage and that should be enough to have a good summer camp program. If I have the right horses, they'll fit for therapy sessions too, if I do them."

M&M frowned when she glanced at the clock on her kitchen wall. "Right now, I need to get out to the barn and started riding. I have three horses here for training."

Susanna grinned. "Remember when I used to come out here and hang around, willing to do anything just to be around horses?"

M&M smiled at the memory. "Yep, I remember."

"Well, I have a couple of hours to spend out here, so give me something to do."

M&M could see that she meant it, so she sent her to exercise the feisty dun gelding on a lounge line before she saddled him. "You'll save me time and possibly a tumble in the dirt," she assured her friend.

Thirty minutes later, Susanna handed off the gelding and took the big chestnut filly back to the wash rack to rinse her off before putting her in a turnout paddock.

M&M glanced back to see her friend checking water buckets then getting out the wheelbarrow and fork to pick out stalls.

"I am *blessed*," she told herself.

Before noon, she had her rides done and was making iced

tea to share with Susanna.

"So, this afternoon, I'll sit down with Jerry and work on our camp plan some more. He's pumped about being a *counselor*, you know," she told Susanna.

"Well, I'm looking forward to being a part of it. So's Tiffany."

Susanna glanced at her watch and jumped to her feet. "Gotta go, Mom's with the twins and she has a noon appointment somewhere."

"Thanks," M&M called to Susanna as she dashed out the door.

She was in the barn saddling the pony called Patches when Jerry got home.

"Hey, Mom!" he yelled to her from the kitchen door, "Do we have cookies?"

She hollered back, letting him know to look in the refrigerator for lemon bars and milk, then led the pony out into the sunshine.

Patty's mom drove up to the arena and the little girl jumped out and raced toward the barn.

"I brought carrots for her!" she told M&M. "Is it okay?"

"Absolutely. Horses and ponies usually love carrots, but why not let your mom hold those carrots until after your lesson, then we can take off the bridle and give them to her."

Patty nodded and handed the little bag of carrots to her mom, who had hurried from the car.

M&M took charge of the child and the pony and soon had them circling around her in the center of the riding arena.

After a few rounds, she encouraged Patty to prod the pony into a trot.

"This is fun!" the child squealed as she bounced along.

M&M thought so too. She just wished all her sessions were so pleasant. She had a couple of teenagers coming next hour.

Wildflower Wednesday

As promised, when Patty's lesson ended and she was back on the ground, M&M removed the bridle and slipped a halter over the pony's head. Then she held out her hand to show Patty how to feed carrots without getting bit.

As they walked back to the barn together, Patty's mother asked about lesson schedules for the summer.

"I'm just now working on plans to have summer day camp sessions at Pine Park. I'm not sure if there will be enough children in Patty's age group to have a session."

"But I can come ride, can't I?"

M&M assured her, "Even if we don't have a camp class for you, I'll always make sure you can come and ride."

The little girl beamed her thanks and skipped back to the car.

Jerry saw her as he was coming out, and when he got to M&M's side, he said, "She's certainly a happy looking little kid."

"She's a delightful little girl who loves horses. She wants to come ride this summer."

"Do you think you'll have kids that little for camp?" he asked.

"I don't know. But our agenda—yours and mine for tonight—is to start planning for camp. I'll need all the help you can give me in setting it up."

"Okay, but what do you need me to do *now*?"

"Your usual routine—lunge line for Stormy, then turn him out in the paddock, give the pony a quick grooming and start the stall cleaning. You know the drill."

"Yeah, but what are you gonna be doing?" he asked.

Just then a bright red convertible whirled into the drive, and he recognized the driver.

"I'm surprised those snobby girls came back. I hope they act nicer here than they do at school. Good luck with them, Mom. I'd rather clean stalls than talk to them any day."

M&M straightened her shoulders and went to meet the teens. When she reminded them that they had signed up for a lengthy session that included horse management one actually turned up her nose about brushing and saddling the horse she would be riding. The other one complained that "Horses stink when they sweat. Are they gonna be that hot when we ride?"

"That's pretty much up to you," M&M answered.

Clearly, neither girl understood the reply. They whined their way through a light grooming of their mounts, needed help with the "heavy" western saddles, and one couldn't lift her leg high enough to get her foot into the stirrup. M&M directed her to the mounting block and suggested that she would manage better in jeans that weren't quite so tight.

The riding session didn't go particularly well either. The girls didn't seem to care about the horses or improving their minimal riding skills. When M&M told them, "Time's up for today," they seemed as relieved as she felt. She didn't even direct them to unsaddle the horses and put them back in stalls, even though it was part of the horse management session. She just took reins in each hand and told them goodbye, knowing full well they wouldn't be returning.

She made a face at Jerry when he came around the corner of the barn.

"Told ya," he said with a grin.

Mother and son finished the evening chores and headed to the house for supper, with Jerry still talking about "those snooty girls."

"Forget them. We have more important things to discuss."

As they ate, she told him they needed to figure out a summer camp program.

"We have the offer of several horses to use. That's great, *but* more horses mean more feed, more stalls to clean, more bedding to put in those stalls—you get the idea."

"Yeah. It's gonna mean bigger bills to pay. So, how much money will camp bring in?"

"I regret to say that I don't have any idea. Here's how you can really help. You're better on the computer than I'll ever be. Can you check out some horsey type summer camps and find out what activities they offer and how much they charge?"

"Sure, Mom. And while I do that, why don't you think about ways to cut down maintenance?"

"What do you mean?"

"Well, do the horses have to be stalled all the time? We have paddocks with access to sheds. Then, I wouldn't have so many stalls to keep clean."

When M&M nodded, he continued, "And couldn't part of a horsey camp, as you call it, involve kids learning to take care of horses, like doing some of the grooming, cleaning tack and filling feeders. Not that I mind doing all that, you know."

"Very clever!" M&M told him. "Go get on the computer."

M&M was pleasantly surprised when he came back to the kitchen table with the facts and figures he'd gathered in just over an hour.

"Look at this, Mom! People pay *lots* of money for their kids to spend the day not just riding, but doing all the other things that go along with having horses."

When she and Jerry finished going over the information he'd gathered, M&M breathed a sigh of relief. She *knew* they could have a profitable summer at Pine Park.

Chapter 11

Jerry kept talking about summer camp the next time Brian came to ride.

When they took their refreshment break, Brian wanted to know more.

"You sound like you're looking forward to it.," he said to both Jerry and M&M.

"We are, or at least I am," Jerry answered. "I love horses, everything about them, even the grubby work of grooming and keeping stalls clean and all that. I love the smell of the leather when I help clean tack. I think it's gonna be fun to share that with younger kids."

Brian smiled. "You *are* making it sound fun," He paused and then turned to M&M, "Do you think I could come over and watch, maybe help out in some way?"

Doug Wilson stared at his son, and Brian noticed.

"Yeah, Dad. I really do like horses, a lot. And I always like coming here."

M&M spoke up, "Sure you can come, Brian. And be careful about wanting to help. I never turn down volunteers."

Brian grinned and paused before answering, "But I don't want to just hang out or be in the way. I wanna be part of it."

M&M glanced at Doug, hoping for an approving nod before saying, "We'll find some tasks for you, depending on how strong you are by the time school is out and camp starts. You be thinking about what parts of horsemanship appeal most to you—what you would want to share with little kids."

Doug took the opportunity to remind Brian that he had to get his grades up above average or he'd be doing summer courses to catch up. He also tossed in the pledge Brian made to keep all his physical therapy appointments and working on the exercises.

"I can do all that, Dad. I will. You'll see."

When the Wilsons left, M&M asked Jerry what he thought about the conversation.

"I was kinda surprised. I didn't know Brian liked horses or being here *that* much. I guess it makes me feel good though, like we really *are* helping him."

"Me too," she answered. "But now, we have to come up with some ideas for how he really can help with summer camp."

*****

Brian had drifted off to sleep, but he stirred halfway to Longview. He sat up straight and started firing questions to his dad.

"So, do you think they really meant it, that I can help at summer camp?"

"I'm guessing they did. I haven't known Ms. Johnson or her son to be anything but honest."

"Then I have something to look forward to this summer."

"Just remember you have to do your part—about school and therapy and everything. That reminds me, you have a counseling appointment coming up with that Dr. Clay in Marshall."

"Do I hafta do that?"

"Yep, I'm afraid so. It's part of the package that your 'team' put together, and we agreed to it."

Brian sulked the rest of the way home.

But when they got out of the truck, he had another idea to toss at his father.

"Dad, could I start swimming in the pool? The PT guy says water exercise is good."

"Son, I just had Jessie uncover the pool. The water is still cold. And I'm not sure you're strong enough, yet. Let's wait."

The disappointed teenager hung his head, then jerked it up with yet another idea.

"So, how about if you turn on the pool heater. And I can start just by doing those stretching exercises and stuff, not in deep water. Somebody can watch me and pull me out if I sink."

Doug Wilson was shaking his head when he noticed the impish grin on Brian's face, just before he began to laugh.

"What's so funny?"

"I just remembered something Mom told me. You were a *lifeguard* at the city pool when you were in high school. So, why can't *you* watch me, or even swim with me?"

"Make an *A* on your next algebra test and it's a deal."

Brian laughed again. "Better turn on the pool heater."

After Brian went to his room to finish his schoolwork, Doug really wanted to thank the Johnsons for helping bring his son to this point. He punched in the number, and feeling awkward to still call her Ms. Johnson, he just said, "Hi, this is Doug," when she answered.

"Is everything okay?" she asked.

"Better than okay. I just wanted to thank both you and your son for helping Brian. He's actually laughing now, promising to get his grades up and wants to start swimming."

"Water exercise is supposed to be wonderful," she volunteered.

"So he told me. Won't keep you any longer, just wanted you to know how much I appreciate all you've been doing." He hung up before she had a chance to say anything.

He checked and found Jean in the kitchen and asked if Jessie was around.

"He's out somewhere in the flower gardens," Doug nodded and went to find him.

He caught sight of him trimming the tea roses around the gazebo and walked out to have a talk with his longtime employee and friend.

"Jessie, Brian has asked about starting to use the pool, so could you check the chemical balances and turn on the heater tomorrow?"

"Sure thing, Mr. Doug. It's wonderful to see that boy come back to life. He looks better every day,"

"Yes, he does, and it *is* wonderful. And I thought I told you awhile back to stop calling me Mr."

"I know, but you're my boss, and I respect my position here."

"And I'm glad to have you and Jean. You're like part of the family. We'll have to figure out this name business."

Doug laughed then. "I'm having a problem about somebody's name too. The woman who has helped Brian by doing those sessions with the horse—I feel like I know her well enough to stop calling her 'Ms. Johnson,' but...."

Jessie wondered aloud, "Do you know what her friends call her?"

"Yes, she has a silly nickname. I just can't quite bring myself to call her M&M."

He went back in the house shaking his head over such an independent adult woman with such a childish name.

Inside he found Brian in the kitchen with Jean. She had just baked cookies for him, and he had a mouthful.

As soon as he washed it down with his milk, Brian said, "Dad, I've been thinking. The Johnsons have been *so* nice to us, and we always have some kind of snacks and drinks after I ride, why don't we invite them over for lunch or something, sort of a thank you."

"That's thoughtful of you, and yes, we can do that."

He turned to Jean, "Are you up for cooking a meal for a couple more people?"

She chuckled and nodded, "You know I am."

Doug told her he'd do the inviting next time they were over at Pine Park and let her know when their new friends would be coming over.

First, they had to get through that counseling appointment that Brian dreaded. It was set for the next morning.

*****

Doug dreaded the appointment too, fearful that it would set Brian back in some way. Both of them were quiet on the drive over to Dr. Clay's office.

An hour later, they were back in the truck and Brian was smiling.

Relieved, Doug asked, "So, it wasn't so bad, huh?"

"No, nothing like I expected. Dr, Clay is *nice*. He made me feel like a normal, real person instead of a lunatic."

"Good. So, I guess you won't mind so much seeing him once every few weeks, whatever your 'team' over here recommends."

"No, it's okay. Dad, could we stop by Pine Park and invite Brian and his mom to come for lunch sometime soon?"

"Don't see why not," he answered as he turned the truck down the highway leading to Pine Park.

When they arrived, M&M was in the arena on a horse that seemed to be doing everything possible to unseat her.

The big chestnut gelding jumped sideways, then tried to buck. When she pulled his head up, he reared. She threw her weight forward, sending him back onto all four feet, then pulled him in a tight circle. The horse was breathing hard and sweating when she brought him to a stop.

"Think it over, big boy. You'll like me better if you do what I ask."

Wildflower Wednesday

She had the horse trotting smartly along the rail before she noticed Doug and Brian standing by the gate.

"Wow! She really can ride," Brian said as she approached.

"Sorry, I didn't see you here 'til just now," she called to them as she halted the horse.

"You were pretty busy with that bronc," Doug replied. "Clearly, we are interrupting your work. We just stopped by to invite you and Jerry to come over to our place for lunch, whatever day works for you. We want to thank you for everything. As Brian pointed out to me last night, you offer cold drinks and snacks all the time. It's our turn."

"That's really nice, but not necessary," she said.

Brian looked disappointed so Doug said, "Not necessary maybe, but we *want* you to come. I promise, Jean is a great cook and is already looking forward to preparing a meal for you."

"Then, thank you. I'm afraid the only day of the week that will work is Sunday. Is that okay?"

Brian beamed and Doug nodded, "Sunday it is. I'll send you directions to the house and look for you about noon."

They waved and left, leaving M&M again talking to her uncooperative mount.

Chapter 12

Jerry was so excited Sunday morning that M&M had to remind him about filling water buckets and hay nets at the barn.

In their pickup, Jerry said, "Gosh, Mom, we hardly ever go anywhere for fun. I can hardly wait to get there and see the Wilson's house and eat something different. You know."

"I *do* know. We don't get out much, and I work you so hard you don't have much of a social life."

He laughed then. "It's not *that* bad. You let me have friends over, and I go on the judging team trips and do some fun stuff with the band."

M&M stopped talking as she carefully watched her GPS and followed directions to the address Doug had given her.

When they reached the turn, both she and Jerry gasped in surprise. The gated entrance was bordered by massive brick corner supports. The entire property appeared to be surrounded by heavy metal fencing.

Doug had told her about the security gate, and given her the code numbers to punch in, but she'd never expected anything so elaborate. The long drive led to a stately brick two story with columned front porch.

"Gosh, Mom, they live in a mansion!" Jerry exclaimed as they pulled closer to the house.

M&M had no idea where to park, but she slowed as she approached the three-car garage.

Just then Doug stepped outside and waved to her. He called

Wildflower Wednesday

out, "Come on up to the front of the house, it's a circular drive."

By the time she had stopped her truck, Brian was carefully maneuvering his way down the porch steps. "Come on in," he told them.

Doug had gone back inside and was standing at the massive front door when they reached it. He, too, welcomed them inside.

A bit overwhelmed, M&M briefly felt like backing out the door and going home to change her clothing. Then she realized that both Doug and Brian were casually attired in jeans and polo shirts, much like Jerry was wearing. She let out an audible sigh of relief and Doug asked, "Did you have trouble finding us?"

"Oh, no. You gave excellent directions. I guess we just weren't expecting such a huge place. Your house looks like a southern mansion."

Doug grinned, "Lyndsey was an interior decorator. She liked the look. Brian and I aren't into formality, so I hope you won't mind that we'll be having lunch out back in the gazebo."

M&M, relieved that they weren't about to be seated in a formal dining room, nodded and said, "That sounds lovely."

Doug led the way through the house to the back porch which overlooked formal gardens. He pointed down a winding stone path to the gazebo and asked Brian if he wanted his walker or the motorized wheelchair.

"Nope! I've practiced going on the path with my cane, and I can do it."

The foursome proceeded slowly so Brian could keep up. When they reached the gazebo, M&M noticed that he chose to sit down and catch his breath, but he gave her a smile and a thumbs up when she asked if he was okay.

Doug smiled too. "I didn't know you've been working so hard at getting around outside. Good job."

Then he turned back to M&M and Jerry and said, "The formal garden was Lyndsey's idea. I'm more of a country boy, so I got Jessie to plant something different for me."

He pointed down the hill to a field filled with bluebonnets, bordered by Indian paintbrush, poppies, and other native wildflowers. "Looks more like Texas, doesn't it?"

She nodded. "It does, and it's beautiful. I forget from one year to the next, how much I love the Texas wildflowers in the spring,"

"Who's Jessie," Jerry wondered aloud.

"You'll be meeting him later. He's our landscaper, among other things," Doug answered.

"And his wife, Jean, is our housekeeper and our cook, among other things," Brian added. "She made lunch for us. I don't know what we're having, but I know it'll be yummy."

M&M was intrigued to hear that the woman had prepared a meal for them on Sunday, normally a day off for almost everyone.

Seeing her puzzled look, Doug explained, "Jessie and Jean live on the property. They have a cottage near the pool, which you can't see from here. I'm sure Brian is going to escort you to the pool later, since he is already bugging me about swimming."

"Isn't it too cool?"

"Not anymore," Brian answered. "I got Dad to turn on the pool heater the other day. Now all I have to do to get to swim is make an *A* on my next test."

M&M grinned and whispered to Doug, "Bribery works."

They were all seated at the round glass top table enjoying the mint tea when a golf cart approached. The driver, a rather heavyset woman with a broad smile, pulled right up to the edge of the gazebo and stepped out.

Doug introduced them and Jean said, "I'm so glad to see friends coming 'round here, and I hope you like what I've cooked up for your lunch."

"You know we will," Brian said.

Jean had the entire meal in the back of the cart, all in covered dishes. She handed out plates, silverware and napkins and encouraged the foursome to "Come and get it," as she took lids off the food.

"Wow! My favorite," Brian said when he saw the fried chicken.

M&M inhaled and turned to Jean, "It not only looks delicious, it smells heavenly. Thank you for preparing such a delightful meal for us."

"My pleasure," Jean answered as Doug gave her an approving nod.

She waved, stepped back onto the golf cart and left them to their lunch, with a promise to bring out dessert later.

Jerry said, "This is great," more than once, and M&M volunteered that both of them loved eating something she hadn't cooked in a hurry after a day in the barn.

She was pleasantly surprised to notice that Brian was eating a plateful of chicken.

Doug noticed and told her, "Brian's got his appetite back, thanks to you and Goldilocks."

"I'm not sure we can take credit for it, but it's good to see. Brian, you are looking stronger every time I see you."

"I am, and I'm working to be better every day. That's one reason I want to get into the pool. Water exercise is supposed to be a good thing."

Brian turned to Jerry, and asked, "Do you like to swim?"

"Sure."

"Then sometime maybe you can come back over and go swimming with me."

"Okay."

The boys finished their food and Brian asked if he could show Jerry the pool.

Doug paused, then agreed with the reminder that going into

the water was still off limits.

When Jerry and Brian made their way down the path, Doug turned to M&M and told her, "You *do* get credit for the wonderful change in Brian. Until I took him over to Pine Park, he wasn't interested in anything. He's so much better, more like my Brian was before...."

M&M felt a mixture of guilt and gratitude. "Doug, I told you then, and I'm telling you now, I was not and am not a therapist, but I am happy to see such improvement in Brian. And if I've helped make that happen, I'm grateful too."

Doug asked, "So, now that you've seen the success with him, are you thinking about starting an official equine therapy program?"

"I don't know. Maybe. I'd like to. But there's some cost and time involved in getting certification. I can't think about that right now. I think you know I'm setting up a summer camp program to boost my income."

"Will you still be able to do some training and private lessons?"

She wondered why he asked. "Yes, of course. I'll have to. I wouldn't think of giving up any of my clients or students, but if you're wondering, I'll always make time for working with Brian."

"How do you do it?"

"Do what?"

"Working hard, as hard as any man I know—taking care of your horses, your barn, training horses and riders, and being a good mom."

"Doug, I'm doing what I love. And it's all I know. So, I just keep putting one foot in front of the other."

"I admire you for that."

Just a little surprised, and uncomfortable with the compliment, M&M asked, "Do you think we should go check on the boys?"

"No need. Brian is as good as his word. He won't go into the pool until he gets that *A*. Let's give them a chance to spend time together, they seem to be getting on well."

M&M had to agree to that, so she sat with Doug and enjoyed the incredible view from the gazebo.

"You're quiet today," he observed.

"It's just that I'm not barking orders to kids or horses," she said, "And honestly, I'm somewhat overwhelmed and don't know what to say about your beautiful estate."

He laughed, "Estate! Is that what you call it?"

"I guess," she stammered, "It's just, well, a bit overwhelming."

Doug laughed again. "It just not what you expected from a pushy ol' guy like me, right?"

"Something like that," she admitted.

"Well, I should explain a bit about this 'estate'. The acreage was my idea. And I wanted a big house, plenty of room for kids and their friends, that kinda thing. The dressed-up version—including a formal dining room, the furnishings and décor, were all Lyndsey's doing."

"Are you okay to talk about her?" M&M asked.

"Sure, now I am. It was a while in coming. I loved her, I miss her, but I've accepted that she's gone."

"That part I understand."

"Well, by now you may have guessed that Lyndsey and I were a team, totally different people yet we made a great partnership. I was a farm boy, went to college two years because my parents wanted me to. I determined after two years of mediocre grades that nothing I learned there was going to help me and I was, therefore, wasting my parents' money, so I quit."

He went on to tell her that he was always drawn to the land, so he went to real estate school and became an agent specializing in farm property.

"I tried my skills at upscale ranch homes, and that's when I met Lyndsey. She was just getting started as a decorator and had staged a house for one of my clients. I was stunned at how different she made the place look and how quickly it sold."

"And the rest is history, right?"

"Yeah, pretty much. We both loved our work, and soon loved each other. Like I said, we were a good team."

Doug paused. His voice quivered when he said, "I don't get to talk about her much. Thanks for being a good listener."

*****

Jerry took one good look at the pool and just said, "Wow!"

"What?"

Taking his time to look at the intricate tile work, with dolphins, sea turtles and starfish highlighting the bright sea blue of the pool, Jerry finally said, "This is the most beautiful swimming pool I've ever seen. And it's *huge*."

"Yeah, it is big. My dad said he wanted it big enough to *really* swim in it. My mom wanted it to be pretty. She liked fancy stuff. She picked out all the furniture and everything for our house."

Jerry didn't say anything else and Brian finally asked, "Something wrong? You seem really quiet."

Jerry threw his hands up in the air and said, "All this has me just about speechless. I guess I just didn't know ya'll lived in a mansion."

Brian looked shocked at the term. "I've never thought of it like that. "It's just where we live. It was a lot better when my mom and my brother were here." He choked up then and shook his head, "Let's talk about something else."

Jerry agreed and the talk turned to horses and Brian's desire to ride like a cowboy.

"Do you really want to learn to ride broncs or something?"

Brian shook his head. "No, just be good on a horse, you know for fun. Maybe go on trail rides. I always wanted to go to a dude ranch for vacation. I think my dad did too. We just didn't get around to it."

He paused, remembering a trip the year before. "We did go to the Grand Canyon, and we rode mules down to the bottom. It was fun."

"Where do you go on vacations?" Brian asked.

Jerry laughed. "We call it a 'working vacation' when we go to a big horse show or sale and stay two or three days. It's sorta a vacation, but it's also part of my mom's work to keep Pine Park in business."

"Is *that* fun?"

"Part of it is. We usually stay in a place with a pool, and get to eat out, and there are usually quite a few people we know." Jerry thought aloud, "You must think I have a boring life."

"Why would you think that?"

"Because, you live in this mansion, with your own pool, and that entertainment area we walked by, I bet you can watch movies in there."

"We can. Maybe you can come over and see a good movie sometime," Brian grinned. "We even have a popcorn machine."

Jerry looked envious until Brian added, "It's just stuff. It was more fun when my brother was here."

Then he asked Jerry, "Ever wish you had a brother?"

Jerry shook his head, "I guess I never thought about it. It's always just been me and Mom. My dad died when I was real little. I really don't remember him, just know what Mom and our friends have told me."

He looked up to see his mom and Doug approaching. "Here comes Mom," he told Brian. "I bet we'll be leaving now because there are hungry horses and barn chores waiting."

He heard M&M telling Doug how much she'd enjoyed the

lunch and visit. He seconded that when they came closer, and Doug Wilson said, "It was a pleasure to have you both here, and I hope you'll come again."

As they drove down the long driveway, Jerry turned back for a last look and said, "Gee, Mom, they live in a mansion."

She chuckled. "I believe Mr. Wilson prefers to call it an estate."

Chapter 13

 Brian and his dad went back out to the gazebo to enjoy the view while they ate supper. Jean had brought them leftover fried chicken and made pimento cheese sandwiches for them before going to her own home.

 "This is good," Brian said as he munched on his sandwich.

 Doug happily agreed, "Jean's a good cook, and it's also good to see you have your appetite back."

 "I feel better too, and it was really neat to have Jerry and his mom over here for lunch. Do you think they had a good time? Can we have them over again?"

 "You've got a lot of questions run together there. I liked having them here too, and I think they enjoyed themselves, and certainly we can invite them over again sometime."

 Brian frowned and Doug noticed. "What's wrong?"

 "Nothing's *wrong*, it's just that Jerry seemed to think we live in a mansion, and that it made everything great."

 "We do have a nice house, Brian, and we're fortunate to be able to have everything we need or want."

 "I know, Dad, but...."

 "But what?"

 Unexpectedly, tears began to fall when Brian answered, "The house, the pool, everything was a lot more fun before...." He paused, struggled for control, then continued, "Now, it's just the two of us, and it's lonely here and it makes me miss them more."

Doug reached out, half-hugged his grieving son and said, "I know."

"Dad, could we move?"

Surprised, Doug answered as honestly as he could at the moment. "I guess we could. But where would we go and what would we want to be different?"

Brian had a quick answer. "Everything."

He continued, "I'd like a smaller house, so we didn't seem so alone. And I wouldn't mind living in Marshall. I could probably go ride every day."

Now shocked, Doug asked, "Brian, would you really want to leave your school, your friends here?"

"I think I would. My friends don't even know what to say to me, so they don't come around much. The soccer team guys are mad at me 'cause I can't play anymore."

Doug didn't know what to say. After a lengthy silence he told Brian, "You've given me a lot to think about."

When they went inside to go to bed, Doug was still thinking about all Brian had told him.

He realized that he had some of the same feelings about their current home. It seemed empty and sad without Lyndsey and Thomas. Maybe a different location would be good for them. Or would they just be trying to run away? He wasn't sure.

The next morning, he still wasn't sure, but he waited for Brian to join him for breakfast before he left for his office.

"Son, I've been thinking about our conversation last night. I definitely will consider relocating, but I do wonder if it would be a healthy move, emotionally, you know, for us. Can I go with you to your next counseling session? We can talk with the doc about it."

Brian nodded, "But could we talk to Dr. Clay instead of that guy here? "

"I guess so. But why?"

"I like him better. He doesn't tell me what I ought to be thinking. He just listens and helps me see things better in my head, you know."

Doug departed for his office with a reminder to Brian to study hard and get that *A*.

He drove to work wondering just how complicated it could be to move to Marshall.

When he arrived, he called Sam Cunningham into his private office.

"What's up, boss?" Sam asked as he came through the doorway.

Doug hardly knew where to begin, but he knew he could trust in both the confidentiality and the recommendations of his office manager. "Sam, I'm considering opening a satellite office in Marshall, and relocating there for purely personal reasons."

Sam abruptly sat down. "Wow! You know how to get a guy's attention first thing on a Monday morning."

"Okay, so how doable is it for me to run Wilson Real Estate from there instead of here, or would I need to commute daily?"

Sam paused before answering, "I think it's doable, certainly. I'm pretty sure you can expand your business in the Marshall area too, which would keep you busy there part of the time. I don't see why you'd have to commute back and forth on a daily basis, but your employees here certainly would need to see and speak with you on some kind of regular basis."

Doug smiled and continued, "Okay, we've established that the move is possible."

Sam merely nodded.

Then Doug continued, "Next question. You've been to my home. How marketable is it?"

"Tough question. It's a beautiful, desirable piece of property. I'm sure a lot of people would love to own it. I'm not sure how many of them can afford it. It might sell quickly, might not."

"I respect your opinion, and I appreciate your honesty," Doug told him, "And that's why, if and when this move takes place, I'll want you to be in charge of this office, *really* in charge."

When his employee remained quiet, Doug added, "Of course, you can expect an increase in salary to go along with the extra headaches."

Both laughed at that and Doug told Sam to arrange for an appraisal of his estate. Then, he added, "Get a couple of our best agents to do some hunting for available property in or near Marshall."

Sam asked, "What kind of property?"

"Two kinds, I guess. I'll need an office in a good location and then a residence on a few acres."

"Boss, if you're looking for something comparable to your current home, I don't know that you'll find something 'move in ready'. Would you consider building a new home?"

"Well, first of all, I don't think Brian and I want or need anything so big or so fancy. But sure, I'd be up for building another house. Might be fun."

With all that information whirling around in his head, Sam Cunningham excused himself to get started on the requests.

Doug reached for his phone, then stopped when he realized that he was about to call the Johnsons. Surprised at himself for wanting to share the news with them first, he opted to call home instead.

When Brian answered, he said, "Just wanted to let you know, I'm working on what we talked about yesterday. There may soon be a for sale sign in front of the house, if you're serious about moving."

He had to assure his son that he wasn't joking before he got the response he wanted. Brian was laughing and asked, "When can we go house hunting?"

Doug ended that call and made another one, this time to the Johnsons.

When M&M answered, he said, "Hi, just wanted to let you know that you and your son are costing me more money than I counted on."

Her puzzled response had him quickly explaining, "Brian likes being over there so much that he wants to know why we can't move to Marshall. I haven't come up with a good excuse, so we may soon be living in your neck of the woods."

He ended the call with, "Just wanted to let you know. See you tomorrow. Bye."

*****

M&M shook her head in disbelief. Surely Doug Wilson was joking. Why would he even consider *moving*? He had a thriving business and a beautiful home in Longview.

Later in the day, she mentioned the call to Jerry. "I think he was just kidding, but it's a weird joke."

"Maybe he wasn't joking, Mom. Brian told me that their fancy house was 'just full of stuff' and it was lonely and sad there without his mother and brother."

"Oh. But his business office is there. And all their friends."

Jerry just shrugged and went to the refrigerator in search of a snack.

"Guess we'll find out more when they come for Brian to ride tomorrow." She shifted her thoughts to the next session and asked Jerry, "What do you think about Gwen for Brian's next mount?"

He chuckled, "I think it's about time he rode something bigger, more his size, but Gwen isn't even here."

"Susanna called and said they are ready to wean the foal,

and she'll be bringing Gwen over today. So, I can introduce Brian to her, let him get used to the idea of switching from Goldilocks to her."

Jerry had a feeling that Brian wasn't going to like the idea. He was right.

*****

The riding session went smoothly, with Brian continuing to show more balance and strength. After he dismounted, M&M told him she wanted to show him another horse in the barn. While Jerry took over unsaddling Goldilocks and returning her to her stall, M&M led Brian and Doug to another stall and said, "This is Gwen."

The elegant gray mare, still fretting for her foal, was pacing around the stall. She came to the door and reached over to nuzzle M&M, then pawed impatiently.

Brian, leaning on his cane, said "She's *huge*. And what's wrong with her?"

M&M explained that she had just been separated from her baby, a part of the weaning process, and she would calm down and be her sweet old self in a few days. "In a week or so, she'll be ready for you to ride."

"But she's *huge*."

Jerry approached and said, "She's really more your size, tall as you are. And my mom always says, 'the more horses you ride the better rider you'll be.'"

M&M encouraged Doug and Brian to follow her to the little table in the shade, where they could enjoy lemonade and cookies. Once seated, she told them a little about the horse. "She belongs to my friend Susanna, and she is here on loan for you and for summer campers."

"She's that gentle?" Doug asked.

M&M nodded. "She is one of the kindest horses I've ever handled, and she comes with quite a story."

Wildflower Wednesday

She went on to tell them about how Susanna and the veterinarian had gone to rescue her, and she was so starved and weak they struggled to get her into the trailer and bring her to Pine Park.

Jerry added, "Yeah, and then we thought she was gonna die before she got strong enough to stand up and walk around."

"That *is* quite a story," Doug agreed.

"It really is. Get Susanna to tell you the *whole* story sometime."

Brian changed the subject, "Did Dad tell you we might move over here?"

"He mentioned it," M&M answered.

Jerry told Brian, "It'd be neat to have you for a neighbor. I can introduce you around next year at school and all that."

With their boys chattering about teen activities in Marshall, M&M asked Doug, "So, you're serious about moving?"

"I am. We are," he said, "Just look at how enthusiastic Brian is about coming over here. It was *his* idea."

*****

When the Wilsons said their goodbyes and got into the truck, Doug asked his son, "Are you up for a ride around town?"

"Sure. Why?"

I have directions to a couple of properties we can look at, one's for an office, which probably won't interest you, but if we're gonna move, I'll need an office over here."

"Gosh, Dad. You're *really* working on us moving. Sure, I'll go with you to look at places for your office, or for us to live."

His enthusiasm proved contagious, and Doug was soon parked in front of an office building that looked more than adequate for his needs. "This looks okay," he told his son. "It's a good location too. If the interior looks as good as the outside, I'll see about working a deal to lease with option to buy."

He started up the truck and headed to a residential area on

the outskirts of town. His agents had given him addresses of two homes, both on three-acre sites.

"What do you think?" he asked Brian as he pulled into the driveway of the first home.

"It reminds me of our house now, with the columns on the front and all. I'd rather have something *different*."

Relieved, Doug answered, "Me too."

The second home was red brick, sprawling ranch style, with a matching barn and white fenced corral.

"I like this one better!" Brian exclaimed as they drove closer to the house. Then they saw a brightly painted SOLD sign in the front yard.

"Guess we missed out on this one," Doug said, "But they'll be others."

Then he asked, "Is this the type of house you like?"

"I think so. I hope we can have a barn and horses. Maybe more than three acres."

Doug was glad to hear that he and his son were thinking along the same lines. He also knew that the place they were seeing in their dreams might not exist.

"How would you feel about us building a house?" he asked.

"That would be neat! But wouldn't it take a long time? I'm kinda hoping I can go to school in Marshall next fall. You heard what Jerry said about showing me around."

"I'll go back to my office and get some of my agents busy looking around for more houses. Maybe we can find something just right and move-in ready."

He did just that. By the time he and Brian had finished their meal, Sam Cunningham was at the front door with a briefcase filled with information about Marshall houses for sale as well as the property evaluation for Doug's current residence.

"Thanks, Sam. I didn't expect even you to get this done so quickly."

Wildflower Wednesday

"No problem, Boss. Now I'll be getting on home. See you in the morning."

Brian was bouncing up and down in his chair and reaching for his cane when Doug got back to him,

"Take it easy, son. I don't want you to fall outta that chair and hurt your leg."

"I'm just so excited, Dad. Can I see the pictures and stuff about those places for sale?"

"Sure," Doug said, as he sat back down and shoved their used dinner plates to the side. He spread the papers out so they could study listed homes. There were ten of them, but only three that both Doug and Brian thought looked promising.

"I'll call on these first thing in the morning, make appointments to look at them. Do you want to go too?"

"Sure I do." He paused. "Dad, can I ask you something?"

"You can ask me 'bout anything. What is it?"

"We've never talked much about money in our family. It seemed like there was enough for whatever we needed or wanted. But that was when Mom was working too, and I'm just wondering, you know, if it'll be okay, moving your office and buying a place."

"It'll be fine. My real estate company will support us, and I expect this place will sell for more than enough to buy what we want in Marshall." Doug hesitated, then added, "You're right, we don't talk much about financial things and maybe we should. I have not brought this up before, but you have the right to know that there was a very large monetary settlement because of the accident that took your mom and brother."

"Did you sue the guy?"

"No, I didn't. I didn't intend to either, although I guess his insurance company's legal team expected me to. I knew no amount of money would bring them back, and our medical insurance covered most of your medical bills. At the time, I wasn't thinking about anything except you getting well."

"So, how come you got a big settlement anyway?"

"Lawyers handled the whole thing. All I did was say okay and sign some papers."

Doug hesitated again, then thought he might as well tell Brian the rest. "I want you to know, just in case you're worried about not getting a full scholarship to play soccer in college, there's enough money for four years of college wherever you want to go."

"*No!*" Brian screamed. "I don't want that money. It's like it has their blood on it. Like it makes what happened to them okay. It's not okay and it will *never* be okay." He buried his head in his hands and sobbed. He cried long and hard.

Doug, also moved to tears, stood from his chair and stepped closer to wrap his arms around his son and they wept together.

They cried themselves out, had to stop and catch their breaths, then remained in a sadly silent embrace.

Finally, Brian spoke again. "I know it's wrong to hate, but I'll always hate that man for what he did to them, and to me."

"He was impaired, Brian. He wasn't intentionally careless."

"What do you mean *impaired*? Was he drunk?"

"No, alcohol was not involved. It was a medical impairment. I don't know exactly what happened because I never bothered to find out. It just didn't matter then. Do you want to know?"

"I don't care. It's still not okay."

Doug didn't know whether to be relieved or worried. He was grateful that Brian was no longer *totally* blaming himself for the fatal accident, but he didn't want him to have so much hatred for another human, any human. He decided a conversation with one of the counselors would be a good next step.

He changed the subject back to the insurance payment. "Well, the money is there in a separate bank account. You don't want it and fortunately, I don't need it, so maybe, later on, we

Wildflower Wednesday

can figure out something special to do with it, maybe something to honor the memory of your mother and brother."

Brian nodded as tears trickled down his cheeks.

The next morning, Doug called and set up appointments to visit the three homes he and Brian liked.

Then he called M&M. When she didn't answer, he left a voice mail message, "Just to let you know, Brian and I will be looking at *for-sale* properties near Marshall today."

Then he wondered why he had felt the need to let the Johnsons know they were house shopping.

He called home and told Brian about the appointments and asked about his schoolwork.

"Dad, I just got my report card online. I'll show it to you when you come home for lunch. And about that test, I made an A. So, when can I go swimming?"

"We'll talk about that at lunch too," Doug told his son, and disconnected the call with a smile on his face.

He checked with Sam Cunningham and his personal secretary, saw that everything was running smoothly there, so he left early and headed home for a leisurely lunch.

Brian was waiting under the umbrella table by the pool.

"I asked Jean to bring our lunch out here," he explained. As soon as Doug sat down, Brian shoved his tablet over to him and said, "Just look at my grades."

Doug's eyes grew wide. "Good job, son. You've almost got straight *A*s again. I'm proud of your hard work."

"So, when do I get to swim? And who's going to be my swimming buddy or lifeguard or whatever?"

"No time to swim today. We have appointments to see houses after lunch, probably won't get back home until late afternoon." He paused, "How about tomorrow? And I can be your swimming buddy and see how you do in the pool. Okay?"

"Great. Do you really have time to come swim?"

"I'll make time. And after I check you out, maybe you can invite a friend or two over for your next time in the pool."

"Thanks, Dad."

Father and son devoured their sandwiches and cookies, washed everything down with iced mint tea and got into the truck, headed to Marshall.

Brian utilized the GPS to direct them to the first location. Turning into the drive, he said, "This place looks neat. It's like a modern farm, with horses and everything. Look, there's a chicken coop!"

They moved slowly up the long gravel driveway, taking in the sights of the little farm. It reminded Doug of his childhood on a big farm. When the house came into view, he was disappointed to see that it showed signs of age and disrepair.

"This one isn't gonna work, is it?" Brian asked.

"No, but since I made an appointment with an agent, the thing to do is for me to get out and talk with him. There he is on the front porch, waving at us."

Doug suggested Brian just wait in the truck while he went and spoke with the agent. He explained that he wanted something more up to date, left his business card and returned to the truck.

"Sorry, son," he said. "I should have had my people check closely on age and condition of these places. I bet the picture of this house, the one we looked at and liked, was taken about 15 years ago."

Disappointed, Brian replied, "Yeah, and I bet it hasn't been painted since then."

They visited two other properties and were again disappointed. One was what Doug called a "pretend ranch" a nice enough house with a little barn and shed to house tools and implements. He was laughing as he looked at the outbuildings.

"What's so funny?" Brian wondered.

"These buildings are too small to be useful. I'd want a barn big enough for at least a couple of horses, and a storage area that will hold more than a lawn mower."

The third property was a real ranch, geared to running a sizeable herd of cattle. "This," Doug said, "Is more ranch than I want."

They turned toward home in silence, and Brian dozed off before they got halfway there.

Doug knew his son was tired and disappointed, and promised himself to plan better for their next excursion.

When he got Brian into the house to rest, he checked in at his office. Sam wanted to know how they liked the sale properties.

"Didn't," Doug said, rather curtly. "Sam, next round of info, be sure the photos are current. We are looking for something upscale and move-in ready."

Sam answered, "Boss, it sounds like you want a casual version of what you have, maybe with a horse barn and pasture instead of those formal flower gardens."

"Something like that."

Sam promised to have the agents search again, and to give Doug some new prospects as soon as possible.

He had questions too, "I know I mentioned it before. Have you thought about building a house? That way you can get exactly what you want. And how soon are you going to list your place here?"

"Since you and I both think it may take a while for the right buyer to come along, I'm inclined to think go ahead and put it on the market."

His office manager assured Doug that he would get the photographer out there and have a sale brochure printed right away.

Chapter 14

The next morning right after breakfast, M&M called Susanna. "Hi. Do you have some free time this afternoon?"

"I can probably make some. Why?"

"Brian will be coming for his next session, and I'd like you to be his handler today. I introduced him to Gwen and he's nervous about her. I thought maybe you could tell him more about her, help make the transition easier for him."

"Sure, and if it's okay I'll even wear my breeches and ride her while I'm there."

"Good. See you later," M&M said as they ended the call.

She'd just finished her lunch when Susanna arrived. "Come in and have a cold drink before you go saddle up," M&M told her.

While they were sipping drinks, M&M told her friend she was puzzled about some recent messages from Doug Wilson. "He says they are looking at homes over here. They're talking about *moving* to Marshall."

"So?"

M&M rolled her eyes. "Susanna, Jerry and I were over there for lunch last week. They live in a mansion—with formal gardens, swimming pool and everything else you can imagine. And Wilson Realty is in Longview. Why on earth would they want to move over here?"

Susanna shrugged, "Don't know. Maybe they want a fresh start, a change, after what's happened to their family."

Wildflower Wednesday

"Maybe. Jerry said Brian told him something like that, said the place was kinda lonely and sad without his mom and brother."

"That's probably your answer then. And I've noticed that Brian and Jerry seem to have connected. They're acting like friends, and I imagine Brian can use a good friend." Susanna stood up and said, "And now, *my* friend, I am going to ride sweet Gwen and hope she isn't mad at me for sending her away from her baby."

They both headed to the barn. M&M had another horse to ride before Brian's session, so she saddled him up and joined Susanna and Gwen in the arena. Jerry came in from school just in time to get Goldilocks groomed and saddled for Brian.

When the Wilsons pulled into the drive, three horses were circling the arena.

M&M waved to them and asked Jerry to tie Goldilocks by the gate and take her mount to the barn. "I'll be right back," she told Susanna. "I'm going to get the cookies and lemonade out. Join us over at that little table so you can tell Brian more about your mare."

Susanna nodded and cantered Gwen to the gate, dismounted and led the horse to the table where Doug and Brian Wilson were waiting.

She motioned for them to sit down. "I came to see Gwen today, and couldn't resist having a ride on her," she explained. Then she told them more about how Gwen had been rescued and proven herself a winner in the show ring after her rehab. "She's a wonderful horse," she assured Brian, "And M&M asked me to bring her over for you to enjoy before summer camp time."

Seeing his doubtful expression, she assured Brian, "You're gonna love her."

Then, seeing that Jerry and M&M were ready to start the

session with Brian, she sat down by Doug and started to chat.

"M&M tells me you're thinking of moving over here," she began.

"Brian actually suggested it," he explained. "And the more I thought about it, the better it seemed. I think both of us will enjoy having something of a fresh start, being somewhere without so many sad memories."

"Well, how's the house hunt going?"

He shook his head, "Not great, so far. We're now talking about building a house, but it seems Brian really wants to be over here to start school in the fall. I'm not sure how we can accomplish that."

"Well, good luck.," Susanna said as she glanced at her watch. "Wow, I've got to get going, by the time I put Gwen up and get home, my babies will be awake and giving their daddy a hard time."

Doug waved goodbye as she drove away, then turned and watched his son ride the little palomino. M&M was right, he thought. Brian did look too tall for that horse. He also looked confident and secure, a vast improvement from his first few sessions.

When his ride was over, Brian even went with Jerry to groom the horse and put her in a turnout paddock.

M&M joined Doug, took a seat in the shade and told him, "That boy of yours may really have the makings of a cowboy. I'm amazed at how far he's come in such a short time."

"Me too. I appreciate all you've done to help him, not just the physical aspect, he's just all around a happier young man, more like the old Brian."

They chatted comfortably until the boys joined them for some lemonade. Then Doug said, "We've got to be going. Brian and I have yet another place to look at today. If he's not too tired."

Brian said, "I *am* tired, but I want to see the place. It probably won't take very long, and then I may sleep on the way back home."

As they left, Jerry told his mom, "Brian talked about moving over here. He's really excited about it. I hope they find a place."

*****

While Jerry and M&M were taking care of barn chores, Doug and Brian were looking at what was being marketed as a country estate. Doug liked the exterior, but the gaudy interior of the house just made him laugh. "This looks like something in a movie," Brian said.

"Yeah, a *bad* movie," Doug replied.

They soon agreed that the changes to make the house acceptable would be pricey and probably take months for completion.

"If we have to take that long to move, we might as well build what we want," Doug told his son.

With that thought in mind, he drove home thinking of the names of architectural designers who might draw up some plans for them.

*****

Days later, every agent at Wilson Realty had given up on locating something to suit the boss, and they were now searching for building sites. An architect had submitted several house plans for consideration. Doug and Brian had agreed on a plan they liked, but Brian was sulking.

"What's the problem?" Doug asked him.

"Dad, it'll take months and months to get this house built, and that's after we find a piece of land to build it on. You *know* I wanted to be in Marshall for school in the fall."

Doug said, "Maybe we can apply for some kind of advance transfer, since you *will* be a resident there. I'll check into it."

And, in hopes of cheering up his son, Doug added, "And

Sam called earlier and said he has info on a couple of farm properties for sale. I'll check them out tomorrow. He also has an appointment with a couple who want to look at this place tomorrow." When he got no response, he added, "Things will start happening, you'll see."

Doug's words proved more prophetic than he expected.

His office manager brought the prospective buyers to the house and they stayed more than two hours, looked at everything in the house and on the grounds and the woman declared, "We love it!"

Her husband told Sam, "We'll have an offer on your desk by morning."

Doug left Brian at home with his school assignments and went to Marshall to see building sites.

The first one was a virtual forest, located on a poorly maintained gravel road. The next one was actually an old farm, and the owners were eager to move to a nearby city to be with their children and grandchildren. An agent met Doug in front of the farmhouse and told him that he had just shown the place to another family and that he expected an offer.

Doug Wilson looked at the man, decided it wasn't a sales tactic, and said, "Show me around. I need to see if there's a good building site for a house, plus room for a barn and probably for a swimming pool. "

They walked over the portion of the acreage that was cleared. The rear portion was a pine forest, and when they approached it, the agent told Doug, "The owners, Mr. and Mrs. Hawthorne, have a rather unusual stipulation about this part of their land. The adjoining land belongs to a professional horsewoman, and they have always given her permission to ride on the trails through the pine woods. They want that to still be an option for their friend, and they want it in the contract."

The agent continued, "The other folks I've shown this place

too haven't been too crazy about granting that request., but I've checked out the neighbor. She's responsible and professional so I can't see that it would be a problem."

Doug Wilson started to laugh. "Would that professional equestrienne happen to be Ms. Johnson at Pine Park Stables?"

"Yes. How did you know?"

"Just a guess. A lucky guess. I know Ms. Johnson. I'm sure we can get along as neighbors."

"Then you're interested in this place?"

Doug Wilson rarely did anything on impulse, but he felt this was so right that he answered, "I want this property, and I'll pay full asking price. No problem with the trail riding permission. He handed over his business card to the astonished agent and said, "My office manager will bring you a formal contract in the morning."

He could hardly wait to get home and tell Brian that they had a place to build their new house, and it was close to the Johnsons.

As he'd expected, Brian was happy with his news.

Then, the first complication arrived with a call from Sam Cunningham. "Hey, Boss. I've got good news and I've got bad news."

"Let's hear it," Doug answered.

"Well, as promised, those prospective buyers delivered an offer and it's a good one. They're paying full price and it's a cash deal."

"So, what's wrong with that?"

"Nothing, that's great. The problem is they want possession in a month. No negotiation."

"What! Brian and I have no place to go. I don't see how we can make it happen that fast." He thought for a moment. "Tell you what, Sam, just let me 'sleep on it' and I'll have a reply, an official one, in the morning."

When the call ended, he relayed all the information to Brian.

"What are we gonna do, Dad?"

Doug frowned, shook his head, looked skyward and silently prayed for guidance.

"I don't know. I'm not sure the Hawthornes can be out of the farmhouse in 30 days. I had thought you and I would just stay here while our new house is under construction. Now that won't work"

Brian asked his dad if he remembered the little camping trip they took in a rented motorhome.

"Sure, I remember. Seems to me, you and I liked the little house on wheels pretty well. Your mom wasn't quite so crazy about it."

"Well, couldn't we rent one of those campers and live over there and watch the house going up?"

Doug was astonished at his son's suggestion. "I think that might work. Tomorrow I'll check out availability of campers while you do your schoolwork. Great suggestion!"

"Dad, there's just one thing we haven't talked about."

"What's that?"

"What about Jessie and Jean? Where will they go when this place is sold?" Brian's bottom lip quivered when he added, "I can't hardly think about them not being with us. They're like part of our family."

"Well, I've talked to Jessie a bit, and you know he now has established something of a landscaping business on his own, plus what he does for the real estate company. He and Jean are talking about finding a little place of their own. Don't think they've had much luck so far."

"Oh," was Brian's dejected response. Then he perked up, "Dad, would they want to live in that farmhouse where we're moving? We could still have them with us, and maybe Jean will keep cooking for us."

Doug was again astonished at Brian's ideas. "Well, I'd sure like that and maybe they would too. Let's ask them, right now."

He called Jessie's cell phone and asked, "Could you and Jean come over to the big house? Brian and I have an idea we want to share with you."

He presented the suggestion to the couple, Jessie nodded and looked to his wife for a reaction and she burst into tears. "Oh, *yes*! *Yes*! *Yes*!" she replied. "My heart has been breaking, thinking of not being with my Wilson family. I'm sure we will love that farmhouse and being nearby. And, of course, I'll keep on cooking for you."

When Doug went to bed that night, he was sure all four of them would fall asleep with smiles on their faces.

Chapter 15

M&M was surprised when the Hawthornes came around to see her so early in the morning.

"Hi!" She welcomed them and invited them into the house. Mr. Hawthorne shook his head and said, "Can't stay. We just have some good news—wanted to tell you in person."

"Good news is always welcome. What's up?"

"Well, you know, we've been wanting to sell our farm and move to be near our kids," Mr. Hawthorne began. "Now we have a buyer for our place! He seemed to fall in love with the property, plans to build a big house over there, and when we told him we wanted you to still be able to use the trails in the woods, he was fine with it."

Mrs. Hawthorne smiled. "We think he'll be a nice neighbor for you, and I think he knows you." After a pause, she added "Name's Wilson."

M&M was too shocked to say anything, but finally managed to tell the Hawthornes that she would miss them but was happy that they would be able to make the long-wanted move.

When they left, she called Doug Wilson and accused him of sneaking around behind her back.

His response was also one of shock. "I didn't know I needed your permission to buy a piece of property," he said curtly and ended the call.

Jerry had wandered into the room and heard the exchange. "What's the matter, Mom?"

M&M snapped at him. "I don't know what's wrong with me. I just got *so* mad feeling like I'm being manipulated somehow. I'm over it, already. See." She smiled.

"Well, then you probably owe *somebody* an apology. I think it's neat that Brian and his dad will be our neighbors. I really like them."

M&M had said she was over being mad, but she couldn't quite get past feeling like everything in her world was suddenly out of her control. She was glad to see Susanna drive up while she was still doing barn chores.

"What brings you out here so early?"

Susanna told her she was running errands, just stopped by to bring Gwen a carrot. Then she frowned. "What's with you? Look ready to take on a bronc and whip it into shape."

M&M managed to grin and admitted, "I just had a surprise announcement and somehow it really got under my skin." Then she explained the visit from her neighbors and her reaction to their news.

"Okay, so I'm with Jerry. *Why* are you upset about this?"

M&M shook her head. "I can't explain it. I think I just feel out of sorts because I don't seem to have much say about anything. And Doug Wilson is so *controlling,* and I don't like feeling like he's running my life." She asked her best friend, "Am I being silly?"

"Honestly, yes."

Susanna gave her a hug, delivered a carrot to Gwen and departed, leaving M&M to ponder her reaction.

By noon, she admitted to herself that Jerry was right. She owed Doug Wilson an apology. But how was she going to explain her explosive response to the news that they would be neighbors?

She didn't have much time to think about it. As she started to the barn for the next horse in the training lineup, Doug

Wilson turned into her drive. He was out of his truck and striding in her direction, and she couldn't even seem to move.

"Okay, let's have it," he almost shouted. "I don't know how, but I've managed to make you angry. What's up?"

A totally mortified M&M felt tears spilling down her cheeks as she stammered, "I'm sorry. I don't even know why I got so mad. I think I just felt out of control of everything."

Doug started to put his arm around her shoulders, seemed to think better of it, and took a step back. "Okay, I thought you and I had a good understanding about helping each other by you working with Brian and my financial backing. Then, our boys seem like they're becoming friends."

When M&M remained silent, he continued, "So, I thought it would be okay for us to be neighbors."

He paused, then said, "And if you're thinking that because I'm in real estate, I'm going to clear that pine forest and turn it into a crowded neighborhood of houses, rest assured, I have *no* intention of doing that."

She managed a bit of a smile. "I hadn't even thought of that, or I would have been *really* mad."

"Okay, so I already gave my word to those folks, you'll still have riding privileges on the trail through the woods. In fact, you and Jerry can come over to see me and Brian anytime."

M&M nodded. "Again, I'm sorry I reacted so badly. Welcome to the neighborhood." She extended her hand and he took it, squeezed rather than shook it.

"I'll let you get back to your work," he said, turned and left.

*****

Thirty minutes later he was back in his office making phone calls. He made an appointment for movers to come give an estimate on packing and storing his furniture and household goods. Then he called an RV dealer and inquired about rental and sale options. He checked in with Brian and learned that he

Wildflower Wednesday

had completed his schoolwork, so he headed home to pick him up. He knew Brian would love going to shop for a camper.

On the way to the dealership, Doug explained that he needed lots of input about what furnishings they would want in their new home. "I don't want to pay to have a bunch of stuff packed up and stored and then just get rid of it when the new house is ready."

He and Brian agreed that they would not want some of the formal furniture, and that Jean could be a big help in deciding about the household items.

When they turned in to the lot, Brian said, "Gee, Dad, I didn't know there would be such a variety of campers here.

A salesman was at the truck door by the time they got out. Doug explained that they were undecided about rental vs purchase, and he told the man why they wanted a camper. First, they looked at the rental fifth wheels and motorhomes, and Doug was disappointed,

He said, "If these were horses, I'd say they'd been used hard and put up wet."

The salesman nodded and led them to a row of new fifth wheel campers. Doug explained that he and his son expected to live in the camper for the months it would take to build a house. "Then, if we buy something, we might want to keep it and take a trip once in a while."

They were then shown several motorhomes, and Brian immediately spoke up. "Dad, I like *this* one. It has two TVs and enough of a kitchen for us and comfy beds and—"

Doug interrupted, "Okay, I see lots of good features here. But remember, we will be *living* in it for a *long* time."

He asked for a brochure to take home. "We'll think it over. Get back to you tomorrow."

On the drive back to the house, Brian kept telling his dad that they could have a great time in that motorhome.

When they got home, Brian was tired and headed to his room to rest. Doug made calls to check on the timing of moving out of his place and into the farmhouse.

By supper time, he was happy to tell Jessie and Jean that they would be able to get into the farmhouse when they left their current home. Now, all he had to do was buy an RV and do whatever was required to park it by the homesite.

The next morning, Doug went to the RV dealership and bought the rig Brian liked.

Chapter 16

Doug was working twelve hours a day, setting up his new office in Marshall while overseeing Sam's leadership at the Longview location, lining up lists for the movers to store their furniture and household goods, and trying to spend quality time with his son.

They were on the way to Marshall for a riding session when Brian told him, "Dad, I haven't even thanked you. I'm sorry, I guess I've been a brat."

"Whatever are you talking about?"

"I'm talking about you doing so much for me. I know you're working extra hard, but you always take me over to ride, and you're moving your office and everything...."

Doug smiled and assured his son, "I'm just glad I can do all this, for *both* of us."

They turned into the drive at Pine Park to see Jerry already in the arena with Gwen. M&M was carrying an ice chest to the little table under the nearby trees. The truck was barely stopped when Brian stepped out, hurrying to the arena gate. Doug went to carry the ice chest for M&M.

He grinned at her as he took it, "I need to make myself useful, and clearly Brian doesn't need my assistance. He's practically running to the arena gate."

"It's good to see, isn't it? I can hardly believe he's the same boy that came here pale as a ghost and weak as a newborn."

They walked together to the gate, and M&M went into the

arena to join the boys.

"Take Gwen on over to the mounting block," she told Jerry. Then she added, "Brian, eventually you will be able to mount Gwen from the ground, but for now, we will continue to use the mounting block. As you can see, only Jerry and I will be in the ring with you today. Your team has decided that you don't need additional help or supervision, and Jerry will be a very short-term horse handler today."

Brian's eyes widened at her words. "Do you mean I'll get to hold the reins and everything?"

She nodded. "That's exactly what I mean. But Jerry will lead off and then step away. He'll move back to the horse's head, or beside you at any time either you or I think he needs to."

Brian was beaming when he told Gwen, "Walk on."

M&M reminded him about how to handle the reins and after one circle she signaled for Jerry to unsnap the lead from Gwen's bridle and step away from her head. Horse and rider proceeded to circle around M&M at a walk, and then a trot. M&M only had to remind Brian once to keep his heels down.

When she saw that he was tiring, she told Brian to stop his horse and Gwen obeyed his "Whoa," before he even tightened the reins.

Brian was grinning and Jerry and Doug were actually applauding when Gwen went to the gate for the dismount. M&M was pretty happy too.

"That was awesome," she told Brian. "Now, part of being a cowboy is taking care of your horse, so you go with Jerry to unsaddle Gwen and turn her out in the paddock."

She and Doug watched as Brian, still using a cane, managed to keep up with Jerry as they went to the barn.

"Let's get ourselves a cool drink and sit in the shade," she suggested. "The boys will be along in a little while."

When they sat down, Doug told her he was really amazed at

his son's progress.

"He's so excited about moving over here," he added. "And I know it seemed weird or abrupt to you, but I think it's going to be great for both of us to have a different place to call home. Brian is already talking about changing schools, riding horses, making new friends." He paused, then continued, "You and Jerry have been good for him, and for me. Thank you."

M&M smiled, "You and Brian have been good for us too, and good to us, so the thanks is mutual."

Brian and Jerry came and sat with them and began to chatter about the motorhome that would soon be parked on the other side of the pine forest.

"Did Dad tell you that Jessie and Jean are coming too?" Brian asked. "It's so neat! They're going to live in the farmhouse, and Jean will still cook for us."

Jerry spoke up, "Invite me over when she does fried chicken again. It's the best!"

M&M was a little surprised at the remark and said, "Nothing like inviting yourself."

"Why not?" Doug said. "We're going to be neighbors."

Brian added, "And, I'm going to invite myself over to ride a horse even after my sessions are over, unless Dad buys me one of my own."

M&M laughed. "That sounds like a hint if I ever heard one."

She assured Brian that he would be welcome to come ride one of the Pine Park horses.

"And Jerry can come swim, as soon as we have a pool," Brian said. He turned to his father. "Hey, Dad, I asked him to come swim but we're gonna move soon." He looked from his dad to M&M, then he asked, "Can he come over to Longview and swim before we move?"

Both boys then added a "Please," leaving their parents to do nothing but agree.

By the time Doug and Brian departed for home, the foursome had agreed to have a picnic by the pool after the boys' swim. M&M said, "I just have to check my calendar to be sure what day we can get away from the barn for a few hours."

Doug told her he would call later to verify the day.

Jerry was so excited about the plans that he reminded his mom to check the calendar before they even got back to the house.

"I can't believe I'll get to swim *this* early in the season, 'cause their pool is *heated*. I wonder if the pool they build over here will be heated too. And I hope Jean cooks fried chicken for that picnic."

He kept on and on until M&M had checked her calendar, figured out that they could go to Longview Wednesday *if* Jerry promised to give her some extra help with horses and barn chores before they left *and* after they got home."

"Sure thing, Mom," he responded.

When Doug called, he and M&M agreed on Wednesday for their pool and picnic time.

"We'll just let the boys swim until they get tired and hungry, then eat," Doug told M&M.

Jerry bounced with excitement when his mother confirmed the plan. "I've never been swimming before summer!" he told her.

M&M surprised herself by also looking forward to the outing to Longview.

She and Jerry rushed through the afternoon barn work to get cleaned up and started to the Wilson's place.

As she drove, Jerry kept her entertained, talking about how he and Brian might get to go off the diving board, or play with the multitude of float toys he saw by the pool.

"Just remember to be careful of Brian, he's still not back to full strength," she cautioned.

Wildflower Wednesday

Jerry thought for a minute, then said, "Okay, Mom, maybe I should let Brian lead the way and let him tell me what we can do in the water."

"Good idea," she told him as she turned the truck into the long drive to the Wilson home.

When she pulled up in front of the house, Brian and Doug were waiting to welcome them, and they all walked to the pool together.

Brian said, "I already have on my swim trunks, under these sweatpants."

Jerry answered that he was wearing his under his jeans. In no time, both had removed top layers and carefully walked down the steps into the big pool.

With Doug's cautionary, "Be careful," Brian waved, grabbed two pool noodles from the edge and tossed one to Jerry. The teens were soon floating, splashing, laughing and talking.

"Clearly, they don't need us interfering in their fun, so let's have a seat and get something to drink out of this cooler Jean sent out."

"How thoughtful."

"She is, always, and she's been rummaging in the kitchen since noon. No telling what she's planned for our picnic."

"I'm sure it will be delicious. Thanks for asking us over again. Jerry has been so excited about swimming in your heated pool."

"We, Brian and I, are glad to have you. We enjoy your company, even without the horses."

They smiled at each other and Doug said, "Really, I'm glad we've become friends."

When she said nothing, Doug asked, "We *are* friends, aren't we?"

M&M grinned and nodded.

"Good. Well, there's one thing we need to clear up. I know

you've said your friends call you M&M, and since I need to stop the 'Ms. Johnson' bit, I need to call you *something* else and M&M just doesn't work for me. Tell me again, what does M&M stand for, besides that chocolate candy?"

She chuckled, "My name is Mary Miranda. I was named for my mother, Mary, and my Aunt Miranda. As a child, the grownups called me Mary Miranda, to avoid confusion, I guess. It's just a lot of name."

"It is," he agreed. "Would you object to me shortening it to Miranda?"

She shook her head. "Not at all. Just know that it may take a while before I get used to it."

"Okay then, Miranda, let's finish our drinks and take a walk before our picnic is delivered."

Following his lead, they strolled out to the gazebo so M&M could look over the field of wildflowers.

"The flowers are still beautiful," she said.

Doug walked down into the field and carefully picked a big handful of the bluebonnets and paintbrush.

"Since you like them so much, take these home."

M&M was too surprised to say anything except "Thank you."

"Won't you miss all this?" she asked Doug as they walked back to poolside.

"Yes and no. I've been happy here, but both Brian and I think the change will be a good one. And I intend to recreate the things we love most here in the new house we're building. Since you love wildflowers, I'll tell you that I've already asked Jessie to order seeds to create another field of them near the new house."

"I'll look forward to seeing that," she said. "What else do you plan to re-create, as you call it, at the new place?"

"We'll have a pool, although probably not as fancy as this

Wildflower Wednesday

one."

By then, they'd reached the pool and found two boys wrapped in towels.

"We're starving," Brian informed them just as Jean arrived in the golf cart.

She laughed and ordered him, "Prove it. I want *no* leftovers," as she pulled two big picnic baskets out of her cart.

She was gone before the boys could dig through the packaged food to see what all they had to eat.

Brian was delighted when he discovered that the cold food included assorted sandwiches, deviled eggs, and fresh fruit. There was also a hot pack of freshly fried chicken."

"She obviously knows what you like," Doug observed as he passed paper plates and napkins around the table, then said, "Dig in."

Brian and Jerry didn't have to be told twice. They filled their plates, hoping to have some of every item in the baskets. Doug and M&M watched while their boys continue to eat long after they had finished.

"That was delicious," M&M told Doug. "Please thank Jean for us."

He chuckled. "The empty baskets will be the best thanks of all, but I'll tell her."

"Mom, maybe when they all move over to Marshall, maybe if we're real nice, she'll cook for us too," Jerry wished aloud.

At her puzzled look, Doug told M&M, "I guess you haven't heard the latest about our moving plans. Brian and I will be camping in a motorhome while we watch the house going up, and Jessie and Jean will be moving into the farmhouse as soon as it's vacated by your current neighbors."

"Wow!" M&M said, "Then they're moving with you?"

Jerry looked at her with a smile. "I thought you knew that, Mom. Brian already told me."

"Well, it sounds like good news all around," M&M responded.

Realizing the time, she then reluctantly told Jerry, "I hate to tell you, but our barn work is waiting, and we need to get back to it before dark."

As they rose to leave, Brian said, "I wish Jerry could stay and spend the night. We could watch a good movie or two."

M&M shook her head. "I'm sure he wishes he could stay too, but our deal is he has to be my helper since we took part of the day off to come over. I'm sorry, but that's still the deal."

Jerry added, "Yeah, I'm sorry too, but thanks for thinking of it, Brian."

"Maybe another time," Doug suggested.

M&M and Jerry again thanked him, and they left, waving as they went down the drive.

On the way home Jerry told his mom, "It'll be neat to have them for our neighbors, but what are we gonna do for fun. Brian has the pool and movie room and stuff now, but living in a motorhome without any of that might not be so great."

"For one thing," she answered, "Brian really seems into riding, so he can come ride as often as he wants to, and you'll need to take him around other kids so he can get acquainted."

"Yeah, and he says he wants to help with summer camp. Do you think he can?"

"We'll find something for him to do."

Chapter 17

It wasn't quite daylight when M&M awoke with a start.

"I'm not ready," she told herself.

"Ready for what?" asked her sleepy son as he stumbled into the room.

"Camp! It starts today. I'm not ready. I'll *never* be ready."

"Well, a bunch of kids are gonna be out here in a few hours, ready or not."

"Why are you up so early?"

"You were talking in your sleep, Mom, and pretty loud."

"Sorry I woke you up."

"It's okay, I'm too excited to sleep. Brian and I have been looking forward to this for weeks.

Mom, he's really up for it. I think he wants to be a camp counselor as much as I do."

She just nodded and went to turn on the coffee pot.

Two hours later she breathed a sigh of relief when her volunteer staffers started arriving. Suddenly she was glad that everyone had insisted on coming early to meet the campers on their first day.

She just hoped the smile that lit up her face told them how happy she was to have their help because she simply could not find the words.

As the kids arrived, Tiffany sorted them into groups by age. The youngest four went with Jerry and Brian to the tack room to see saddles and bridles. The middle schoolers were getting an introduction to horse grooming with Susanna as M&M led her junior high campers through the barn aisles and introduced them to all the camp horses.

The full line-up included Patches and another pony called Peanuts, loaned by a former student. The big horses were Gwen and Sarge, the retired mounted patrol horse. His owner said if Sarge was happy at Pine Park, M&M could call him hers. Goldilocks was stalled next to Sun Ray, another palomino that looked like her somewhat taller twin brother. He was also loaned by a client.

Across the barn aisle were two Quarter horses, a plump bay gelding appropriately called Butterball, and a buckskin named Gunsmoke. On down the aisle were the two blacks, Charcoal and Peppy. Colorful pintos Spot and Snoopy completed the roster.

The campers petted every single horse while M&M rechecked her list before assigning a horse to each youngster in her group.

An hour later, groups and leaders switched places. The older kids were mounted and riding in the arena, while other groups were getting grooming lessons with Jerry or tack cleaning with Brian, Susanna and Tiffany had moved to the arena to assist riders as needed.

M&M wore a genuine smile by lunch break time. Every camper had been on a horse. Not one had been frightened or injured. They were all seated on picnic blankets, and Tiffany had passed out hand wipes and cold drinks when the pizza delivery truck arrived. Everybody cheered.

After lunch, leaders again took charge of their little groups. All campers left knowing something about cleaning tack, brushing horses, dressing appropriately and how to start and stop a horse.

When camp was over for the day, Jerry helped clean stalls

and turn horses into paddocks, while M&M finished up by filling hay nets, water and grain buckets.

It was just before dark when M&M went to the house, bone tired but happy. Jerry had made sandwiches for them and told her the hot tub was ready and waiting.

"You are the *best* son ever."

He grinned when she added, "And you're a pretty good camp counselor, too."

*****

By the end of the week, the sessions were running so smoothly that M&M didn't hesitate to say "yes" when Doug called and asked if he could come over to observe.

"I've been nervous about Brian being in the middle of it, but I didn't want to embarrass him by coming and hanging around."

She laughed, "He'll probably be too busy to notice your presence. And Doug, he's doing a great job with the kids."

*****

Before the campers arrived Monday morning, she mentioned to Brian and Jerry that Doug wanted to come see how camp was going.

"He probably would have been over before now, but he's been busy getting all our stuff ready to put in storage and load up our motorhome," Brian volunteered.

Then the kids started coming and M&M forgot all about Doug's visit until midway through the morning when she glanced toward the arena gate and saw him there. She was too busy directing horses and riders to even acknowledge his presence until the next break between classes. Then she told him he'd find Brian in the barn, either in the tack room or at the crossties.

When he hesitated, she motioned him to go. "Brian knows you're coming over, and he seemed okay with it."

Doug gave her a grateful smile before heading to the barn.

*****

When he got to the tack room door, Doug stood back and watched his son showing four youngsters how to care for the tack and teaching them the names of all the saddle and bridle parts as he cleaned them. He then explained that some parts needed to be oiled to keep the leather soft and pliable.

Doug was amazed that Brian knew so much about the equipment and tickled to see how he had those kids happily wiping down leather reins and polishing bits.

He stepped out of the doorway as the session ended so campers and counselors could take their snack break. Planning to stay on the outskirts, he lingered at the barn door until Tiffany yelled at him.

"Hey, Mr. Wilson, come on over and have some refreshments. There's plenty for everybody."

Still hesitant, he walked slowly until he caught the scent of freshly baked cookies, then wondered who in the world had baked cookies.

He didn't wonder for long. A cute little girl came up to him with a filled bakery box.

Not at all shy, she said, "Hi, I'm Katy, and my mom baked the cookies this morning. She doesn't like doing stuff with horses, but I do, so she bakes cookies for camp."

He chuckled and reached for a cookie as he thanked her.

M&M motioned him over to the chairs with the other adults and said, "I see you've met Katy. She's our youngest, and possibly most enthusiastic camper."

Susanna added, "Just you wait, M&M, she's gonna be just like me, hanging out in the barn all the time."

At Doug's puzzled look, Susanna explained how she had come to Pine Park for lessons and became M&M's *shadow*. "That was a lot of years ago," she added.

M&M chuckled. "Yeah, and you're still hanging out at my

barn, and I'm *so* glad."

Doug realized that these women had a lot of history together, and he was just hearing a little of it.

Grateful to be welcome, he decided to stay and watch another session. Before leaving to check in at his Longview office, he congratulated M&M on running such a professional camp.

"I'm in awe at how much you're teaching these kids, and I had no idea Brian knew so much about horse equipment and care. You are a great instructor!"

"Thanks, but it's easy because I am sharing what I know and love with a great group of youngsters. They clearly love horses and *want to* learn."

"Incredible," Doug said to himself as he got into his truck.

Hours later when he returned to Pine Park to pick up Brian, Doug used the same word again as he drove back to Longview. "It's incredible, what all you've learned in such a short time. I had no idea you knew so much about horses or horse gear."

"Well, Dad, I really *do* like horses and riding has been *so* good. I asked to do the camp stuff as sort of a thank you to the Johnsons. I sorta cheated to learn all the stuff about tack and grooming."

"Cheated?"

"Well, the kids think I have known all this stuff, but I borrowed a book from Jerry and studied about all things horse. I had to memorize the parts of the saddle and bridle and all that."

"You worked that hard just to be at camp?"

"Yeah. And then I found out it was really fun sharing with the littler kids."

"I'm proud of you, son." After pausing, he then added, "Gotta change the subject though."

"Okay, What?"

Doug took a deep breath, hesitated, glanced at his son, "Moving time is here. Movers can take the furniture to storage tomorrow. Jean has the household stuff all sorted and we've put everything we need, except our clothes, into the motorhome. It's waiting in the driveway."

"It's gonna seem weird, isn't it, to drive off and leave it?"

"Yeah, it is. It's a little sad, too."

"Dad, do you feel like we're saying goodbye to Mom and Thomas all over again?"

"I guess so, in a way," Doug admitted as a single tear rolled down his cheek.

Brian sniffed, found a tissue, blew his nose. "I didn't think it'd make me cry."

Doug reached over and rubbed Brian's shoulder and assured him, "It's still a good change for us."

Brian nodded and blew his nose again.

When they walked into the house, Brian's nose refocused. "Fried chicken! I smell it!"

Jean came out of the kitchen to tell them, "I'm fixin' an early supper for you, figured it oughta be something special since I won't get to cook for you 'til we get over to the farmhouse."

"I'll call you as soon as it's ready. Won't be long," she told them as she turned back to the kitchen.

"Leave it to Jean to cheer us up," Doug said. "I'm so glad she and Jessie are going to move with us."

"Me too. How soon will they move into the farmhouse?"

"Just a few days, I think."

At Doug's request, Jessie and Jean joined them for supper at the kitchen table and Jean's excitement about the move proved contagious.

Before she brought out dessert, they were all laughing and talking about moving and all their plans for the new location.

Doug asked Brian if he could get his clothes ready, and got

Wildflower Wednesday

an affirmative answer, so father and son left the table to start sorting through their closets.

Two mornings later, Doug was driving the motorhome, towing his truck to Marshall in time to deliver Brian to Pine Park for camp.

"It's a good thing Pine Park has this big driveway, or I'd never be able to turn this rig around without unhooking the truck."

"You seem to be handling it okay. Are you coming back to get me after camp?"

Doug nodded. "But I'll leave this thing on its parking pad and come in the truck, like always."

"See ya later," Brian said as he climbed out of the truck and hurried to the barn. It was just minutes until starting time.

"Hey, Jerry!" he called out as he entered the big barn.

"Down here, saddling horses. Come help me."

Brian went to the crossties and starting brushing Goldilocks, still his favorite horse. "I know I'm too big for her, but she's special. I hope I get a horse of my own that I like as much."

"You're planning to get a horse?"

"Well, I hope so. Dad hasn't exactly said he was going to get me one, but he does plan to have a barn by our house. Hey, we're almost officially neighbors. Our house on wheels is parking over there today."

Jerry was just starting to tell Brian about all the things he hoped they could do together when they heard car doors slamming in the drive.

"Campers are here," Brian said.

The boys didn't have another chance to talk all day. Younger kids kept them busy.

Brian waved goodbye as he stepped into his dad's truck.

"Tired?" Doug asked.

"Yep. Tired *and* hungry."

"Me too, and I haven't quite figured out the camper cooking equipment yet. How about we go get burgers and fries at that drive-in? We can have an early supper and eat some of that cake Jean sent with us later."

"Sounds good to me," Brian answered just as the first clap of thunder made him jerk straight up in his seat.

"Wow! That was loud and *close*."

As his dad drove, Brian checked the weather app on his phone and reported, "This says powerful thunderstorms are likely all evening. Flood watches, too."

"We sit high enough not to worry about flooding, and we'll just stay inside tonight."

Father and son made a run for the motorhome when they got to the place they now called home. They toweled dry quickly and sat down to eat their supper as rain poured in torrents.

By dark, the rain had let up, and they thought the storms were over. But within minutes, thunder startled them, lightning flashed and the ground shook beneath their camper.

Doug looked out the window just as Brian yelled, "Dad, lightening struck the farmhouse. It's on fire!"

Chapter 18

Doug immediately called 911, reported the fire and gave directions to the property. It was minutes that seemed like hours before he heard the blaring sirens as firetrucks approached.

Firefighters attacked the blaze with everything they had, but the farmhouse was fully engulfed in flames before they rolled up.

The captain spoke with Doug as part of his crew prepared to depart. "I'm sorry, sir, the structure was too far gone before we even got to it. I'll be leaving some of my men and equipment here for a few hours to keep an eye on the hot spots, just to be safe."

"Thank you," Doug said as his tearful son snuggled next to him.

Just as the first truck cleared the drive, Brian saw a pickup racing toward them. When the driver hit the brakes, two figures fairly flew out of the truck, and ran to them.

Brian recognized M&M at the same time she said, "Oh! Thank God you two are safe. We heard the sirens, then thought we saw flames through the pine trees."

Doug, astonished to see that both M&M and her son were still in their pajamas, assured them, "We're fine. Lightening stuck the house and it's gone. I don't know how I'm gonna tell Jessie and Jean."

"Oh, Dad, they're *gonna* be *so* upset. They were planning to move in day after tomorrow. What'll they do?"

Doug just shook his head. "First, we have to break the news to them. Then we'll sit down and try to figure out a solution, a good solution."

M&M, likely realizing her attire was somewhat inappropriate, backed away and told them, "We were just scared when we heard the sirens. Glad you're okay."

She waived Jerry along with her as she headed back to her truck.

Brian commented as they drove away, "Nice of them to come check on us."

"Yep, and we *are* okay, so let's try to get some sleep."

Brian was soon snoring softly, but Doug couldn't manage to put his mind to rest. He rehearsed, over and over in his mind, what he would say to Jessie and Jean.

At daylight, he was up making coffee in the little kitchen area. Brian was soon by his side.

"Didn't mean to wake you,"

"It's okay, Dad. I think it's pretty hard to move around in here without being heard."

Doug nodded.

"I guess there's no way Jessie and Jean can move in here with us."

"Afraid not."

"Then what *can* they do?"

Doug shook his bowed head. Then lifted his chin and declared, "First thing, I have to go see them, have a man to man talk with Jessie. We'll figure something out."

*****

M&M was sipping her coffee as she cooked breakfast for Jerry.

He was pacing around the kitchen and fretting about the burned-out house. "Mom, it's just terrible that Jessie and Jean were about to move over there. Now they'll have no place to go."

"I know. It's terrible for them, and for Doug and Brian. Jean and Jessie are like part of the Wilson family."

"I know, and Brian *loves* them. It seems like he's had enough bad stuff happen without this."

M&M slid a plate of pancakes and sausage across the counter and told Jerry. "Sit and eat."

A stack of pancakes disappeared before he said another word. Then, "Mom! I have an idea. I know Mr. Wilson will eventually figure out a place for them over by their new house, but that's months away. Why can't we ask Jessie and Jean to stay with us, just for a while?"

"*Wha*t?"

"We could invite them to stay with us."

Astonished, M&M answered her son, "Jerry, we hardly have room, or furniture suitable for even overnight guests."

"But, Mom, I could sleep in your office. One of my twin beds would fit in there. Then they could have my bedroom. I bet they could put their own bedroom stuff in there."

"You'd do *that*?"

"Sure. Why not? Jean might even cook some for us, too."

M&M laughed. "Leave it to you to figure out a way to get plenty of that fried chicken."

"Gee, Mom, that would be a bonus, but I really want to help out the Wilsons like they've helped us. And I like Jessie and Jean."

"Okay, I'll think on it."

She hesitated. "Maybe I'll talk to Doug about it, but they may have this all resolved without our help."

*****

Doug was looking for a resolution as Jean wept and Jessie continued to shake his head in disbelief.

Trying to reassure them, Doug said, "You *know*, I will

eventually have a place for you right by our house, but for now...."

"Maybe we're not meant to be there," Jessie broke in.

Jean's sobs grew louder at that.

"Okay," Doug offered. "I'll tell you what. I'm going to my office and get my staff to start looking for places we can rent, hopefully close to me and Brian. I'll let you know as soon as they have something to show you."

He left before they could refuse the offer.

Wilson Realty employees were accustomed to unusual requests from their boss, so Doug didn't hesitate to have them start the search.

By late afternoon, he had a short list of rental properties that might suit Jessie and Jean. The bad news was, none were conveniently located near Doug's motorhome and building site.

He hated having to report that news to his son who had gone over to Pine Park to hang out with Jerry.

When he drove up to get Brian, he was invited to join the boys and M&M for lemonade and conversation.

Brian immediately asked, "Did you find a place for them to move?"

Doug shook his head, "I had everyone in my office hunting rentals that might work. They came up with a few possibilities, but none of them are close to us."

"Well then, we have a suggestion," M&M said.

"Dad, just listen to this!"

Jerry was too excited to stay quiet. "We, Mom and I, want them to come stay with us until they get a permanent place."

Doug didn't believe what he was hearing. *"What?"*

Then the other three were all talking at once and he heard bits and pieces of, "I can move out of my bedroom if—" "We really will be glad to have—" "It'll be close to us."

He could give nothing but the honest response, "I don't

know what to say."

Then M&M *did* know what to say, "I think we need to get Jessie and Jean to come out here and show them around, see if they think this will be comfortable for them."

Doug, still surprised at the suggestion, agreed, and said he would bring them out to Pine Park as soon as possible. "Thank you for your generous offer," he added.

"It was actually Jerry's idea," M&M confessed, "But the more I thought about it, the better it seemed."

Doug told Brian they needed to go to the motorhome, so he could cook up something for supper and make some calls.

*****

Although saddened with the housing problem for Jean and Jessie, Brian was still able to giggle at his father's attempts to cook their supper.

Doug laughed as he admitted, "We clearly need Jean's presence in a kitchen as close to us as possible. I'll get them out here tomorrow to talk about the Johnson's idea."

"Do you think they'll be okay with it?"

"Honestly, no. At least not at first. That's why I'm not telling them much, just get them out here and let them see for themselves. Maybe the Johnsons can help convince them to at least give it a try."

Brian listened when his dad called Jessie and suggested, "I've got at least one possibility for you and Jean. Why don't you two drive out here tomorrow and let me show you what's available. We can meet at my new office in Marshall, and I'll show you to the place I have in mind."

When the call ended, Brian said, "Gee, Dad, you sure didn't tell him much."

Doug nodded, "No, because I figured he'd balk at the idea of staying with anybody except us. I do hope you noticed, I didn't lie, I just didn't reveal much information."

"Yeah, Dad, I got that."

*****

Brian was still helping at camp when Doug went to meet Jessie and Jean and drive them to Pine Park. He was talking with the younger campers when Doug drove them up to the Pine Park barn.

"Why are we here?" Jessie asked, just as M&M looked up from her spot in the center of the arena and waved.

Doug said, "I thought you might like to see Brian at work. He loves helping these little campers. The kids will be leaving in a little while."

If Jessie and Jean thought it strange to be at a horse camp instead of looking at rent property, they said nothing. Doug knew he'd done a good job of distracting them when Jean remarked about how healthy and happy Brian looked.

Jessie added that he hadn't been around horses in years and just now realized how much he'd missed them.

Surprised, Doug said, "I didn't know you had any experience with horses."

"Sure, I grew up on a farm. I had a sweet cow pony that I always rode to help my dad pen the cows and check the fences and stuff like that. It was a good way to grow up."

"Well then, if you want to look around Pine Park, M&M would probably give you a great tour of the whole place as soon as camp is over today. Let's just wait a bit."

They watched while parents drove up to collect their children. As Brian and Jerry waved goodbye to the last boy, M&M came to the truck to say, "Welcome."

Doug told her, "I just found out that Jessie has a real fondness for horses. Why don't you show him around Pine Park?"

"I'd love to as soon as we all go to the kitchen so I can pass around glasses of cold lemonade. I need some myself."

Wildflower Wednesday

They all walked toward the house, with Doug hanging back and whispering to M&M that he hadn't told Jessie and Jean about the idea of them sharing quarters.

She gave him a puzzled look, hurried to catch up with the others and ushered them through the back door into the kitchen.

"Have a seat," she told Jessie, Jean and Doug as she poured glasses of lemonade and handed them around the table. "Brian and Jerry will be here shortly. They're putting horses out in paddocks for the afternoon."

"Our Brian sure looked happy out there," Jean remarked.

"He's been a great help with the kids, and he does seem to be having a good time."

"So," M&M began, "It seems that nobody has yet told you why you're here today. First, I want you to know how very sorry I am that the house burned."

As tears trickled down Jean's cheeks, she continued, "I can just imagine how disappointing this must be and the timing is awful. Jerry and I have an idea, a solution, at least temporarily, for you to remain near Brian and Doug. They are fine with it, so I hope you will be too."

She glanced at Doug for a nod of approval and when she got it, M&M continued, "Jerry and I would like for you to come and stay here with us."

"We couldn't possibly impose on you like that," Jean protested.

M&M assured her, "It's not an imposition. We have room. I know this kitchen isn't what you're used to, but—"

Jessie interrupted then. "Listen, Ms. Johnson, you are very generous to even offer such a thing, but we aren't charity cases. I do have a job, and we can afford to rent or buy our own little place."

Doug spoke up then, "Well, the places that the realty team

found aren't located close by, and Brian and I very much want you with us. We'd have you live with us except the motorhome just won't accommodate four people. I assure you that we will rebuild a house on my new property, which, by the way is just on the other side of that little pine forest." He pointed to the woods, "But you need someplace to go *right now*."

Brian and Jerry came in just then and interrupted the conversation with their own comments.

"Are you gonna come stay here?" Jerry asked as Brian went and hugged Jean and told her, "I sure hope so. You'd be nearby and can still cook good stuff for me. Dad isn't so great in the kitchen."

Tense as they were, all the adults chuckled at that.

"It seems to me that we need to think about this, talk about how it might work for everybody," Doug suggested, thinking that Jean and Jessie were too overwhelmed to have much of a discussion or make a decision. When he said, "Why don't I drive you over to the building site for a look at our camper," they both nodded and left without another word.

As they rode back to his office, Doug assured his longtime friends and employees that the idea had come from the Johnsons, and he had been as surprised as they were.

"*Please*, at least consider it, if it's even for a very short time. You'll have a place to go and be able to stay nearby to keep Brian well-fed. Jessie, it would be handy for you to be close to do the start-up landscaping at the building site too."

Jessie shook his head, "I just can't see us acting like house guests. It's too much like taking charity."

Jean was teary-eyed again when she reminded both men that she really wanted to be with *my Brian*.

Doug planted the seed for a working partnership with, "Look, Ms. Johnson is working as hard as she can to keep her place and she could sure use help of any kind. I know you could work out some kind of deal to help her—household duties as well as outside. Jessie, maybe you could be of some help around the barn. That boy of hers works like a farm hand every day."

"Me and Jean, we'll talk about it," Jessie promised as they got out of the truck.

Doug called M&M as soon as he let them out and went to the house.

"Tell Brian I'll be back over to pick him up in an hour or so."

"Okay. How did they seem? I thought you would have told them about the idea of them staying here before you came over."

"No, I figured it would come better directly from you."

"Well, did it?"

"Too soon to say. Jessie said they'd talk about it."

*****

Two evenings later, Jessie and Jean drove over to Pine Park to sit down with M&M and discuss the possibility of sharing her house.

"We didn't tell the boss we were coming over here," Jessie said.

"Why is that?"

Jessie volunteered, "He is always more than generous with us, and we don't want him paying our way for everything."

"And we don't want to impose on you," Jean added.

"Okay you two. Listen. This was Jerry's suggestion and I agree with him. We know how important it is to both Doug and Brian to have you with them. They have been more than generous in helping us out too, and we'd like to return the favor." She laughed. "My son also had an ulterior motive with this idea of his. He *loves* Jean's fried chicken and figures she'll cook some for him if she's here."

All three chuckled at that. Then Jean said, "Of course, I can cook chicken for him. Or whatever else he likes."

An hour later, they had outlined a plan that all found

acceptable. Jean was going to act as cook for both the Wilson and Johnson families. Jessie was going to pitch in and help around the barn.

He assured M&M that he knew how to lead horses in and out of stalls and paddocks, clean and bed stalls and fill hay nets. "I'll enjoy doing it," he insisted, "And besides, we have to contribute to Pine Park if we're gonna stay here."

Jerry came in from the barn and shouted "Hurray!" when he learned about the agreement.

He told Jean and Jessie that he was turning his bedroom over to them and he could have it cleared out and ready for their furnishings in a day.

Jean hugged him and thanked him for giving up his room to them.

He responded, "It's a great trade for some of your fried chicken"

Chapter 19

M&M could scarcely believe how quickly and easily her house was rearranged.

Just three days after she, Jessie and Jean had agreed on how they could share living quarters and responsibilities around the house and barn, Jerry had moved his bed and chest of drawers into her office and put the rest of his furnishings into the nearby storage shed. Jessie had followed up by putting their bedroom furniture in place and asked if some of Jean's cooking utensils could go into the kitchen.

M&M laughed out loud. "Certainly, tell Jean to make room for whatever she needs. I can put some of my stuff in the storage shed. I know my kitchen will seem inadequate to her after the big kitchen at Doug's place."

"Don't you worry about my Jean. She can prepare a good meal anywhere with a couple of pots or skillets."

M&M thought she proved it two nights later when Jean cooked the first dinner for six. The adults had, by then, determined that all could manage their own breakfasts, Jean would make what she called picnic or sack lunches for everybody each day and then cook an evening meal that they would share, seated around the kitchen table at Pine Park. It was, as Doug pointed out, larger than the little dinette in his RV.

When they finished the meal with a rich butterscotch pie topped with whipped cream, M&M assured Jean that having her in the kitchen was "the best thing ever." Jerry agreed and hopped up to clear the table.

"That was *so* good, I'm volunteering to do the dishes," he said. Brian got up to help him.

Astonished at the boys, M&M grinned, "Yep! Best thing ever."

She continued to think so as Jessie pitched in around the barn, cutting down on the time and energy she spent in cleaning, bedding and feeding chores.

After the first week, Doug came over, found her alone out in the tack room and pointedly asked, "Is everything going okay, having Jean and Jessie over here?"

"Doug, it's actually wonderful. They are *so* helpful, both of them. I'm not used to having help, and I guess I'd better not get used to it, but it's sure nice."

She thought he looked relieved, but he didn't say so, just, "I thought it very generous of you to even offer to share your house with them."

She smiled. "You know the saying, 'If both parties think it's a good deal, then it's a good deal'."

"Well, I guess I'm the third party in this, but I see it as a good deal too. I still get the benefit of having them nearby."

Changing the subject, she asked, "How's everything going over at your building site?"

"Seems slow to me. I'm having the burned-out building cleared away and first stakes are going up for the new house."

"Is it hard, living in that little camper?"

"No, it's okay. I like being close to Brian, and I'm not there most of the day—most of my time is at one or the other of my offices. I'm glad Brian can come over here, even when it's not camp time."

"He's always welcome here. You know, our boys seem to really get along well."

"Yes, they do. Let's take them out for something fun. How

about dinner and a movie?"

"It would give Jean a night off, too. Sounds good."

"So, what kind of movie, or meal?"

She chuckled and admitted, "I don't know anything about the latest movies. Why don't we let the boys pick one?"

"That could be risky, but I guess we can survive anything for a couple of hours."

They agreed to ask Brian and Jerry for preferences, then checked the time. By then, they needed to get to work.

Hers involved saddling a young mare in for training before getting camp horses ready.

She didn't give another thought to movie going until they all met for supper and Doug asked the boys, "Is there a good movie on around here?"

Jerry answered first, "I think there's a good one on at the downtown theater."

Brian asked, "Why?"

Doug answered, "Just thinking. Miranda and I want to take you guys to eat out and see a movie."

"*Who* is Miranda?" Brian and Jerry asked in unison, causing her to laugh loud and long.

When she caught her breath, she explained that Doug didn't find M&M a suitable name for an older woman.

"That's not *exactly* what I said," he protested, and she laughed again.

They all agreed on an Italian dinner followed by the remake of a popular old western movie.

"We can go tomorrow night," M&M said. "No camp the next day."

"Sounds like Jean gets the night off," Jessie said, and Doug nodded.

*****

Doug was astonished when both boys ate every bite of

their salads, spaghetti and garlic bread, then asked if they had time for dessert.

"Okay, guys. Sure, you can have dessert. I forget that you are both bottomless pits. You must really work up big appetites working at horse camp."

"Yes, sir," Jerry answered. "And it's a treat for us to eat in a restaurant,"

When their waiter came around with the dessert menu, the adults shook their heads, but Brian and Jerry ordered pie ala mode and again consumed every morsel.

Glancing at his watch, Doug told them, "Time to go if we don't want to miss the start of that movie, but not to worry, I'll get you some popcorn."

Two hours later, all four were discussing the merits of the remake of a favorite movie as Doug drove them home.

When Jerry and his mom got out of the truck at Pine Park, she said, "That was fun. Thanks for thinking of it."

"We'll do it again sometime," Doug answered, then waited in the drive until he saw that both were safely inside their house.

As he headed to the motorhome, Brian added his thanks. "I really had fun tonight. I'm glad we all get along so well, and I'm glad we're moving over here."

He paused then, and Doug thought his voice choked up before he added, "Dad, I still miss Mom and Thomas, but somehow it's not as lonely over here."

"I know."

Doug Wilson fell asleep thinking how glad he was that Brian had suggested the move to Marshall.

He awoke thinking how complicated his life had become with two business offices to run.

As they ate breakfast, he told Brian, "I've got to go over to the Longview office this morning, then come back to the one here for a couple of hours. Want to come along?"

Brian shook his head.

"You know I don't want to leave you here alone."

"Okay, drop me off over at Pine Park. I can hang out with Jerry. Or pester Jean into baking me a few dozen cookies."

Relieved by the suggestion, Doug agreed, and they were soon on the way.

Brian was opening the truck door before it rolled to a complete stop and Doug didn't even go ask anyone if it was okay for Brian to be there. He saw Jean's bright smile as she waved from the back door.

With his son happily and safely spending the day at Pine Park, Doug could turn his thoughts to his business. As he drove to Longview, he rehearsed his office meeting speech to his staff.

He was beyond surprised when everyone stood and applauded upon his entrance.

Sam Cunningham said, "Good to have you back here, Boss,"

Doug couldn't remember when, if ever, that his employees had seemed that glad to see him.

Sam explained it when they were alone in Doug's office. "We're so glad to see you happy again. It must be contagious."

Doug hadn't until that moment realized how his state of mind had affected his employees. They had been loyal even when he was distraught, demanding, probably unreasonable.

"Sam, I've been so fortunate to have this group of people work for me and with me, and I need to tell them so. Let's get that meeting started."

When all the employees assembled in the big meeting room, Doug was able to tell them, "Thank you, all of you, for your compassion and your hard work for Wilson Realty. I'm happy to tell you that my son Brian is doing amazingly well. The secondary office in Marshall is almost organized thanks to those of you who have helped train new employees. Wilson Real Estate is still thriving, and our success will be reflected in year-end bonuses for all of you."

When that announcement was met with gasps of surprise followed by applause, Doug concluded the meeting with, "Now, get out there and list some new properties, or sell a farm. Go!" He laughed and waved as they left.

He was still smiling as he drove back to Marshall.

He swung the truck into the Pine Park drive to check on Brian before going on to the Marshall office.

"Hey, Mr. Wilson, we're all out in the barn," Jerry yelled as he stepped out of the truck.

He found the boys and Jessie watching as M&M quickly put a vet wrap on Patch's left foreleg.

"What happened?"

"The ponies got into a kicking match in the paddock," Jerry explained, "Jessie broke it up before it got too bad."

M&M straightened up and added, "Yeah, good thing he did, or poor little Patch might have needed the vet."

"So, the pony will be okay?" Brian asked.

She nodded, "Yep. Thanks to Jessie's quick thinking, Patch probably won't even miss a day of camp."

She led Patch to an empty stall as Jessie was telling them Jean probably had lunch sacks ready to pass around if they were hungry.

"Let's go," Brian said as he and Jerry headed for the house with Jessie close behind.

Doug waited to walk with M&M.

She told hm, "The boys are still talking about how much they enjoyed going to the movies."

"I had a good time too. I was just thinking, we ought to do it again sometime soon."

When she nodded, he added, "And I was thinking, maybe sometime, the two of us could go to dinner or something."

She looked surprised and asked him, "Do you mean like just

you and me?"

"That's what I mean."

"Doug, I don't *date*. I haven't ever thought about it."

"Wait a minute! Who said anything about a *date*? I thought two friends could go out to eat together without putting another name to it. We *are* friends now, aren't we?"

Relief flooded her face. "Yes, of course we're friends."

"Good! Then pick out a place you'd like to eat, and let me know what you decide. Deal?"

She nodded as they stepped into her kitchen.

Chapter 20

Brian could hardly believe how soon camp would be over and school would be starting. He almost hated to think about the changes ahead of him. Helping with camp had been fun. The kids liked him, and he was able to move normally, ride reasonably well and do his share of the tasks expected of camp counselors. He was troubled to realize he had no friends his own age except for Jerry. He wasn't really looking forward to being the new kid at school. Just as he shook his head to clear it of negative thoughts, Jerry hollered, "Breakfast is ready. Get a move on."

He scurried to the kitchen just as Jean was placing a platter of hot biscuits filled with sausages in the center of the table. "Help yourselves," she told the boys, and they didn't have to be told twice.

He joined Jerry in thanking Jean. "We know we're supposed to get our own breakfast," he said, "So you're *really* nice to fix ours."

"Yeah, but we need to hurry up and eat," Jerry urged, "Mom and Jessie are already out in the barn starting chores."

Both boys left the table with an extra biscuit in hand, and as they walked, Jerry told Brian, "Band practice starts next week, and it's early in the morning, before it gets hot, but if you want to tag along, I can introduce you to some kids and sorta show you around campus."

"Thanks. I want to go."

Thoughts then switched back to campers and horses. Brian

Wildflower Wednesday

helped groom and saddle mounts for the first class scheduled in the arena, then went to the tack room to organize his supplies. He had taken one western bridle apart to surprise the camp kids with a little test. When they came in, he said, "Today is test day."

Seeing their surprised faces, he softened the news. "No, you won't get graded, this is just to see how much you remember about bridles. He held up the headstall and asked, "Who can name this part?" and little Patty was first to answer. The kids took turns identifying the bit, reins and curb strap, then explaining the part each played in signaling the horse. Then he asked for a volunteer to re-assemble the bridle, and all hands shot up.

"Wow! You guys have learned a lot."

"That's because they had a good teacher," M&M announced from the open doorway. "Now it's time for you to go to your next session. That will be grooming tips out by the crossties. Jerry is waiting for you there."

As the campers left, she added, "I really meant it, Brian. You've been a great teacher and helper for camp."

He grinned and repeated her words, "That's because I've had a good teacher. In fact, *two* good teachers, you and Jerry. And next week he's gonna take me to school and teach me the ropes there."

"You'll do just fine," she encouraged, and Brian so hoped she was right.

*****

M&M called on everybody to help plan for a special last day of camp. She knew she would be in the center of the arena directing the young riders as they performed for their parents. She had printed little graduation certificates for each camper, and Tiffany made rosette ribbons to decorate them. Jean baked sugar cookies in cutout shapes of boots and horseshoes for refreshment time. Brian and Jerry put their heads together, struggling to think of a contribution.

Finally, Brian said, "I know. Let's each have a bucket of treats—carrots or alfalfa cubes—so the kids can take them to the horses when they say goodbye."

"That's a good idea. What made you think of it?"

"I remember how I fell in love with Goldilocks when she took a treat from my hand."

And on that final day of camp, every camper took treats to their favorite horses. Some hugged them.

Some had tears in their eyes as they said goodbye. Brian did too. His dad was standing nearby and noticed. "You okay?" he asked.

"Yeah. I just know it's hard to say goodbye." Then he smiled. "I never thought working with kids at a camp would be so much fun, or that I'd hate to see them go."

M&M overheard as she approached. "It is bittersweet, isn't it?"

Jerry joined them then and added, "Yeah, it's been a good summer, in lots of ways. But now, Jessie sent me to tell all of you that Jean has a special late lunch ready for us. Let's go eat."

They were soon seated around the table, too busy eating to talk until dessert was finished.

Then Doug said, "I hope camp met your expectations. Do you think you'll do it again?"

M&M nodded, "It was better than I expected. My finances are good enough that I *might* be able to get PATH certification this fall. Jerry and I will be putting our heads, and our lists together later, to see exactly how to proceed. I certainly couldn't have done so well without a lot of help, and you, all of you, have been wonderful. Thank you just doesn't get it."

"I'm the one who needs to say thank you," Brian said, "I was pathetic when I first came to Pine Park, and I'm almost a regular kid now."

"I'll second that," came from Doug.

Then Jean and Jessie started to praise M&M for sharing her house and she threw up her hands, laughed and silenced them all with, "Okay, that's what friends do. We help each other."

As they went back to their motorhome, Brian told his dad, "You know, I really meant what I said, about how riding and working at camp helped *me*."

"I know. You've come such a long way."

Chapter 21

Brian was almost asleep when his cell phone chimed. He picked it up to hear Jerry. "Hey, I've got band practice in the morning. I know it's early, but do you wanna go? You'll get to meet a few kids before school starts."

"Sure, I'll go."

"Great. Mom has to drop me off. We'll come over and get you. It'll be about 6:45."

Brian fell asleep thinking about meeting some Marshall kids, and awoke thinking more about being the new kid.

"I guess I'm a little nervous," he told Doug as he finished his cereal and rose to go out and meet Jerry.

"Hey, glad you're coming along," M&M welcomed him when he stepped up into her truck.

"Me too. I'm glad Jerry asked me. He's the only teenager I know over here."

M&M let them out near the school stadium, and they started walking to the track where the band members were gathering.

"I'm a little nervous, meeting a bunch of new people. I hope your friends don't think I'm a weirdo or somethin'"

"Why would they?"

Brian shrugged and Jerry reassured him. "Now, if they'd met you back when I did, they might think you're a miracle man or somethin' cause the first time I saw you, you could hardly stand up, and look at you now!"

"Thanks, but I still feel a little out of place, you know. I used to be something of a jock, and now...."

"And now you're the new kid at school. I get that. Now come on and let's get the first introductions out of the way."

Jerry led the way to the band director and said, "Hey gang, this is my neighbor, Brian Wilson. He just moved to Marshall."

Several just said, "Hi." One of the boys introduced himself as Wayne and started kidding Brian, "By the end of the week, it'll be time for a test to see how many of our names you can remember."

A petite blonde girl told him her name and asked if he would be playing in the band.

Brian was engaged in active conversation by the time practice started and he took a seat in the stands to watch his soon to-be classmates play as they marched.

A few minutes later, other boys gathered in midfield and were soon following orders for jumping jacks, sit ups, then push-ups. Brian guessed they were members of the football team, confirmed when band practice ended and Jerry called out, "Hi Coach!" to the man directing drills.

"They're in the middle of their warmups, probably waiting for us to get off the track so they can run sprints. I'll introduce you to some of the players another time," he told Brian.

They spotted M&M's truck on the parking lot and hurried to load up and head for home.

"Your friends were nice and friendly," Brian told Jerry. "Thanks for asking me to go along. I'd like to do it again."

"Next practice is Thursday morning."

M&M interrupted. "Brian, do you think your dad could provide transportation if I'm out of town?"

"I'm sure he can."

"Outta town? Where are you going?" Jerry asked.

"It's not for sure yet. Lots of details to work out, but I may go to one of the PATH certified centers to work on some training requirements."

"Mom, that's awesome! But ... *how* can you be gone from Pine Park? And I thought the application process was expensive and...."

"Don't get too excited yet, son. Like I said, there are details to work out, mainly ones that involve you being okay in my absence."

"Mom, I'm not a baby!"

Brian tried hard, but he couldn't help but laugh.

"What's so funny?" Jerry demanded to know.

"You sound just like me when my dad tried to be so careful not to leave me alone."

"It's what parents *do*," M&M informed them.

The boys continued to alternately chuckle and whine about being treated like helpless little kids until they pulled up by the Wilson's motorhome.

Doug came out to meet them and Brian immediately volunteered, "Jerry might need a 'trustworthy companion' for a few days. Can I volunteer?"

"What *are* you talking about?"

Both boys were giggling before M&M could even begin to explain her pending trip to PATH headquarters.

Doug shushed them with a stern look and suggestion that they permit him to have "an adult conversation" with M&M.

By then, she was laughing too. "It seems my friends have been busy behind my back, making all kinds of recommendations and requests so that I can get special consideration to become a certified PATH instructor. I'm working on taking a quick trip to headquarters for testing and training, *if* I can make satisfactory, safe arrangements for my kid and horses."

"Well, Brian and I will love having Jerry with us, although

the sleeping arrangements may be less than luxurious, and I know Jessie and Jean will do whatever is needed."

She smiled her thanks before Doug continued, "I'm not much of a hand with horses, but these guys and Jessie can surely take care of the basics."

"They can, but I need to make calls and arrange schedule changes for some horses coming in for training, plus be sure my bank balance can stand the shift."

Brian got out of her truck still grinning at the prospect of spending more time with Jerry.

As he and his dad went into the motorhome, he said, "Dad, I had a great morning, met some nice kids. I think I'm really gonna like living over here."

"Well, I hope so, since construction starts on the house next week, and my office in Marshall is already doing well."

"That's great!"

"Brian, there's something we need to talk about, seriously talk about."

"What?"

"Transportation."

"What do you mean?"

"I mean, what if I can't always be available to drive you to wherever you need to go?"

"Gee, you and Ms. Johnson seem to kinda take turns taking me and Jerry places. And I know Jessie will give us a ride."

"That's not what I'm talking about and I think you know it."

Brian hung his head. His lower lip trembled. He mumbled, "I guess I do know."

"Son, I had hoped never to have to have this conversation with you, but now, well, I think it's time."

Brian felt tears forming as his dad continued, "I haven't pushed you about driving, but you can't live in fear of it. You've got to get back behind the wheel sometime."

He hesitated briefly, then continued in spite of Brian's tears, "I think that time is *now*."

Brian shook his head. "No, I can't. Every time I think about driving, it's like I feel that truck hitting the car and turning us over. I don't ever want to drive."

"Okay, then it's time for us to discuss this with somebody smarter than me. Do you want to see the counselor in Longview, or talk with Dr. Clay?"

"I don't want to drive!"

He began to sob while Doug talked, "Son, I can't make you drive, but I can make you face your fear of it. I'm going to get an appointment with Dr. Clay, since you seem to like him, and we will go to him, together, as soon as he can see us."

As a child, Brian had never been spanked, rarely been scolded, but he thought then that he knew how it felt to be whipped.

His father's shoulders sagged as he stepped outside to make a phone call. When he came back into the motorhome, Brian was still sniffling.

"Okay, we can get in to confer with Dr. Clay in a few days. Now, let's talk about something else.

How do you and Jerry plan to hang out together while his mom is gone?"

"I don't know, but this trip is a really big deal for her, and I guess she won't go unless she's sure Jerry will be *looked after*, whatever that means."

"I'll check with her a little later, reassure her that I'll do what I can to help with that."

Chapter 22

M&M was in the kitchen telling Jessie and Jean how she hoped to make the trip to PATH headquarters when Doug walked in.

"I know I'm interrupting, but it's intentional. Brian filled me in, and I'm tossing my hat in the ring as a helper."

"Thanks, Doug, but it just seems *so* complicated. I have a barn full of horses out there and a teenager who still needs a bit of parental supervision."

"Okay, I have a teenager too, and they get along, so how about letting me parent them both for a few days."

Jean interrupted, "I can help with those boys. They'll be well fed, their clothes will be kept clean, and we'll let them sleep here, or camp in the motorhome, but one of us will be with them."

"The horses, some of them aren't even mine."

"From what your friends are saying, most of them could be, if you want them," Jessie added. "And about taking care of them, I know the basic stuff, and that boy of yours knows everything about managing your barn. All you need to do if see that there's plenty of feed and bedding on hand, or ordered, and leave the name and number of your vet, just in case we need him."

Doug grinned, "Well, it all seems to be settled, Miranda. All you have to do is get yourself to that PATH place and pass those tests."

She wore a smile as she dropped into the nearest chair. "I

don't know how to thank you, all of you."

Jerry walked in just in time to hear Doug say, "Just go."

"Mom, it's great that you have the opportunity to work on certification for Pine Park. It's one of the things that'll keep the farm going in the right direction. I vote with Mr. Wilson. Just go."

She nodded.

Ten minutes later she was in the barn, followed by Jessie and Jerry. With notebook in hand, she went to every horse and talked about any special feed or handling. She even asked Jerry if he could ride Sarge at least every other day.

"You know, he's being given to us because he didn't do well turned out to pasture. It seems he needs to have a job."

"I got it, Mom. What about Gwen?"

"Susanna wants to take her home. The kicker is, she'd like to bring the filly over here to get some extra handling, lunge line lessons. Susanna just hasn't had the time to spend with her."

"No problem. I can work with the filly."

She nodded, "I know you can. The rest of the school horses are due a vacation—you know, some turn out time."

Jessie spoke up, "I can sure put horses in and out, keep their stalls clean. Between us, Jerry and I will see to their feed and water twice a day.

Jerry added, "And Brian wants to help, *really*, and I'm nominating him to be the head groom. He knows how to use a brush and curry comb as well as anybody."

"Okay, guys. You've convinced me. I'm going for that certification. Now, if I just don't flunk the tests."

"Mom! That's not gonna happen. You're the best horsewoman ever."

She grinned her thanks, "You're probably a little prejudiced."

"When do you leave, and how will you get there?" Doug

asked.

"First of next week, and I'm flying. Tiffany found me a cheap ticket. Of course, it means I'll be leaving at dark thirty in the morning and returning in the middle of the night, Shreveport airport."

"I'll give you a ride, both ways," Doug offered.

She opened her mouth to protest, changed her mind and said, "Thank you."

*****

Three mornings later, Doug arrived at her door promptly at 4 a.m., took the luggage from her hands and walked her to the truck. He opened the door for her before loading her suitcases into the back.

When he slid behind the wheel, she started to thank him. "Doug, getting up this early to drive me to the airport was more than thoughtful. I don't know how to thank you."

To her surprise, he reached over, patted her hand. "No thanks necessary. Like you've said, friends help each other. You didn't have to set up a program just for Brian, but you did. You gave me my son back."

She protested, "But you paid me, paid me very well."

"Just stop it," he insisted. "We're not gonna be keeping score about who did what for who, are we?"

"No, you're right. We *are* friends."

"And don't' forget, now we're neighbors too."

She nodded and sank back for the ride to the airport.

When they reached the terminal, Doug insisted on taking her luggage to check out, then walking her as far as security allowed. She started to thank him again and he silenced her with a quick hug and said, "Good luck. See you next week."

He drove back to Marshall realizing that, to his surprise, he was going to miss Miranda Johnson.

When he stepped back into their motorhome, he found

Brian rummaging in the refrigerator. "What are you doing up so early?"

"Looking for a quick breakfast. I promised Jerry I'd come over and help with the barn chores. They always start early, and now he really has to because his mom is gone, and he has to go to band practice. I might tag along with him again if it's okay."

"Sure, it's okay. Let me find the frozen waffles and pop them in the toaster. Pour us some juice."

As they finished eating, he asked, "How are you going to get to school grounds and back?"

Brian shrugged, shook his head. "I don't know for sure. I think Jessie is taking us and picking us up. Jerry just has a learner's permit, so he can't drive his mom's truck with just me in the front with him."

"I see."

"See what?"

"I see the need for both of you boys to get some practice behind the wheel so you can provide your own transportation."

Brian paled, "Dad, I don't want—"

"This is about *need*, not want, and we will be seeing Dr. Clay to help you out with this."

Brian changed the subject to, "Can you drive me over to Pine Park? It's a long hike through the woods."

"I can. This time, but here's just one example of why you need to be back driving." He paused, then added, "What would you think about having one of those four-wheeler things? They aren't approved for streets and highways, but it would be a good way to go between here and Pine Park."

Brian brightened, "That might be neat. Could Jerry use it too?"

"We'll see. Right now, we'd better get you over there to help in the barn."

They found Jerry filling hay nets and Jessie filling water

buckets.

"Am I too late to help? Brian asked.

"Not hardly," Jerry told him. "You get to take the pony out to the paddock and brush Sarge while I fill the grain buckets for Jessie. Then it'll be time to go."

Doug saw the boys were focused on their tasks, then checked with Jessie about getting them to school grounds and back.

"I got it covered. Me and Jerry already talked about it. I'm his driver on band practice days, and if Brian wants to come along, I'll see he gets there and back too."

"Okay then. I'll be at my Marshall office until noon. Tell Jean she doesn't need to fix my lunch. I'll grab a bite downtown and check back mid-afternoon."

As he drove to work, he reminded himself to call a farm equipment store and ask about those four-wheelers.

*****

Brian and Jerry talked all the way to the school grounds.

"I really like the kids I've met so far. It won't seem quite so weird, you know, going to a new school if I at least know a few names and faces."

Jerry nodded, "I think you'll like a lot of things about our school. For the most part, the teachers and the kids are really nice. We haven't talked about it much, but I guess you'll find you have things in common with classmates. Are you into joining clubs?

"Not really. Are you?"

"No time for any more extra stuff since I do band and the horse judging team for FFA. That means most of the kids I hang with are into horses. There are a few serious musicians in the band, but I'm not one of them. I just like to play the drums and march."

When Brian didn't say anything for long minutes, Jerry

asked, "What kids did you hang out with in Longview?"

He shrugged and tried to laugh, "I guess I was something of a jock, mostly ran around with the rest of the soccer team. Emphasis on *was*, I can't play anymore."

"I bet you'll find something else that you like, and can do," Jerry said, and Jessie added, "Sure you will. Smart boy like you will have new friends and new activities in no time."

"Maybe. I hope so," Brian answered as they arrived by the football field.

He and Jerry stepped out of the truck and waved goodbye to Jessie just in time to greet two girls from the band.

"Hi!" said a petite redhead, "I'm Joanne. We saw you with Jerry the other day. Are you going to be attending Marshall High?"

Brian nodded.

"Will you be playing in the band with us?" asked the other girl.

He chuckled. "No, and you wouldn't want me to. I have absolutely no musical talent."

"Maybe you'll be in one of my classes," Joanne said as she picked up her instrument and went to line up for marching practice.

Brian told Jerry, "Wow, I was afraid she was gonna ask questions I couldn't answer."

"It's like Jessie said, you'll find things to do."

"I hope so," he muttered as he went to sit on the bleachers and watch the band members march around the track while the football boys stretched and warmed up in the center of the field.

An hour later, he and Jerry were climbing into Jessie's truck and he mentioned, "I watched the football team practice, and they looked less than enthusiastic. What's with that? Doesn't Marshall have a good team?"

Jerry shook his head, "I don't know. We had a great team

last season, but several starters were seniors. Maybe the younger guys don't have much experience. I'll try to pay attention next time or ask Coach. He'll probably be my history teacher."

They were soon back at Pine Park and found Doug waiting with an invitation.

"I called around and got some info about those four wheelers. Let's go take a look."

Jerry started for his house, but Doug stopped him, "No, I want you to go too. Brian and I already talked about one of these things being handy for getting from our place to yours."

When Jerry hesitated, Doug added, "I already cleared it with Jean. She knows I'll have you back before lunch, both of you. I'll be going back to work and stay at my office while you take care of everything here."

With that information, both boys climbed into Doug's truck, surprised but excited about what they were going to do.

At the dealership, Doug quickly explained his needs to the sales manager and they were led into a row of parked four-wheel vehicles and picked the one they liked. The salesman demonstrated it and then asked if they wanted to try it out. When they hesitated, Doug insisted. "Come on guys. You both will be using this thing to get back and forth. You have to give it a test drive. Climb in and take it around the parking lot."

Brian stood back, so Jerry climbed behind the wheel and said, "Get in."

He took two turns around the lot, then stepped out and encouraged Brian to try it out, "It's a piece of cake. You'll like it."

A silent, pale Brian sat behind the wheel and with shaking hand, started it up. He drove ever so slowly around the lot once, then brightened, smiled, and went a little faster.

"It's okay. I can handle it," he told his dad when he braked to a stop.

An hour later, they were on their way back to Pine Park with the newly purchased four-wheeler and load ramps in the truck bed.

"Wow! It's gonna be neat that Brian can just come over anytime now," Jerry said.

Chapter 22

Jerry tried not to worry about keeping everything at Pine Park operating just as it would if his mom were there. Jessie was a big help and kept offering to take on more of the chores if necessary. Brian came over every day and did what he could, surprising all of them with his increasing strength and stamina.

When he asked about riding, Jerry said, "Let's be sure it's okay with your dad. If he says yes, then you can ride Sarge. We're supposed to keep him happy, and that means letting him think he's working."

Brian was so excited at the prospect that he talked his dad into it, and Jerry thought it made both his new best friend *and* the old horse happy.

As Jessie drove them to the field the next morning, Brian asked him, "Do you think your mom will be pleased with how we managed at Pine Park?"

"I sure hope so. We've all tried to do it just like she would." He paused. "I think we've done fine. I guess I just miss her. I don't think I've ever been away from her for longer than a weekend, and that was for a band trip or a horse judging competition, so I was too busy to miss her so much." He hesitated before whispering, "I guess I sound like a baby."

"Nope," Jessie assured him, "You're just being honest, and there's nothing wrong with loving and missing your mother."

Brian added, "I know I'd *really* miss my dad, especially now that there's just the two of us."

"Here we are," Jessie said as he braked the truck. Both boys climbed out and waved goodbye before starting for the track.

Brian sat on the bleachers and watched as the band marched and played, and the football boys stretched and started their warmups.

When the band came off the track, Jerry passed the players as they got ready to sprint, and said hi to the coach.

When the coach absent-mindedly nodded, Jerry asked, "What's up, Coach? The whole team looks so down. Are you making practice *that* hard?" he half-joked.

He was surprised at the coach's response. "To tell you the truth, I'm probably more down than the players. You know we lost a lot of starting seniors, and now we are a young inexperienced team without a kicker."

"What do you mean, without a kicker?"

"I mean, *none* of them, not a single one, can kick the ball 20 yards. We keep drilling, they keep trying, but it looks almost hopeless. Unless they get much better in a hurry, we might as well say we don't have a team this year."

"Gee, Coach. I'm sorry to hear that. Maybe one of them will be a fast learner."

The coach snorted and walked off behind his players.

On the way home, Brian said, "I saw you talking to the coach. He looked kinda mad."

"I think he's more *sad*. He told me none of the boys on the team can kick a ball more than 20 yards, so they might as well not have a team."

Jerry paused in thought, then asked, "You used to play soccer. Can you kick a ball?"

Brian shrugged. "I guess so. I haven't been practicing. No reason to."

When they got back to Pine Park, he told Jerry, "You've made me wonder if I can still kick. I know it won't hurt me to try. Do you have a ball, any kind of ball around here?"

"Sure, we keep balls in a box in the corner of the barn. Sometimes kids need something to play with while their brother or sister has a riding lesson. Why?"

"I thought I might practice kicking, just to see if I can. But I'd rather do it over here than at our place. I don't want my dad to think I'm going to try to play soccer. He'd have a fit."

"Why?"

"Because, I have a steel plate screwed into my leg, and I can't risk breaking it, or taking a hard blow to my head because I had such a bad concussion."

"But you can still kick a ball?

"I think so. My kicking foot is on the good leg. Go get me a ball and we'll find out."

An hour later, Jerry was watching Brian kick an old soccer ball from one end of the arena to the other. When he stopped to catch his breath, he was sweating profusely, but wore a big smile as he sent Jerry a thumbs up sign.

Then, checking the time, they both rushed to the barn to finish grooming and stall cleaning chores before lunch.

When they sat down to eat, Jessie and Jean both asked how things were going with the horses and barn chores, reminding them that M&M would be home in two more days.

"I'll be glad when she gets back, but I think everything's okay," Jerry answered, then turned to Brian, "Are you gonna ride Sarge today?"

"Yep, if Jessie or you will watch me. That's the deal."

"I'll watch you," Jerry volunteered, "That'll give me a break before working with that youngster and starting the feed routine."

He crossed his fingers *and* whispered a little prayer that Sarge and Brian would get along fine. He knew even a slight mishap would send Brian's dad into a protective rage.

He'd worried, even talked to his mom about it. She'd reassured him, explained that she too was the single parent of one child, so she understood Doug Wilson's attitude.

She'd told Jerry, "If you'd had the kind of injuries Brian had, I'd want to wrap you up in padded blanket and never let go."

He cringed at those words and went to help Brian saddle Sarge.

The horse was clearly happy to be the center of attention and pranced smartly when they led him to the mounting block in the arena.

"What's with him anyway?" Brian asked.

"I hope he's just feeling good about getting out and going to work."

Brian marched up the steps and swung into the saddle and Sarge didn't move until he was given the cue to walk. Jerry breathed a sigh of relief and thought Brian did too.

Brian walked and trotted the horse, stopped him, changed directions, and continued without a bobble. When he stopped again and asked Sarge to back, the old horse tucked his nose and went in reverse until Brian released pressure.

"Let's see if he knows the side pass," Jerry suggested and told Brian how to hold him in place and cue by pushing with one leg. Sarge showed them he knew that move too, both directions.

"He's sure a nice horse," Brian said. "I hope to eventually get one of my own, one that has manners like Sarge."

"I'm sure Mom can help find the right horse for you when you and your dad are ready. Let's put this guy out in the paddock, and I'll get to work with that filly."

Brian agreed and soon went to the house, then returned to help with barn chores. As they worked side by side, they talked about the schedule for the next day.

"I have band practice again in the morning. Wanna go?"

"Sure. I'll see if Jessie will drive us, then Dad can go to his office whenever he needs to."

"Your dad sure is busy, keeping up with two offices. It's nice that he offered to pick up Mom at the airport."

Brian said, "Yeah. Do you think your mom and my dad, you know, *like* each other?"

Jerry laughed. "I know they got off to a bad start, with your dad wanting Mom to do therapy for you, and she didn't think she could, and all that. I know they argued, made each other mad. I even heard my mom yell, which she never does. He paused, then added. "Yes, I think they're friends now."

"I mean maybe they might be, you know, *more* than friends."

"Yuck. No way! Mom has always said the two of us was enough for her."

"Well, I can't imagine my dad being romantic with *anybody,* and especially not so soon, or with somebody so different from my mom."

"Then why'd you ask the question?"

Brian shrugged. "Don't know. Just a weird feeling, I guess."

"Forget it."

Brian nodded. knowing it wasn't a subject he would bring up again.

*****

The next morning both boys had something entirely different to discuss.

Brian again watched while Jerry marched and played with the band, and the football team launched into pushups, sit ups and jumping jacks, all without enthusiasm.

When both the band and football boys were leaving the field, Jerry made a point of introducing Brian to the coach.

"Coach, Brian is my neighbor, transferring over here for school this year, and *maybe* he could help you out."

Brian looked surprised as Jerry continued, "He played soccer in Longview and he can really kick a ball. I saw him yesterday."

"Is that right, Brian?" the coach asked.

"Well, yes sir, me and Jerry were just foolin' around with an old ball yesterday, and I still know how to kick."

"Would you consider trying out to be our team kicker, or are you just interested in soccer?"

Brian hung his head and hesitated before answering, "I can't play soccer anymore. I got hurt in an accident and have a metal plate in one leg. I can still kick the ball, but I don't know much about football, and I don't know how I can help your team."

The coach asked if he would come out onto the field for a few minutes and show him how far he could kick and how well he could place the ball.

He shot Jerry a dirty look before agreeing to do as the coach asked.

The coach held a football, explained how he would hold it and where he wanted Brian to kick it. A smile lit up his face when Brian put that football every place he asked, kick after kick. The few football players that hadn't left the area were watching and started cheering when the coach said, "That's good enough. Brian, we'd sure like to have you on the team."

Brian didn't know how to answer him. He finally said, "I'm flattered, sir. I really want to fit in here, and I'd love to play sports again, but I honestly don't know if my dad will agree to it. He's afraid of me getting hurt again."

"Maybe I could come talk to him about it," the coach offered.

"Maybe," was the best Brian could say to that, already imagining his dad's reaction.

Just then, he spotted Jessie's truck in the parking lot and

said, "There's our ride. Gotta go."

On the way back to Pine Park, he told Jerry, "My dad is gonna want to ground us both for even suggesting this. I don't know if I should thank you or be mad at you."

"Neither. It sounds like your dad will be the one to decide that too."

An awkward silence prevailed all the way to Pine Park, as the boys climbed out of the truck, Jerry said, "Brian, I'm sorry if I did wrong. If your dad gets mad, I'll take all the blame. I don't want you to get in trouble."

Brian's answer was an unconvincing, "It'll be okay."

There was no further mention of the idea for the next twenty-four hours. All thoughts were focused on M&M's homecoming.

Jean picked Jerry's brain about favorite foods so she could prepare a welcome home dinner. Jessie and the boys made extra efforts to have the barn and the horses looking their best. Doug said nothing, but actually seemed to be looking forward to his midnight drive to the airport. The boys asked to go too, but he reminded them that they needed a good night's sleep, because barn work wasn't going away just because the "boss lady" was coming home.

*****

When her plane touched down on the runway, Doug was waiting, only slightly embarrassed to hold up a little sign the boys had made that said, "Welcome Home!"

When M&M spotted him, she started laughing and hurried towards him.

"You don't have to tell me, Brian and Jerry made the sign. How'd they talk *you* into bringing it?"

He chucked and admitted, "It was either promise to bring this sign or bring *them*, and I thought they needed a good night's rest. Those boys have worked *so* hard to keep everything just the way you want it. But you'll see that for yourself. Tell me about your trip."

"Doug, it was better than I'd dreamed. The director at PATH headquarters was wonderful, very accommodating to what I'll call my special needs."

At his inquiring look, she explained, "I had limited time to be at headquarters, not to mention limited funds. I got a scholarship of sorts, plus they brought in extra staff to do my training and testing in the shorter time frame."

"That *was* nice,"

She beamed then. "It was better than nice. I passed all the tests, meaning I am a certified teacher and after inspections and visits from other PATH staffers, Pine Park should become a certified center."

"That's awesome! Congratulations!" he said as he hugged her, then helped her into the truck before loading her luggage into the back.

"Under normal conditions, I'd say I should take you out to dinner to celebrate, but since it's almost two a.m. and you're no doubt exhausted, I'll do that another time."

"Thanks, Doug. I'm too exhausted to celebrate right now anyway," she admitted as she buckled her seat belt.

Minutes later, she was slumped over and snoring softly.

Doug let her sleep until he had the truck parked near her door. Then he nudged her gently, "Wake up, Sleeping Beauty. You're home."

Jean met them at the door and walked her to her room while Doug brought in her luggage.

"See you tomorrow," he said to both women as he went out the door.

Chapter 23

Doug went to both offices before noon, grabbed a sandwich at his favorite Longview café and hurried to pick up Brian at Pine Park in time for his session with Dr. Clay.

Eyes downcast, Brian dragged his feet through the dust as he came to the truck, climbing in slowly, he didn't offer a greeting until Doug said, "Okay, son. I know you don't particularly want to go talk to Dr. Clay, but I don't know any better way to handle your reluctance about driving."

His lips trembled when he answered, "I know, Dad. It's just hard. I wish we lived back in the old days. I could just ride a horse to school."

A smile brightened his face then when he said, "Or, maybe I could learn to drive a buggy. You know, like Doc did in Gunsmoke."

Doug had to grin at his son's attempt at humor. "We can see about you learning to drive a horse attached to a buggy, but that won't take the place of a motorized vehicle in this day and age."

"I know," he sighed.

They soon arrived at Dr. Clay's office and were immediately shown into a cozy little conference room.

"Since there are two of you, I thought we'd be more comfortable in here," Dr. Clay explained as he came through the other door. "Want something cool to drink?"

Doug looked at Brian, who shook his head.

"I think we're good, Doc. Thanks."

"Okay then." Dr. Clay turned to Brian, "You look like a very different young man than the one I first met just a few months ago. I get reports from your sessions at Pine Park and your physical therapist. Dr. Hood has signed off, saying you no longer need supervision from an orthopedist. Thanks to your dad, I've even seen your grades for the last semester."

When both Brian and Doug remained silent, he continued, "Good job, Brian!"

Brian just nodded.

"So, what brings you here today?"

Doug waited for his son to speak, but to his surprise, Brian burst into tears instead.

"Whatever it is, I can see you're in distress. Just take your time, Brian, and tell me when you're ready."

"It's my fault, I made him come."

"*Please*, Mr. Wilson. Let Brian tell me."

So, Doug watched for what seemed like hours, but actually only minutes, as Brian struggled to compose himself and speak clearly.

Finally, he began, "I'm scared to drive. I don't ever want to drive a car again. I start shaking just thinking about it. Dad says I *have* to."

Dr. Clay asked ever so softly, "Do *you* think you have to?"

Brian sniffled and nodded. "I know my dad is right but...," his voice trailed off as he began to cry again.

Doug found it so painful to watch that he wished he hadn't forced Brian to come, and he stood as if to leave.

Dr. Clay motioned him back into his chair and suggested, "Brian, this conversation seems to be as painful for your dad as it is for you. I'm going to suggest," he continued, "that both of you talk about steps to take to get past this hurdle in your recovery. Talk to each other, and to me, and let's see if we can't make some progress."

Wildflower Wednesday

Both Brian and Doug managed a grin when Dr. Clay added, "Nobody expects you to drive in the Indy 500, you know." He suggested, "Baby steps," then asked Brian what the first one might be.

"I think I already took one," Brian ventured. "I drove a four-wheeler, just a little slow circle around a parking lot, though."

"That's a start," Dr. Clay responded. "Next, maybe you could try that in a car or truck, not in traffic."

The conversation continued along those lines until Doug glanced at his watch, realizing they had already stayed past their appointment time. He stood again, and this time Dr. Clay nodded approval and helped end their session on a positive note.

"Why don't you try some of these things we've talked about, then come back to see me in a week or two."

Doug thanked him and they left with Doug wondering if he'd done the right thing, forcing Brian to face his fear. His son, his *only* family member, looked like a whipped puppy.

He was relieved that Brian fell asleep on the way home. At least they didn't have to talk any more about driving.

Back in the motorhome, they both needed what Doug called "refueling" and snooped through their little pantry and refrigerator for snacks.

Doug readily agreed when Brian told him, "Good thing Jean is cooking for us. We don't have a lot of good stuff here."

Then they both heard a car approaching on the gravel drive to the motorhome. Looking out the window, Doug was surprised to see not one, but a line of cars and trucks coming toward them."

"What the heck? Somebody must've taken a wrong turn. I don't recognize any of these vehicles. He stepped outside just as the first car stopped, the driver rolled down his window and asked, "Is this the Wilson place?"

"It is. I'm Doug Wilson. How can I help you?"

Just then Brian stepped out of the motorhome and called out, "Hello Coach."

Puzzled, Doug asked, "So, how do you know my son?"

He noticed that the long line of vehicles in his driveway were no longer moving and the occupants of those vehicles were emerging and walking towards him.

Brian spoke up first, "I met the coach when I went with Jerry to band practice and he introduced me around. The football team was practicing too, so I met some of these guys."

Coach Bradley stepped out of his car and told Doug, "We've come to talk to you about Brian joining our team this season. We really need a kicker and he's *good*."

As the coach spoke, the boys came closer, until they were clustered around the two men, while Brian remained on the motorhome steps.

Doug frowned, looking from his son to the group gathered around him and asked, "How do you *know* he's good? And do you *also* know that he was critically injured and carries a steel plate in one leg?"

"Mr. Wilson, your boy told us he had been injured, couldn't play soccer anymore, but he also showed us he can still kick a ball anywhere he wants it to go."

Doug's fists were clenched, his faced clouded in anger when Brian interrupted, "Dad, what happened was, the guys were thinking they wouldn't even have a team without a kicker, and Jerry told them maybe I could kick for them—"

"So, *Jerry* is responsible for this," Doug all but roared. "There's no way Brian can play football. Not only does he have a leg that can't stand another harsh blow, he's had a severe concussion and can't risk another one."

Mortified that he was about to spill tears, Brian just shook his head and murmured, "Sorry," and went back inside.

Wildflower Wednesday

The boys and their coach left without another word, but Doug had plenty more to say.

He called Pine Park and when Jean answered he shouted, "You tell Ms. Johnson and her son to come over here *right now!*"

She apparently relayed the urgent sound of the message because M&M and Jerry drove up within minutes.

"What's going on?" she asked as she climbed out of the truck. Then, noting Brian's pathetic look asked another question, "What's wrong?"

"I'll tell you what's wrong! Your son got Brian all but signed up to play football. *Football!* Do you even realize how absurd that is? He can't even play soccer anymore, can't risk his damaged leg or having another concussion. What in heavens name were you thinking, Jerry?"

Jerry paled at the accusation and tried to apologize.

"Stop!" Brian yelled from the open door of the motorhome. "Just stop! Jerry was trying to help me fit in at a new school. I'm the one who showed off that I could still kick a ball. And I'm glad I can still kick."

Before Doug could yell again, M&M stepped to his side and laid a gentle hand on his shoulder. "Doug, I understand your fear for Brian."

"No, you don't."

"Yes, I do. Remember, I too am the single parent of just one child. He's all I have. I *do* understand your protective attitude."

Doug drew in a deep breath, ready to argue the point, but Brian spoke first, "Dad, I know you're afraid for me. I get that. I'm scared too, but I'm more scared of not being *normal* anymore. I'd rather get hurt than not be able to do anything."

Tears streaked Jerry's cheeks as he stepped forward. "Mr. Wilson, I *am* sorry if I put Brian in a dangerous position. I didn't mean to. He's my best friend."

When he turned and ran back to the truck, his mom followed, leaving Doug and Brian alone to finish their conversation.

"Dad, *please,* just think about letting me kick for the team. *All* they need is a kicker. I wouldn't be out on the field except to kick the ball."

"Son, I don't understand you. You're afraid to get behind the wheel of a car and drive, but you're willing to go out on the athletic field and get charged by a team of boys determined to knock you down!"

Brian jerked backward as if he'd been slapped.

At his motion, Doug realized what he'd said and reached to hug his son. "I'm sorry, I didn't mean to say that."

"But you *did* say it, and I guess you've got a point."

After an uncomfortable silence, Brian continued, "I'm working on getting back to driving. How about letting me work at being the team place kicker?"

Doug shook his head, but Brian prodded him, "Fine, then I just won't do *anything*, and we'll both be miserable!"

Brian stormed out of the motorhome and headed through the woods, and Doug was without the words to bring him back.

Chapter 24

Brian rushed along the trail through the woods to Pine Park, stumbling a couple of times in his haste to get to the house or barn and hopefully find Jerry or Jessie.

He was breathing hard when he reached the clearing, but he pushed forward at a faster pace. Then he saw both Jessie and Jerry at the barn door. Out of breath when he reached them, he stumbled forward but Jessie caught him as he began to topple over.

"Take it easy," Jessie suggested, and Jerry stepped up and laid a hand on his shoulder.

"Jerry, I'm so sorry my dad blamed you for the thing about kicking the ball. It's just that he's so determined to protect me that he won't let me do *anything*."

"It's okay," Jerry interrupted, "At least *you and I* know we didn't mean any harm, and we're still friends. Right?"

"Yeah."

Jessie suggested, "You boys have had a rough start to the day, why don't you go in the house and get Jean to give you something cold to drink and maybe some cookies and wise words."

"Wise words?" Jerry wondered aloud.

Jessie nodded, "She always seems to know how to patch things up. Maybe she can help you mend your fences with your parents and the coach."

With renewed hope, the boys headed for the kitchen to get

food and wisdom from Jean.

Brian told her how mad his dad had been, Jean hesitated briefly, "He's just being a good father who loves his son with his whole heart. Give him some time to calm down and maybe you can talk about playing ball."

"But, I wouldn't be *playing* ball, I'd just be kicking it," Brian protested.

"Whatever. Give him time to think it through."

Just as Brian said, "I don't guess we have any other choice."

M&M came into the kitchen and told them, "I don't blame Doug for being upset and angry. I wouldn't want Jerry to take that kind of risk either."

Jerry argued, "Mom, if I got hurt riding a horse, I'd still want to ride, just like you did when you got your foot and ankle smashed. Would you tell me I couldn't ride anymore?"

She threw up her hands in surrender. "None of us want to give up what we love most."

Brian explained, "Sports aren't my whole life. I just want to do what any normal kid can do, not be pampered and babied."

M&M's cell phone chimed, and she saw Doug was calling. She paused, considered not answering and decided she'd rather talk to him on the phone than in person,

"Hello, Doug. If you're looking for Brian, he's over here. Our boys are stuffing themselves with Jean's fresh-from-the-oven cookies."

Brian didn't know whether to be relieved or alarmed to hear his dad say, "I'll be right over."

Jean cleared the table and herded them outside to wait.

Doug's truck soon turned into the drive, followed by several other vehicles. Jerry recognized the coach and some of the boys and muttered, "Oh, no. Here we go again."

Brian wanted to turn around and run for the safety of the house, but Jerry, M&M, Jean and Jessie rallied around him in

Wildflower Wednesday

support.

Then he saw that Doug's lips trembled as he came to them and said, "I'm so sorry for what I said. Brian, it's just that I am *so* scared for you, so determined to keep you safe." He hesitated, then continued, "But I guess that's no way to let you grow up and be who you want to be. As you can see, the coach and half the football team has followed me over here. They have something more to say, and I've promised to at least listen."

Doug motioned and all the vehicle occupants unloaded and came forward. Stopping directly in front of Doug, the coach said, "We regret having upset you, but we want to explain our position, be sure you understand us."

Then, one by one, the football players stepped up, introduced themselves and delivered their thoughts.

"I'm Wayne, senior quarterback for the team. I have scouts looking at me for a college scholarship and it's the only way I'll get to go. But if we don't even have a team—"

"Without somebody who can kick the ball, we won't have a team this season," Coach Bradley interrupted.

Another player added, "We know Brian can kick the ball. We want you to know we only need him to *kick*. He wouldn't be on field for anything else."

Two burly boys introduced themselves as Burt and Jim. Burt told Doug, "Sir, I promise you, I will protect Brian every second he's on the field. Nobody, and I mean *nobody* will get around me to hit him."

Jim added, "And I'll be on his other side. Nobody will get to him."

Yet another player moved forward. "And I'll have his back, Mr. Wilson. I won't let anybody hurt him."

Brian saw the worry lines marring his father's face, and he heard the tremor in his voice when he spoke, "Brian wants so much to be a part of your team and your school. I see that you

- 179 -

want him too. Give us time. Let me think on it. You'll have your answer by first practice of next week."

That news was greeted by joyous shouts of "Hurray!" and "Thank you!" as the team members departed.

The coach remained and extended his hand to Doug, "I thank you, Mr. Wilson, for your consideration, and I salute your son for both his skills and his courage."

Brian breathed a sigh of relief when they were left standing alone in the drive at Pine Park.

"Let's go home, Dad. I'll drive."

His hand trembled as he turned the ignition key and Doug asked, "Are you sure about this?"

He nodded and drove, ever so slowly, down the drive and turned onto the roadway. Perspiration glistened over his upper lip by the time they pulled up next to the motorhome.

"Good job, son. It'll be easier next time."

Brian was trembling when he crawled down from the truck cab. Even so, he looked directly into his father's face, "I *can* drive, and I *can* kick that football for Marshall too!"

Doug couldn't respond, so they walked silently, side by side, to the motorhome. A long uncomfortable silence hung over them until Brian finally spoke, "Dad, I know you're scared about me getting hurt. I'm scared too." He hesitated, then added, "But I'm more scared of being a cripple, or a scaredy cat, or a misfit that nobody wants around."

Doug sank into the couch and answered, "You are making it impossible for me to say *no*, But let me just tell you something. You are not a cripple, and you have more courage than I do, and if there is anybody anywhere on this earth that doesn't want you around, well that person is missing out."

Brian rushed forward and fell into Doug's lap, hugging him until they were both breathless.

Doug found his voice, "I'll be going with you to the next

Wildflower Wednesday

practice. I'll let that coach know I am giving you permission to be the kicker, but that's *all*, and I'll be holding him and all the players responsible for keeping you safe."

And when he went to bed, Doug Wilson whispered a prayer, "Please, dear God, keep my boy safe from harm."

*****

M&M was surprised to hear from Doug early the next morning. He called to say, "I'll be going to watch the rest of summer football practices with Brian, and since the band seems to practice on same time frame, we can give Jerry a ride."

"Does that mean you've agreed to let him be the team place kicker?"

"Reluctantly, but I'm going to practice to remind the coach and players that I expect them to do as they promised, keep him *safe*."

"Doug, I can't imagine how hard this must be for you."

He remained silent, so she shifted the subject to driving. "Could we maybe take turns driving the boys? I was planning on letting Jerry do some driving back and forth. He needs the practice before going for his regular license."

"Now that you mention it, Brian needs practice too, *lots* of it. It'll be a challenge for me to fit in time for that when I'm running between two offices."

"We can figure it out, take turns or get a driving coach. *Hey*, that's an idea. Coach Bradley teaches drivers ed, and he's gonna owe you a favor, a big one."

She glanced at the clock by her bed and jumped to her feet. "Gotta go. Those horses are looking for their breakfast."

"Okay. We can figure this all out over dinner. How about tonight? You pick the time and place."

She hesitated. "It's a deal. Pick me up at 7:00, and since you'll be driving, *you* pick the place."

She grabbed a cup of dry cereal and munched on it as she went to the barn, hoping she wouldn't regret agreeing to dinner with Doug.

Chapter 25

When Doug hung up the phone, he wondered where in the world he would take Miranda Johnson for dinner. He didn't even know what she liked to eat, other than Jean's cooking and hamburgers from the drive-in. He wasn't familiar with the local restaurants either.

As he drove to his Marshall office, he decided to ask some of the local employees for recommendations. He got more answers than he needed, so at noon he called her.

"I'm stuck," he confessed. "I asked co-workers for suggestions and got a long list of good restaurants around here. What do you like to eat?"

She laughed, "I like most everything."

"That's no help."

"Okay, there's a good steak house out on the highway, just out of the city limits."

"Steak it is. I'll see you at seven."

Then he started wondering if he should make reservations, how he should dress, if he should take her flowers or candy or something. At that, he had to chuckle at himself, because no matter what *she* said, he felt like this was a *date*.

At exactly seven he knocked on the front door, to have it answered by no other than his son.

"Hey, Dad. Since you and Ms. Johnson are going out to eat, Jean and Jessie are letting us have a cookout. I'm helping with the hot dogs and Jerry is flipping burgers."

"Sounds like fun, I'll just pick you up when I bring Miranda home."

She came up behind Brian and grinned. "Seems like everything we do requires scheduling transportation."

He gave a low whistle as he walked her to the truck. Seeing her in a silky gold pantsuit and matching shoes was so *different*. "You look lovely," he stammered.

She smiled, "You clean up pretty good yourself."

By the time they reached the steak house, they had worked out a plan for getting their sons some much-needed driving practice while going to and from the school grounds.

Once inside the restaurant, Doug gave his name to the hostess and she took them to a little table by the window, as he had requested.

She seemed surprised that he'd made reservations.

"I just thought it would be nice to look outside while we ate." Seeing the waiter approaching, he asked, "Would you like wine, or an appetizer, or both?"

She shook her head. "I like both, but don't need either."

They both asked for sweet, iced tea and when the waiter departed, Doug asked her to explain.

"I enjoy wine occasionally, but not often, as I am usually driving. And to be honest, I don't need the calories of the wine or the extras." Then she admitted, "I intend on eating a *big* steak."

He grinned. "Me too."

They chatted comfortably throughout the meal, lingered over coffee and, at Doug's insistence, ordered two pieces of cheesecake to go because, "The boys will love it."

Conversation flowed all the way back to Pine Park, and as he parked the truck, Doug remarked, "This has been fun for me, and I hope for you. Let's do it again."

She smiled and nodded just as their sons flung open the

front door and cheered when they saw the sack in Doug's hand.

"What'd you bring us?" Brian wanted to know.

M&M shrugged and told Doug, "Come on in and let's watch them devour *our* desserts."

Doug laughed, assured the boys that the desserts *were* for them and handed the sack over to Jerry. Minutes later, saucers were empty and loaded into the dishwasher.

When Jerry said, "Thanks, Mr. Wilson," Doug answered, "You're welcome, but we've got to do something about this *Mr.* and *Ms.* stuff, don't you think?"

"I guess so. What do you want me to call you?"

"Just Doug will be fine."

"Well, what's Brian gonna call my mom? You call her *Miranda,* but everybody else calls her M&M?"

All eyes turned to Brian as he said, "I'll stick with M&M if that's okay."

She nodded, turning back to Doug, "Thank you for a wonderful dinner."

With *good nights* said all around, Doug and Brian departed for the RV they called home.

On the way, Brian said, "Was that like a *date* with Ms., I mean M&M? It sorta seemed like it."

"I guess it *sorta* was," Doug answered, relieved that Brian didn't add more questions or comments.

Chapter 26

The next morning when Brian saw Jerry, he mentioned the outing. "My dad said it was *kinda* like a date. What does *that* mean?"

Jerry shrugged and shook his head. "Don't know."

"Well, I can't believe my dad likes your mom, you know, like *that*."

Jerry scowled. "What do you mean? What's wrong with my mom?"

"*Nothing*. I like your mom. But she's so *different* from mine."

"Well, I don't think your dad is anything like mine either. Not that I really remember him."

After an awkward silence, Jerry admitted, "I guess I never thought my mom would have a boyfriend. She always said I was her 'little man of the house'. It's *always* just been the two of us."

Jessie interrupted the conversation, yelling for them to come get their lunch sacks. "Jean's got all the sandwiches and stuff packed up. We're going to town to find some kind of fancy cooking pot she wants, but I'll be back in time to help out in the barn."

The boys grabbed their lunches and scurried back out to the barn to groom the horses M&M needed for her first lesson clients of the day.

"Thanks, Brian. Goldilocks looks shiny as a new penny," She told him as she took the reins and led the palomino to the arena gate where Katy waited.

Brian grinned and admitted, "It's still a little hard, handing her over for another rider. I love that little horse."

"Just remember the *little* part." Jerry reminded him. "She's too little for a tall guy like you."

"I know, but ... *how* do I go about finding the *right* horse for me?"

"Talk to my mom about it."

"First I have to get my dad to agree to me having one."

Brian mentioned the idea to his dad when they were back in the motorhome that evening.

"Are you sure you really want a horse of your own? I know you can ride at Pine Park any time you want to, and owning a horse means you will have to take care of it."

"Dad, I know how to take care of a horse. Thanks to Brian and M&M, I can be a responsible horse owner, and yes, I want one of my very own. One thing I've missed growing up was having a dog, or some kind of pet."

Doug sighed. "I didn't realize you wanted a pet. You never said."

"It's no big deal."

"Then let's give it some more thought. I'm thinking you'll be going off to college in another year. What then?"

Brian's reluctant shrug ended the conversation, temporarily.

*****

Jerry was having a like conversation with his mother. "Brian told me he really wants his own horse, but he doesn't know how to go about it. I told him to talk to you."

"If Doug agrees, and *only* if he agrees to the idea, I'll be glad to help him find something suitable."

"You really like Doug, don't you?"

"Of course, I do. Don't you? He's been nothing but generous

and kind towards us and I, for one, know it's a big job, being a single parent."

"Yeah, and I like Brian a lot too. I'm glad they're our neighbors now." He shifted thoughts. "It's convenient too, that we can ride to school together, take turns driving and all that."

She sighed. "That reminds me, school starts next week and you need new shoes, jeans and whatever else you've outgrown. When do you want to do the good old back to school shopping?"

"It'll have to be in the afternoon, or even at night if stores are open. Band practice will be every morning until classes start."

"Let's plan on going out for burgers and shopping one night soon. That way, I can keep up with the barn chores, lessons and training."

"Mom, are you gonna have enough clients needing lessons or horses trained to, you know, make enough money?"

"It looks really promising, I have bookings for both through the end of the year, plus now that I can start therapy sessions soon, we should be okay."

"Oh, I forgot to tell you. There's something *new*, at least to me, in the way of making money with those hayburners of ours."

"What's that?"

"Leasing a horse to a rider who doesn't want the full expense or responsibility of ownership."

"I don't understand. How does that work?

"Let me give you an example. You remember little Patty, and how she loves the pony, right?"

He nodded.

"Well, she is begging to have her own pony, or horse, and her parents really want to give her what she wants, but they just can't. They live in town so they would have to pay a board bill, plus all the other expenses of maintaining a horse or pony—feed, vet, farrier and so on. They have friends in Dallas who

Wildflower Wednesday

lease a horse for their child, and they asked me what I thought about doing that."

He prodded her to continue. "How does somebody lease a horse?"

She explained that she had done some research and learned a lot. "For a family like Patty's the benefits would be that the horse or pony would be available whenever she wanted to ride, or on an agreed upon schedule, and they would pay a portion of the animal's upkeep, but not be responsible for big vet bills in the event of serious illness or injury. I think barn managers that lease horses usually figure a mutually agreeable flat fee per month." She hesitated, then continued, "To me, the emphasis is on mutually agreeable."

"Can you explain that?"

"If Patty's parents decide they want to lease the pony for the next year, I would want to have a schedule where the pony would also be available for a lesson or class two days a week, the other days Patty could come ride, groom and love her as much as she wants, and I would charge what it costs to keep the pony in feed, hoof care and stall bedding."

"I guess that's a win-win situation." Jerry thought aloud.

"Well, I hope so. If I could lease even two or three horses or ponies, I would still have use of them part time, plus the others all the time for lessons and class activities, including therapy. I think it'll be worth trying."

Relief flooded Jerry's face. "So, it looks like we're staying at Pine Park."

She smiled and nodded.

*****

On the other side of the piney woods, Brian and his dad were talking about their home.

"Dad, does it seem like it's gonna take *forever* for this house to get built?"

Doug laughed. "It does seem slow, but it'll pick up as soon as the house is totally enclosed so we don't have to worry about the weather. Roof should be done this week and when they get windows and doors in place, it'll seem more like a house too."

Brian looked doubtful until he added, "Oh, that reminds me, we're due to go pick out light fixtures and cabinets and countertops and floor coverings, maybe even paint colors."

"Gosh, Dad, do you know how to do that?"

Doug gave him a sheepish grin. "Not really, your mother took care of all those things."

"Don't we need help?"

"Maybe, I'll ask Jean or Miranda what they think. Females know about this stuff."

He picked up his cell phone and called the Pine Park number.

M&M answered and responded to his plea for help. "You need to talk to my friend Susanna. I think she missed her calling as an interior decorator. She organized and furnished the legal office she worked in, then did their wonderful house, and helped Tiffany with the SSS office and classrooms. She can do *anything* that requires furniture and décor that's functional as well as attractive."

Doug protested. "I barely know her. I was hoping you and Jean would help us out."

"Well, Jean's probably the one to give you help with anything to do with the kitchen. Sorry, but count me out. If I was going to re-do anything, I'd get Susanna to help me. I'm tellin' you, she's *good!*"

He responded with a half-hearted "Okay" before asking, "Is Jean handy?"

In minutes Jean was on the phone saying, "I'll most certainly help choose all the kitchen equipment, but things like countertops and flooring and colors, those need to be what you and Brian want."

Doug sighed, ended the call, and turned to Brian. "It looks like we're on our own with some of this stuff."

*****

On their way to the school grounds the next morning, Brian was reporting the gist of the situation to Jerry. "Dad and I, we don't know exactly how to go about deciding on things like light fixtures and color schemes."

"Why don't you do what my mom suggested? Ask Susanna. She's really sweet and I know she'll help you out. She likes doing that decorating stuff."

"I'll tell Dad you said that. I think he was kinda disappointed that your mom said no."

"Brian, it's not that she doesn't want to help you guys out. It's just that, well my mom isn't into picking out furnishings. She'd be asking Susanna for help too."

He nodded. "Okay." Then he changed the subject, "I talked to my dad about getting a horse of my own."

"And?"

"Well, he gave me something else to think about. You know how we were both a little touchy about our parents having a romantic interest?"

"Yeah. I still am."

"When Dad told me that if I got my own horse, then what would he do with it when I go off to college in another year."

"So?"

"Jerry, you and I are both starting our senior year. *Forget* about a horse, what are our parents gonna do when we leave home? They won't have *anybody*."

"Guess I'd never thought about it like that," Jerry admitted. "It's always been Mom *and* me."

Jessie, who was driving, just grinned and said nothing. When he left them at the edge of the field, he reminded them,

"M&M will be picking you up today."

As they walked to the center of the field, the teens looked at each other and giggled just to think of their parents in a romantic relationship. "Maybe it wouldn't be such a bad thing after all," Jerry said.

Then Coach Bradley yelled, "Line up and warm up," and Brian jogged to join the team. Jerry went to the sidelines to watch until the band members started to play. He was glad to see how the team members rallied around Brian with welcoming comments.

Then he glanced back at the parking lot and saw Doug Wilson's truck. The driver's side window was down and the sun glistened on something shiny. Jerry chuckled as he realized that Brian's dad was watching the football boys with binoculars, and probably didn't want Brian to know.

Warmed by the sun and their respective practice sessions, both the band members and football players were sweaty, thirsty and tired as they headed off the field. Brian joined Jerry to walk to the parking lot just as M&M drove up.

"How'd it go?" she asked Brian as he climbed into the truck.

"Okay, I guess. Good thing I just have to kick, I sure can't keep up with the guys running or even in warm-ups."

"Yeah, but I watched you kicking, and the coach was beaming."

Brian shrugged off the compliment and reached for the water bottle M&M passed back to him.

"Tomorrow you guys will start practice driving up here and back," she reminded them. "Doug and I just have to get together on which one of us drives each way and each day."

Jerry, knowing Brian was less than enthusiastic about the practice driving, remained quiet until his mom informed them that she wouldn't be at home for supper.

"Why not?" Jerry wanted to know.

"Doug and I are going out to dinner and maybe a movie."

The boys in the back grinned and nudged each other but didn't comment.

When M&M passed through the kitchen and picked up her lunch, she told Jean not to expect her for supper.

Jean smiled. "I already heard you and Mr. Doug would be going out to dinner. You two enjoy yourselves. Me and Jessie will look after the boys."

"I know that, or we wouldn't be leaving them, and I doubt if our dinner will be as good as what you cook here."

"Thank you, but everybody needs to get out once in a while."

M&M waved as she went out the door and hurried to the barn. She had horses to ride, two kids coming for lessons and a determination to finish in time to shower and dress in something better than jeans before Doug came by for her.

Her plans came together nicely until she stood in front of her closet looking for that better than jeans outfit. She sighed and shook her head as she thumbed through her meager wardrobe.

"One of these days, I've got to buy myself something decent to wear out in public," she told herself as she settled on an old favorite pantsuit. At least it was in fall colors and had a coordinating sweater.

She was just pulling on the sweater when she heard the crunch of gravel on the drive, then slamming of truck doors and Doug's voice as he came through the front door, "Hey, Miranda, are you ready to hit the road?"

"Coming," she called out as she started to the front room.

As they said goodbye, M&M noticed Jerry and Brian nudging each other, and Jerry was wearing a silly grin.

"What's so funny?" she asked Jerry. He just laughed and shook his head, then muttered. "Nothin'. Have a good time."

When she and Doug got in the truck, she asked him, "What

was that all about?" and he answered, "Honestly, I don't have a clue."

They chatted all the way to the restaurant, mostly about progress on Doug's house. "It's really starting to take shape. Brian's pretty impatient. He says it's taking *forever*. I think he's encouraged by knowing we will be shopping for fixtures and flooring and stuff next week. I do wish you could help us. Guys aren't good at that stuff."

"Sorry, but this girl isn't good at it either. Like I told you already, Susanna can really help you."

"I hardly know her. Will you put in a good word for me? I hate to just call her up out of the blue."

"It would be fine for you to just call and ask, but I'll let her know you'll be contacting her if it'll make you feel better.

"Thanks."

The restaurant was a new one that Doug heard about from his office staff. "I hope this place is as good as I was told," he commented as he walked by her side to the entrance.

"I'm sure it's fine."

They were soon seated in a little secluded corner and handed leather-bound menus. The hostess told them their waiter would be there soon to take their drink orders.

"Seems okay so far," he said as he scanned the menu. "Looks like steaks are a specialty, but seafood is plentiful too. Which would you prefer?"

When M&M told him, "That's a hard choice" He suggested the surf and turf for two, and that's what he ordered for them. They sipped iced tea and continued to talk about Doug's house, then about their sons.

"Even though I wish Jerry hadn't gotten Brian into kicking for the football team, I'm glad the boys are friends." He paused. "I'm grateful that Jerry has introduced him around. He seems happy and is looking forward to starting classes."

"I understand about the football thing. I know you can't help but worry about him getting hurt."

He smiled his thanks, then changed the subject. "Your plans for Pine Park seem to be working out pretty well. Brian comes home and tells me what's going on at the barn."

"It's fun to have him around. Not only is he helpful with the horses and chores, he seems to love it all."

Doug agreed. "He talked to me about getting a horse of his own, which is certainly doable, but I asked him to think about what we would do with it, or more correctly, what *I* would do with it when he goes off to college."

"And?"

"I guess I gave him food for thought. He hasn't mentioned it again."

"Well, he can always ride any of the suitable Pine Park horses."

Their attention soon turned to massive platter with their grilled steak, lobster tails and shrimp.

"I hope you're really hungry," he told her.

She was laughing as she shook her head. "We'll never be able to eat all this."

Almost an hour later, they put their napkins on the table as Doug said, "Well, we tried."

"And it was delicious. Thanks."

"Thanks for coming. I realized today that Brian was hospitalized a year ago. It's been a tough year for us in many ways. He reached across the table and squeezed her hand. "I'm glad I have you to talk to."

She tried to shrug it off, but saw the emotion in his eyes and answered, "Any time."

They turned down dessert and the offered take home box and headed home.

M&M told him, "I ate so much I should *walk* home."

He laughed at that, then suggested, "It's early. Would you come over and take a look at the house? I'd like you to see how it's coming along."

"But It'll be dark when we get back."

"I have security lights, plus a flashlight in the glove box, *and* my headlights. You'll be able to see it pretty well."

"Okay."

When they got to the site and stepped out of the truck, Doug took her hand. "Let me show you how to navigate through the lumber."

She followed him, expressing appreciation of the floor plan. "It looks so open and spacious."

"Brian and I think it'll work great for us. Do you like it?"

"I do."

As they stepped outside, He pulled her into a hug. "Thanks again, for everything."

"It goes both ways."

At that, he softly suggested, "How about a kiss?"

She jerked away. "Absolutely *not*!"

He backed up. "Okay! Okay, I get it."

He switched the flashlight on bright and led the way back to the truck. Both were quiet on the short drive to her house. Once there, he opened the truck door for her, walked her to the door and called in for Brian. "Come on, son. Time to go home."

"It was a great meal," was all she said as he waved goodnight.

Later, when she was almost asleep, her cell phone rang, and she saw it was Doug calling.

When she answered, he apologized. "I didn't mean to offend you. Sorry if I did. But what's the big deal about a little kiss anyway?"

"It's not what *friends* do," she answered, ending the conversation without a goodbye.

Chapter 27

Doug fell asleep thinking about Miranda and wondering how he could make amends.

He awoke the next morning still thinking about her.

It was his turn to take the boys to the school grounds, so he told Brian, "Get a move on, it's time to grab breakfast and go."

He went by to get Jerry and moved over for him to take a turn behind the wheel, reminding Brian, "It'll be your turn on the way home."

When they arrived, Doug complimented Jerry on his safe driving and told them he'd be back to get them when their practice sessions ended.

He thought about parking at the other end of the field to keep an eye on Brian, then decided he had more urgent business elsewhere.

He drove back to Pine Park and parked as close to the barn as possible, looking for a brown curly topped head to pop up over a stall door. When he saw her, he strode rapidly into the barn, into the stall and pulled her close to his chest. He kissed her, gently but thoroughly, then stepped back. "Now! That wasn't so bad, was it?"

Her eyes glistened with unshed tears, and she struggled to catch her breath before answering. "You've just complicated our friendship."

"Should I be sorry for that?"

She shook her head. "I don't know. I didn't expect to ever hear bells ring or feel my heart pound like that again." She frowned. "I *told* you, it's not what friends do."

"Maybe I want us to be more than friends."

When she didn't answer, he closed in to kiss her again before saying, "Think about *that*."

He left before she had a chance to reply.

He was whistling to himself as he drove back to the motorhome and called Susanna. He didn't waste words about the purpose of his call. "I'm no good at picking out fixtures and flooring and décor for the house I'm building. Our mutual friend told me you were a whiz at that sort of thing. She sorta volunteered you for the job. How about it?"

She laughed. "I assume the mutual friend is M&M." She paused until he said *yes* before answering. "I'm flattered, and of course, I'll help you as best I can. How soon do you need to start making selections?"

He chuckled as he told her "Yesterday would have been good."

"Oh dear, then you and Brian better come over in the next day or so and look through some books I have, give me an idea of what you like. We'll start from there."

They agreed on a day and time and Doug put it on the calendar in his cell phone before leaving for his office.

He started his workday by thanking his staff for the great restaurant recommendation, then talked briefly with each one about their listings and pending sales, checked the time and headed back to the school grounds.

He pulled in just as the band stopped marching and playing. Football boys were heading to vehicles too.

"Timing is everything," he told himself as Brian saw him and waved. Both boys drained their water bottles before they reached the truck. Doug got out and moved into the passenger seat, motioning for Brian to climb in behind the wheel.

"You guys look hot, tired and thirsty."

Wildflower Wednesday

"We are," Jerry answered for both of them.

"Hungry, too," Brian added.

"If you want to go to the drive-in for another breakfast, I'll treat," Doug offered.

Brian hesitated. "But there might be traffic in town. I don't know...."

"There's not a lot of traffic in that area," Jerry offered.

Doug added, "Just depends on how hungry you are."

Brian sighed, knowing he was outnumbered and out maneuvered. He started the truck and turned it in the direction of their favorite drive in.

Once there, he and Jerry ordered breakfast burritos and big juice cups while Doug opted for another cup of coffee.

They were back on the road within minutes and Jerry stayed still until they turned into the drive at Pine Park, then reached and touched Brian on the shoulder. "You really are a good driver."

Jerry got out and headed to the barn as Brian called out, "I'll be over in a little while to help you in the barn."

Doug was grinning as he told Brian, "I've got us some help lined up to pick out all that stuff for the new house. Susanna agreed, and we're going over to her place tomorrow to look at some books or catalogs or something. She says she needs to see what we like."

Two hours later, he had consumed the sack lunch Jean packed for him and was headed to his Longview office. Brian had wanted, as usual, to stay at Pine Park.

On the drive, he was trying to think of some way to dazzle Miranda Johnson. At the office he went directly to see Grace and asked, "What's a nice little surprise I might get for a female friend?"

"Flowers are always nice."

"Flowers, of course, *flowers*. Thanks." He hurried to his

private office and called the only florist he knew personally. "Is there any way at all you can come up with a bouquet, or arrangement, or whatever you call it, of wildflowers?"

His florist friend reminded him that it was not the blooming season for wildflowers, but the wildflower farms in Texas Hill Country always had them in their greenhouses.

"I don't have time to drive to the Hill Country."

Then he heard the good news. "I have a good bunch of wildflowers here, special order for a wedding, and I guess I can spare a few for you. Do you want them delivered?"

"No, I'll come by and pick them up in a couple of hours. Thanks."

He met with Sam, then with his sales associates, before leaving the office. He also stuck his head in Grace's door to say, "Thanks. I ordered the flowers," and then left to pick them up.

*****

Hard as she tried, M&M had done little *but* think about Doug's words and those kisses that preceded them. Until today, she'd never thought she'd have a romantic relationship again. She would have told anyone that, right up until Doug Wilson's kisses left her breathless and wanting more.

His departing comment about being more than friends had surprised her even more than his kisses. She had been totally honest in telling him that he'd complicated their friendship, and had no idea what to do, or say, next.

Those thoughts were still roaming around in her head when he arrived back at Pine Park.

Thinking he was coming just to pick up Brian, she kept riding her new client's horse in the arena. She even ignored his presence when he came to the gate.

Then he opened it and stepped right in front of her moving horse. Reining the big mare around him, she said, "*Whoa!*" to the mare before asking him, "What do you think you're doing?"

Wildflower Wednesday

Doug grinned. "I trusted you not to run me down. I'm just trying to make a delivery."

She was puzzled at that. "I thought you were here to pick up Brian."

"That too, but I brought you something. If you could climb down off that animal for a minute, I'll show you."

She was curious and complied. Doug got her to tie the horse by the gate and follow him to his truck. He reached in and handed out a bouquet of wildflowers.

Surprised, she buried her nose in them. "They're lovely. Thank you, but—"

"No buts, just enjoy them, remember where you got them and keep on thinkin'." She didn't have to ask what he meant.

When she looked up from the flowers she blushed, then noticed Jean and the boys were headed her way.

Doug said *hi* to all and motioned Brian into the truck. "We'll be back for supper."

As they drove away, Jerry wondered, "What's with the flowers?"

Jean was beaming as M&M thrust the bouquet towards her. "Would you please put these in a vase with water. They'll be lovely on our table tonight."

With no further explanation, Jean did as she was asked. Jerry followed his mom back to the arena gate and waited for her to say something more. She didn't.

He shrugged it off and went to start the barn chores.

M&M remained thoughtful and silent throughout the evening meal. The boys reminded her that the first football game of the season was coming up.

"But school hasn't even started yet," she protested.

"Mom! It's like this every year. We start to school on Tuesday and first game is Friday night. Are you coming?"

"I wouldn't miss it."

"I'll be going too," Doug added. When Jessie and Jean mentioned that they'd like to go and see Brian kick and Jerry play the drums, he said, "Great! Maybe we can all go and sit together."

M&M was probably the only one at the table who understood how much he dreaded that game, yet he couldn't stay away.

Chapter 28

The first day back at school proved hectic for both boys and their parents. Miscommunication between M&M and Doug was evident when both thought the other was taking the boys to school.

By the time they figured it out, Jerry was late for his first period class and Brian had to stand in line at the office to get his schedule before finding his way to his first class.

Guilt-ridden adults planned to take the boys to the drive-in for milkshakes, burgers or whatever they wanted after school. Jean heard about the mix-up and said she'd fix a special supper with a big chocolate cake for dessert.

M&M rode with Doug for the after school pick up and started apologizing when Jerry opened the truck door. "I am so sorry. You must have been late for your first class. What a terrible start to your first day back."

Doug greeted his son with, "How'd it go? Did it take you all day to find your way around the new school?"

Brian grinned. "I was in same first period class as Jerry. He showed me around after that. It was fine."

Jerry laughed. "Yeah, and he also had about a half-dozen cute girls wanting to show him to his next class too."

"So, it wasn't so bad after all?" M&M asked.

"Mom, the first day back at school is always hectic. Half the kids are late for at least one or two classes. A few don't find the right room until the next bell is about to ring. It's okay.

Tomorrow will be a piece of cake."

"Speaking of cake, I'm hungry," Brian added.

His dad answered, "That's why we're here, taking you to the drive-in for whatever snack you might want. You know, something to tide you over 'til supper."

"Don't overdo it though," M&M cautioned. "Jean has a big supper planned to celebrate back to school."

They arrived at the drive-in and parked just long enough for Brian and Jerry to get giant milkshakes.

"Tomorrow we have to go early. I have football practice before school," Brian reminded his dad.

"Okay. I'll take my turn getting you to school. I want to watch practice anyway. Okay?"

Brian reluctantly agreed. He knew his dad was still worried about him being part of the football team, but he felt like he'd be the only guy on the team with a parent watching over practice.

*****

When game night rolled around, Jean and Jessie followed Doug and M&M to the stadium and parked beside them. The boys had already been dropped off to warm up for their respective performances.

M&M could hear the roll of the snare drums as she stepped out of Doug's truck. Noticing his grim expression, she took his hand and let him lead her to their seats, with Jessie and Jean coming along behind them. They found their places, sat down, then stood for the anthem and the band's version of the team fight song.

Doug breathed a sigh of relief when the coin toss and captain's choice meant the opposing team would be kicking off. Brian was safe on the bench, He remained there until the other team scored and it was time for the Longview Longhorns to kick off. Brian trotted into position and sent the ball flying to the ten-

Wildflower Wednesday

yard line. The crowd roared as he trotted back to the sidelines. M&M tried not to wince. Doug was squeezing her hand so tight that her fingers were numb.

At the end of the game, the locals cheered the 14-12 win, and the team raised and lifted Brian over their heads in salute. Doug held his breath until the boy was back on solid ground, then joined in the applause.

Then he leaned over and whispered to M&M. "You're probably the only one here who understands why I'm really clapping."

She nodded and cheered for the victorious players.

On their way home, Brian shrugged off the praise from Jerry, Jessie and Jean. "It's just good to be the part of a team," he said.

Jerry assured him that the other team members thought it was great to have him. "I'm glad you moved over here."

"That reminds me," Doug told Brian. "Tomorrow we're going out to Susanna's house to talk about our fixtures and floors and all the other stuff for the house. I told her we'd be there right after lunch."

*****

Susanna was at the front door when Doug and Brian arrived.

"Come on into the den," she encouraged them. "I was waiting out here so you wouldn't need to ring the bell. The kids are napping, so we can just look through some books and you can show me what you like."

They followed her into the cozy den and sat around a table laden with big illustrated volumes. A few minutes into their conversation, she guessed, "You like basic and practical furniture, maybe with a country or farmhouse look to it. Right?"

Doug nodded.

"What about color schemes? Do you want something

neutral that flows from room to room?"

"That sounds okay to me. What about you, Brian?"

Both adults turned to see Brian shaking his head. "Gee, I don't know. I like neutrals, like browns and tans, but I like bright colors too."

Susanna made several suggestions as she turned book pages filled with colored illustrations. Then she offered them refreshments as she told them, "I think I have a feeling for what you want, so let's agree on the day and time for me to go along with you to make selections."

Brian had a mouthful of cookies, but nodded when his dad said, "Saturday will work best for us. You pick a time."

They agreed to spend the afternoon searching out fixtures, flooring, and suitable furniture.

"My mom can come stay with the twins." She laughed then. "Lee and Laura would *not* be helpful in a store or on a showroom floor."

"Thanks ever so much." Doug told her as they went out the front door.

Back in the truck, Jerry commented. "Gee, Dad, it's awful nice of her to help out like this. Aren't you going to pay her, or something?"

Doug shook his head. "I already discussed that with her and with Miranda. I got a big *no* from both of them. Susanna says she is not a professional and won't accept payment."

"Maybe we can take them out to eat or something," Brian suggested.

"Good idea. You always come up with good ideas to help out."

When Brian looked puzzled his dad added, "You know, like suggesting Jessie and Jean come live in the house at our new place."

"Yeah, but that didn't turn out too well. What's their long-range plan now? I know they won't live with the Johnsons forever."

"Well, Jessie told me they're still looking for a place of their own, but not having much luck. Everything they've seen in their price range is too far away from us."

"When our house is ready, couldn't they live in the motorhome?"

"Sure. They could and I'd be glad to let them use it, or have it."

"But I guess that's not a permanent solution. Is it?"

"I'm afraid not."

*****

M&M had finished her morning barn and horse tasks and was back in her office studying her fall schedule when Jerry came in.

"Mom, is everything really going to be okay, you know, about our finances?"

Her smile lit up the little room. "Yes! I've just gone over the scheduling of classes, lessons for the rest of the year. We're gonna be fine." She paused. "At least we're in good shape for a while. I guess how permanent that is depends on how good I am at directing an equine therapy program."

She paused again and frowned. "You know what a great help it is, having Jessie and Jean here. I don't know exactly how we'll manage when they leave."

"I don't even want to think about them not being here. Brian doesn't either."

"I'm hoping Doug has a solution that keeps them nearby."

"Like what?"

She just shrugged.

*****

Doug's thoughts kept straying to Miranda as he sat in the Longview office sorting his mail into appropriate piles. Then he came across a hand-addressed envelope with a return name he didn't recognize. Curious, he opened it and began to read. The letter said:

> Dear Mr. Wilson,
>
> You don't know me. I am writing this letter for my husband because he is unable to write. He is now in the Marshall Manor Nursing Home, where he will stay for the rest of his life.
>
> You see, he had a massive stroke and lost consciousness the day of the accident. He was never ill before that, but now he is in a wheelchair, can hardly feed himself, and cries most of every day. My Leo wants more than anything to let you know how very sorry he is that he caused the accident that took your wife and son. He says he should have been the one who died.
>
> So, as he has asked, I am writing to say he's sorry. He knows what happened is unforgivable, but he still wants you to know that. So, this letter, it's s one of the few things I can still do for him.
>
> Sincerely,
> Agnes Miller

Doug drew a deep breath and felt tears forming as he carefully folded the letter.

"What do I do now?" he asked himself as he got up to leave for Longview.

He thought about that letter all the way to the Marshall office, then tucked it into his shirt pocket as he went to meet the sales staff.

It was lunch time before he thought of it again, and on

Wildflower Wednesday

impulse, he drove out to Pine Park and looked for Miranda. She was headed back to the barn, turned and waved to him as the truck stopped.

"Hey! We wondered what you're up to. Jean still has your lunch in the kitchen."

"I'll go get it in a minute." He motioned her closer. "I need to talk to you."

"Okay. What is it?"

He pulled the letter out of his pocket and shoved it into her hands. "This came today in the mail."

She read it, looked up at Doug with brimming eyes, then read it again. "Oh, Doug. This is *so* sad."

"I know."

"But why did you want me to read it?"

"Because, I don't know what to do about it, if anything."

"What do you mean?"

"I guess I'm wondering if I should share it with Brian. He still has some anger issues about the wreck. The good part is he's stopped feeling like he caused his mother's and brother's deaths. The bad part is, he has expressed hatred toward the driver."

M&M put her hand on Doug's arm as she shared her thoughts. "Doug, Brian is a good-hearted, brave young man. I think maybe seeing this letter will lead him to feel less angry."

"Maybe." He pulled her close enough to hug. "Thanks for being such a good listener." Then he glanced around to be sure no one was looking and kissed her on the cheek. "Come on back to the house and sit with me while I eat lunch." When she hesitated, he added, "Please. Eating alone is no fun."

She nodded. "How well I know. I've done it enough."

They walked, hand in hand, into the house and talked quietly as Doug ate his sandwich.

"Where's Jean?" he asked.

"She and Jessie went to look at a house for sale. It's awful of me, but I hope they don't like it. Jerry and I were just talking about how we don't like to think of them not being here."

Doug chuckled. "Brian and I have had similar conversations."

"Well. What are you gonna do about it?"

"I wish I *could* do something. Brian asked if they couldn't move into the motorhome when our house is done, and they are welcome to do that, but it's not a permanent solution. Believe me, that little camper is fine, short term, but I'd hate to think of staying there forever."

"They are welcome to stay where they are for as long as they are okay with it. I'm surprised at myself for being able to say that, and *mean* it, but I do. I really do. They have been so much help at Pine Park that I can't figure out what I'll do without them." She grinned. "And we love Jean's cooking as much as you and Brian do."

Doug tossed an arm around her. "Well, let's work on another problem I have."

"What problem would that be?"

He chuckled. "I'm wanting to kiss you, *really* kiss you, and I don't want an audience.

Can we go out to dinner, or something, tonight?"

She blushed, nodded, ducked out from under his arm and hurried back to barn chores.

"I'll come by here for you at seven," he yelled after her.

He was leaving the drive when Jessie and Jean drove up and stopped beside his truck. "How was the house hunt today?"

Jean shook her head and Jessie let out a loud sigh before saying, "No good."

"Well, I'd be lying if I said I'm sorry, because none of us want you to leave here."

Jean protested, "But I feel like we're imposing, like we're

Wildflower Wednesday

house guests who have overstayed their welcome."

Doug laughed. "Miranda just got through telling me she didn't know how she'd manage without you and you are welcome to stay right where you are."

He started to drive away, then stopped. "Almost forgot, don't make as big a dinner tonight. I'm taking Miranda out, so you'll just have to feed those two bottomless pits."

Jessie winked at Jean and she grinned as they went inside together.

*****

M&M rushed through her training rides and left a note in the kitchen for Jerry, telling him to groom the yearling and turn the pony into a paddock before starting his regular tasks. Then she called Tiffany.

"Can you spare a couple of hours in the mall with an old lady?"

"What?"

"Tiffany, listen. I know this is last minute, but I am *desperate, really desperate* for a wardrobe upgrade. I am going out to dinner tonight, and I can't wear the same old thing *again*. I'm so used to just wearing jeans and tee shirts. Please, can you help me shop for a couple of outfits. It shouldn't take too long. I have a limited budget."

"This is your lucky day. No SSS classes or meetings this afternoon. Stop by and pick me up whenever you're ready."

"Thanks. See you in about thirty minutes."

A quick shower and change of clothes later, M&M was on her way, hoping her curly hair would finish drying by the time they got to the mall. Once Tiffany was in the truck, she thanked her again. "You always look so beautiful, and I know you have excellent taste in clothes, so I thought you could give me a few pointers."

Tiffany smiled. "I can do better than that. I know where all the sales are, so we'll stay in your budget. Tell me what colors you like and we'll coordinate everything. It'll seem like you have several new outfits with just a few pieces."

M&M nodded as she stepped out of the truck. Walking to the mall entrance, Tiffany asked her, "So what's the rush about this shopping expedition?"

M&M blushed, then stammered. "Well, Doug Wilson keeps asking me out, and I keep saying yes, so I don't want to embarrass him in public by looking like a farm hand."

"So, you really like him, huh?"

M&M nodded and changed the subject. "Which store do we hit first?"

Tiffany led her to the big department store that was advertising a fall sale and started thumbing through racks of pantsuits and blouses. Within minutes, she had pushed M&M into a dressing room with a pile of clothes to try.

"Step out and show me when you get something on that you like. If we don't have the right sizes, I'll go find them. And I need to go look for shoes to match. What size?"

M&M couldn't remember when she'd last bought any clothes for herself other than the necessary under garments and socks. She didn't trust herself to choose flattering styles, so she let Tiffany tell her what looked best on her.

An hour later, M&M was at the cashier's desk, credit card in hand. "This is great, Tiffany assured her. "You have two pairs of classic pants with a coordinating jacket, plus three blouses and a long, elegant skirt. Those shoes you think are so comfortable go with everything. Best of all, every single piece is on sale."

M&M's smile was genuine when her bill barely totaled a hundred dollars. "I can't thank you enough," she told Tiffany as they carried her purchases to the truck.

"No thanks necessary. I had as much fun as you did, maybe more."

Wildflower Wednesday

When they got back to Tiffany's office, she asked M&M to come in. "Just for a minute. I want to show you something."

M&M followed her inside and to the huge closet on one end of the classroom. "I am always shopping for my SSS girls, and I just cram all the stuff in here." She grabbed a long cardigan sweater and a necklace strung with colorful glass beads. "Look at this, perfect colors to coordinate with and dress up your outfits."

"Oh, Tiffany. I have more than enough and I've stayed in my tiny budget...."

"Come on! This is my gift to you, from SSS, for all you've done to help the girls. You can't say no. Wear this necklace tonight. And you might need the sweater, it's getting cooler in the evenings."

M&M just hugged her and left with her new accessories. She barely stayed within the speed limit on the way back to Pine Park. With more barn chores waiting, she wanted a bubble bath before dressing for dinner.

Chapter 29

Doug couldn't help himself, he let out a low wolf whistle when M&M stepped out of her door. "Wow! You look incredibly lovely."

Her smile told him she loved the compliment.

He opened the door and helped her into the truck, squeezing her hand before going around to the driver's side. Moving under the steering wheel and reaching for his seat belt, he looked at her. "You look far more elegant than a piece of chocolate candy, Miranda, and every bit as desirable." When she smiled shyly, he added. "And I love chocolate candy."

Flattered but flustered, she protested. "*Stop* teasing me! I feel silly enough, I haven't dressed up much in so long I don't really know how anymore."

"You look real fine to me. I haven't made a reservation for tonight. Where would you like to eat?"

She shrugged. "Don't know."

"Okay, I just heard about a Chinese place, sounds a bit formal but fun. Are you game?"

She nodded. "Absolutely."

As he drove, he struggled again and again to keep his eyes on the road instead of looking over at her.

By the time he parked the truck, all he could think about was touching her. He hurried around to open the door and assist her down the step. She didn't even protest when he pulled her into his chest, so he kissed her on the cheek.

He felt her tremble. "Are you cold?"

She shook her head, and he pulled her closer and whispered in her ear. "Miranda, I am having trouble keeping my hands to myself. That perfume you're wearing is making me crazy. It's sweet and sensual, just like you."

She pushed at him, stepped back. "Doug, I don't know how to deal with this. I thought the romancing part of my life was over, died years ago with my husband. I'm not deliberately trying to tempt you."

He shook his head, took her hands in his and pulled her close again. "I'm sorry. I think I'm scaring you. It's okay. I'll behave, promise." He hesitated, then pulled her along. "Come on, let's go eat."

The restaurant was crowded with diners of all ages, many laughing as they attempted to eat with chopsticks. Doug and M&M were soon studying oversized menus and choosing dishes they couldn't begin to pronounce.

She was laughing out loud by the time he gave up and just pointed at two entrees listed as specialties on the menu.

Their waiter praised him. "Excellent choices, sir. "I'll have your appetizers out very soon." At that Doug laughed too. He didn't even know appetizers were included in his selections.

"This is *fun*," he said. "I hope the food is equally delightful."

They laughed at each other's attempts to use the chopsticks until Doug reached for a fork. "Give those things up before you spill something on that pretty blouse."

She nodded. "Good idea." Minutes later she added, "The food *is* delicious, even though I'm not sure what I'm eating."

"Thanks for admitting that. Now I'll have to make a confession too. I have no idea what I ordered for us, but I figured I couldn't go wrong choosing the house specials."

They declined dessert but couldn't resist the complimentary fortune cookies. "You first," Doug told her.

She broke the little cookie and slid the message out to read, *"The next year will bring happy surprises to you."*

"Hope that comes true for you. Now let's see what's in store for me."

Doug unfolded the little paper and paused, smiled then read, *"Your heart will be warmed by something today."*

He laughed at her raised brows, handed the waiter his credit card and said, "Let's go. I want to see how soon this comes true."

They chatted on the drive back. Doug pulled into the Pine Park drive and braked to a stop.

"Are you making me walk the rest of the way?"

"Nope. I'm stopping here because I don't want an audience when I kiss you goodnight."

He was surprised when she unbuckled her seat belt and leaned into him. He was even more surprised when her lips parted for his kiss. Both were breathing heavily when it ended.

"Glad you parked out of plain sight of the house," was all she said when he started the truck and drove to her front door.

He was equally glad when the door opened and Jerry came out to greet them and tell Doug, "Brian just went over to your motorhome."

M&M told Doug, "It was a great dinner," and went inside.

Doug remembered the message in his fortune cookie and chuckled. He was whistling a happy tune when he got out of his truck and went up the motorhome steps. His jovial mood switched off as soon as he saw Brian's troubled stance.

"What's the matter?"

Waving a piece of paper over his head, Brian yelled. *"This!* This is what's the matter." He broke down then. Sobbing, he managed to ask, "Why didn't you tell me about this?"

Taking the letter from Brian's shaking hand, Doug tried to explain. "I planned to tell you, to show it to you. I guess I was

Wildflower Wednesday

just looking for the right time. I didn't know how you'd take it."

He reached for Brian to embrace him, but the boy dodged his outstretched arms.

"Don't! Just don't touch me right now. I'm so mixed up. I'm half sad and then I'm real mad.

What's wrong with me?"

"Nothing's *wrong* with you. I had a similar reaction when I read the letter. I ended up feeling so bad for Mr. Miller that I felt I should *do* something, but I didn't know what to do. I was planning on talking it over with you." He paused. "Maybe this is something we should discuss with Dr. Clay."

"You mean you really did plan to share this letter with me."

"Of course. Brian, our relationship may not be perfect, but I have never lied to you, *ever*. I'm not lying now. This is about our family—you and me."

Brian nodded and moved into his father's embrace. Tears trickled down his cheeks. He sniffed, then spoke, "Dad, let's think about what to do, maybe pray about it. Then maybe we can decide something."

"Okay. Let's sleep on it." But sleep was a long time in coming for both.

Chapter 30

Brian and Jerry were the first to sit down for breakfast. Jean put a platter of crispy bacon and link sausages in the middle of the table, then put a big Belgian waffle in front of each boy.

Jerry grinned as he reached for the syrup. "This looks great! Thanks, Jean."

"You boys gotta keep your strength up—marching and kicking footballs and taking care of horses takes a lotta energy."

M&M came into the kitchen, noticed Brian hadn't loaded up his plate and was pushing the cut-up waffle around in syrup. "Don't you like bacon and sausage?"

He glanced at her and mumbled. "Yeah. It's a great breakfast. Guess I'm not very hungry this morning."

Doug came through the door just in time to hear. "The Wilsons had a kinda rough night last night." He looked to Brian for permission before explaining. "We had information about the man in the accident that took Lyndsey and Thomas from us."

Paled and shaken, Brian added, "We don't know if we should do anything about the letter from his wife."

"Do you want to talk about it?" Jerry asked.

Doug and Brian looked at each other and shook their heads. Brian turned to Jerry, "Not unless you can tell us what to do."

M&M spoke up. "Sounds like it's a decision for you and your Dad to make."

Changing the subject, Jerry stood up. "We've gotta get

Wildflower Wednesday

going, it's almost practice time."

Doug knew it was his turn as the driving coach, so he herded the boys to his truck and M&M hurried to the barn.

At Doug's suggestion, Jerry stepped into the truck and slid into the driver's seat. "I'll take my turn coming home," Brian assured them both.

As they walked from the truck to the field, Brian asked Jerry when he might be talking to Ross.

"I don't know. Why?"

"Because you asked him to pray for you and your mom, and I wonder if he'd pray for me."

"Sure. Why don't we go by the church sometime soon, and you can ask him yourself?"

They dropped the subject as they reached the edge of the field and didn't bring it up again until they were climbing back into Doug's truck after school.

Brian hesitated putting the key into the ignition. "Dad, can we go by the church office?"

"I guess so, but why?"

"Ross, the youth pastor there is really nice about praying for people. I just wanna ask him to say a prayer for me, for us. You know."

"Okay."

As Brian drove, Jerry told Doug how Ross has prayed for him and his mom and Pine Park. "He sorta helped me with praying too. I'm still learning, but Ross encourages everybody. He says, "Just talk to God.""

"I think I'm glad you guys have gotten to know Ross."

When they pulled into the church parking lot, Doug sensed that this was something the boys wanted to handle on their own. "I'll just wait in the truck," he offered.

When they went inside, he called the Pine Park land line and asked Jean if M&M was in the house.

When she took the phone, he told her where he was, and why. "That sounds good, Doug, really good. I think your son is going to be okay with this, whatever you two decide to do, or not do."

He ended the conversation with, "Me too," just as Brian and Jerry reappeared.

As they got back into the truck, Brian smiled. "Dad, we can talk about this some more later, but I think we need to go see Mr. and Mrs. Miller."

Doug let Brian drive back to Pine Park, then left for the staff meeting at his office.

*****

M&M welcomed them with instructions to re-bed the stalls she had already cleaned. "Then, one of you can do some light grooming on the horses that are still in stalls."

M&M was curious about their stop at the church, but hesitated to ask. She was hoping Doug would fill her in later.

She didn't see him until almost dark. She was putting grain in bins for the horses. He found her in the feed room and cornered her for a kiss. She attempted to protest. "Doug, I don't want your son, *or* mine to see us making out like teenagers."

He laughed and kissed her again. "Why? Don't you like my kisses?"

Breathless, she giggled. "You know I do."

She grabbed his hand. "Come on, let's go to the house. The boys are already there and Jean probably has our meal ready to put on the table."

As they walked, she remembered to ask, "How'd things go with Ross at the church?"

He shrugged. "Don't exactly know. I waited for them in the truck and when they came back, Brian looked relieved, said we'd talk about it later."

She squeezed his hand, then let go as they went inside.

Wildflower Wednesday

*****

After they got back to the their motorhome, Brian brought up the subject of the letter from Mrs. Miller. "You know, Dad, I was still mad at him, blamed him for the wreck, but now...."

"What?"

"I don't know, it seems like his life is so sad, and his wife sounds sad too. I think I want to meet them, let them know, you know, that I'm okay."

Too astonished to reply, Doug just nodded.

Brian needed a response. "Dad, do you think it would be okay to go see them?"

"I honestly don't know." He hesitated. "How about if I call Mrs. Miller tomorrow, try and feel her out about a visit?"

"Okay."

Doug fell asleep wondering what in the world he was going to say to Agnes Miller.

*****

The next morning, he was still uncertain about even making the call, much less what to say.

He waited until 9:00 a.m., thinking Mrs. Miller would surely be awake, and the boys were at the field. He didn't think he wanted a listening audience for the conversation. He had already gotten her phone number and punched the buttons almost hoping she wouldn't answer.

She did. "Hello."

"Mrs. Miller, this is Doug Wilson. I got your letter." He heard only a sharp intake of breath, so he continued. "I'm truly sorry to hear your husband is so unwell. I know he didn't mean for the wreck to happen. I want you and your husband to know that." He waited, but she still said nothing. "So, my son has also read your letter, and he has suggested that we meet with both of you." He again waited for a response.

Finally, she whispered. "I don't know what to say. I never

expected you'd want to see him, or us. My Leo is sure that you hate him for what happened."

Doug shook his head. "Honestly, there was a time when my son did hate him, but that's before he understood how and why it happened. He's the one who suggested we meet you and Leo."

There was a long pause before she answered, "I think I need to talk to Leo, try to explain that you and your son are coming to see him. I'm never sure how much he understands."

Doug suggested then that he would call her back in a day or two and see if and when they might visit with her and her husband.

He disconnected the call feeling for the first time in months that he was blessed. He still had one fully functional family member.

When he summarized the conversation to Brian, they agreed to follow whatever suggestion Mrs. Miller might make about a visit.

*****

Doug was surprised when Mrs. Miller called him at the Longview office. He was even more surprised when she told him that she and her husband hoped to speak with him and Brian.

"My Leo, he wants so much to see you so he can say he's sorry, to ask your forgiveness. He just struggles, you know, to get the words out. I hope he'll be able to say what he's feeling."

Uncertain of an appropriate response, Doug said nothing except that he and Brian would be at the nursing home at 10:00 a.m. because Mrs. Miller said, "That's his best time of day."

Doug called the high school office and asked to have Brian excused from classes at 9:45. Checking his watch, he headed for his truck and the commute to Marshall.

"What's goin' on, Dad?" Brian wanted to know as soon as they exited the school office.

"Mrs. Miller said she and her husband are willing to meet

Wildflower Wednesday

with us, want to, even, and she suggested this morning at 10:00. So, here we go."

Brian was quiet on the short drive to the nursing home, and Doug didn't really know what to say or what to expect.

Brian followed him in and to the front desk where a nurse welcomed them. Before he could explain their presence, a tiny white-haired woman approached and softly inquired, "Are you the Wilsons?"

"Yes, we are. You must be Mrs. Miller."

She nodded and motioned for them to follow her down the hall. "Leo is waiting in the little sunroom."

She led them in and went directly to her husband's side. He was slumped over in a wheelchair, buckled in to keep from toppling forward. He was gray. His complexion matched his thinning hair. He raised a shaking, bony hand in greeting, tried to smile. He looked directly into Doug's eyes and stammered, "I'm grateful that you came. I wanted to say I'm sorry. I hope you can forgive me some day."

Before he could react, Brian went directly to the old man's chair and knelt beside him. "It's okay, Mr. Miller. Thank you for saying you're sorry. Thank you so much. I blamed myself, hated myself at first. Then I blamed you, hated you. Now, I know, finally, what it means when somebody says it was an *accident*. It wasn't your fault and it wasn't mine. It just happened."

Both Leo Miller and his wife were crying before Brian finished. Doug wiped his own tears with the back of his hand. He went to Brian and helped him stand before telling the elderly couple goodbye.

As they walked down the hall to the exit, he told Brian, "I'm so proud of you."

"Why?"

"Because you are both wise and forgiving."

Brian smiled. "It's good not to feel guilty and it's even better

not to be mad at that poor old man."
"I agree. Wanna drive back to school?"
Brian nodded as he reached for the keys.

Chapter 31

Doug left Brian at school and drove straight to Pine Park. He wanted to, *needed* to tell somebody what his son had just done.

He saw M&M leading a horse into the barn, so he went directly there, caught up with her just as she had freed the horse and closed the stall door.

"Everything okay?" she asked before he pulled her into his chest and just held on. He knew his heart was pounding and his voice quivered. "It is now."

She must have sensed his need. She just wrapped her arms around his waist and hugged, then rested her head against him and waited.

When he was able to speak, he told her about the visit to the nursing home. With tears dripping, he concluded, "My son is a man. I'm so proud of him."

"Oh, Doug, what a beautiful ending to such a tragic time in your lives. You'll both be better now."

He nodded, smiled, then released her from his grip. "Let's go to the house and find Jean. She
and Jessie will want to know too."
*****

By the time the boys got home from after-school practice sessions, Jean had grocery shopped and planned yet another special meal. As the six of them sat around the table, Doug made a surprise announcement. "We're going to have a big

Thanksgiving dinner around a big table at the new house." Pausing, he looked at Jean as he added, "That is, if our super chef here will prepare the feast for us."

Jean laughed. "I will love doing the Thanksgiving meal for us."

"Are we *really* going to be in the house for Thanksgiving?" Brian asked.

"Yep! I have pretty much gotten a guarantee from the contractor. By mid-November that house will be ready for us to move in."

"Wow!" was all M&M knew to say.

*****

With the house completion rapidly approaching, Jessie and Jean were still on the fence about their living arrangements. Unable to find suitable housing in their price range, they were torn between staying at Pine Park or moving into the motorhome as Doug had offered.

Jessie kept reminding his wife, "Neither option is a permanent solution. We just can't be the Johnson's permanent houseguests, and we can't live in that little camper forever."

She nodded. "I know, but I don't want to move away from the boys, *my* boys."

Jessie smiled. "You've come to love Jerry too. So have I. And I love being around horses again, so I want to stay close by, but those boys are growing up. They won't need us much longer."

Jean frowned. "Maybe *I* need them."

He hugged her and changed the subject. "You'd better start planning that Thanksgiving feast."

*****

Brian inspected the new house every day with his dad. The drywall was up and trim pieces were unloaded and ready for placement when he asked, "What's next?"

Wildflower Wednesday

"Painting of the ceiling and walls, then the floor coverings. The kitchen cabinets and countertops are almost done, and I want Jean to check out the appliances, since she'll be using them more than I will."

"I sure hope they don't end up moving to a place far from here."

"We all hope that, but it's their decision. I would deed them a piece of land, help them build right by us, but I don't think Jessie will go for that."

"Why?"

"Every man's got his pride."

Brian shrugged and changed the subject. "You know tomorrow is your turn to take us to school. Jerry and I have Driver's Ed together last class period, then go to the practice field. So, we'll be coming home late afternoon."

"What do you think about taking Driver's Ed instead of having study hall?"

"I think it's great. So does Jerry. We like driving around with the coach, and we can finish our schoolwork at home—it's quieter and faster."

"You're liking school over here, aren't you?"

"I am. Dad, thanks for moving us here. It's all good."

Doug nodded and put his arm around his son's shoulder as they walked back to the motorhome.

"Dad, are you glad that we came to Marshall?"

"Sure." Then with a sheepish grin, he admitted, "I will be glad when football season is over, and I can stop worrying about you getting creamed on the field."

"Well, we'll have lots to be happy about at Thanksgiving. Even if we make playoffs, the big game will be over before Thanksgiving, and we'll be in our new house."

*****

That big football game came all too soon for Doug. He

couldn't seem to stop worrying about Brian's physical safety although he was constantly amazed at his progress in all areas. His grades were all A's, he was back driving, perhaps not with comfort, but at least with confidence. He had cheered Jerry on when he went to exchange his permit for a full license. It was good to see his son happy again.

He wished him good luck when he and Jerry left for the school grounds. They both had to be there early to warm up. Doug checked his watch several times and finally decided it wasn't too early to drive over to Pine Park and gather the *fan club* as he called Jessie, Jean and Miranda.

He knew they would all be cheering for the Marshall Longhorns, and especially for Brian.

They all came right to the truck and climbed in. "Nervous?" Miranda asked him, then corrected herself. "Sorry, stupid question."

He tried to smile. "It's okay. The good news is this is the *last* game of the season. I know most everybody in Marshall is celebrating because the team made playoffs. I'll just be glad to see the end of football season and hope Brian finishes without a single bruise."

As they approached the football field, he was surprised to see that the parking lot was almost full.

"Wow! It's a good thing we came a little early."

"This is *the* big game. All the kids come to yell for their team, plus everybody's parents and grandparents show up too."

Jessie added, "It looks like the aunts, uncles and cousins also came tonight. Good thing we have reserved seats."

They had to push through the crowd just to get to their seats, then sat and listened to the band warming up instruments while the cheerleaders leaped and yelled to get everybody in the student section on their feet and chanting, "*We want a win!*"

The game started amid wild cheering with fans on their feet

Wildflower Wednesday

throughout the first quarter. At halftime, the score was tied at 14-14 and the spectators sat back and enjoyed the Longhorn band's presentation. After their performance, Jerry sent a thumbs up to his mom and Doug as the drummers took their seats.

"Here we go," M&M whispered in Doug's ear as players returned to the field. Brian was out there for the kickoff and sent the ball sailing to the 15-yard-line, then trotted back to the sidelines. The crowd cheered. Doug breathed a sigh of relief.

Well into the third quarter both teams scored, putting the score at another tie, 21-21. In the final quarter they battled back and forth with both teams unable to advance to the goal. With just seconds to play, the Longhorns had the ball on a fourth down, 45 yards from the goal. The coach called for their last time out and sent Brian onto the field to attempt a field goal.

Every spectator was standing, screaming as Brian sent the ball squarely between the goal posts. As others around him yelled, "We won! We won!" Doug was silently thanking God that his son was still standing upright. Then, he held his breath again as the entire Longhorn team rushed their kicker, hoisted him over their heads and carried him to the center of the field for the trophy presentation.

Doug felt Miranda's arms wrapped around him in a bear hug. She had to yell into his ear to be heard, "Smile. I know you're celebrating for a different reason, but this is a *win-win* deal here."

He grinned then, and hugged her back.

It took them almost an hour to get back to the truck, and just as they climbed in, Jerry and Brian sent a text to Doug's phone, asking permission to join the rest of the team for pizza before coming home.

"Miranda, what do you think?"

She grabbed Doug's phone and sent a text message back to

the boys. *Have Fun. Be Safe,* then told Doug, "I think we're very lucky to have teenagers who actually ask permission to go celebrate with their friends. All we have to do is be grateful for that, then wait up for them to get home safely, hopefully by midnight."

Doug had to laugh. "You're right."

*****

Doug wasn't laughing when he learned that some of the new furniture he'd selected was on backorder and couldn't be delivered until December. Among the missing items were the dining table and matching chairs.

He called Susanna for help, but she begged off. "Both twins have stuffy noses and bad attitudes, I'm stuck with them today, and believe me I'm sorry. Why don't you ask M&M to help out?"

First, he called the moving company and made sure that all the stored furnishings from the Longview place would be delivered the next day. Then he drove over to Pine Park. He found M&M still in the house sipping her coffee and got right to the point of his visit. "I need your help and I mean *today* not someday."

Puzzled, she asked, "What's up that can't wait until tomorrow?"

"I just found out that the dining table and chairs I picked out with Susanna are on backorder, don't know when I can get them, but definitely *not* in time for Thanksgiving dinner."

"So, do you want to borrow my table and chairs? I know the table is small and plain, but—"

"*No*, I don't want to borrow your table. I want you to go with me to find a new one, something close to what I already selected."

"Okay. Why do you need *my* help?"

"Please, Miranda. Don't make this difficult. I'm a guy. I'm not smart about furnishings. Just say you'll go with me to shop."

Wildflower Wednesday

"Why don't you take Susanna?"

"Her kids are sickly. She won't leave them."

M&M saw her chance to tease him and she did. "So, I'm your second choice."

He wasn't amused. "No! You've always been first choice. I asked you to help picking out stuff before. You said *no*. You told me to get Susanna to help."

"Take it easy. I'm just kidding around with you. Sure, if you think I'll be helpful I'll go shopping with you. Can it wait until this afternoon?"

He nodded and left, calling back over his shoulder, "Just give me a call when you're ready and I'll come pick you up."

Right after lunch she sent a text.

He read *Give me 15 minutes to clean up and I'll be ready.* He drove over to Pine Park and went into the house, found Jean in the kitchen pouring through a cookbook.

"I'm looking for a new dessert recipe to surprise everybody on Thanksgiving," she explained.

"I'm going in search of a table for Thanksgiving."

"So I heard. She'll be out in just a minute or two."

"Jean, I don't know how long it'll take us, so we might go out for dinner. How about cutting back on the meal tonight, just cook for four?"

"I can do that, and we'll let the boys know where you are."

He said, "Thanks," just as M&M came into the kitchen, still fluffing her damp curls.

"I heard that part about dinner." She pointed to her jeans. "I'm not dressed to go out."

"You're fine. I'm wearing jeans too. We won't go anywhere too fancy."

As they settled into Doug's truck, she said, "You don't have to buy me dinner because I'm helping you shop."

He grinned. "I know. It's just an excuse to spend more time

with you."

When he parked at the front door of the furniture mall, she asked, "What, exactly, are you looking for?"

"We are looking for a good-sized table with six or eight chairs, not too fancy or formal. I want your help picking something that looks appropriate for a ranch house, and it needs to be in stock, *not* at the manufacturing plant."

He hurried around to open her door and take her hand as she stepped down to the pavement.

They walked through the entire store before she told him, "I really liked that first set we looked at, but I didn't think it was a good idea to choose the first thing I saw."

Taking her hand, Doug turned around and headed back. It took them about 20 minutes to locate the table and chairs.

A salesman hoovering nearby asked, "How can I help you?"

Doug answered, "Do you have this dining set in stock?"

When he got the affirmative response he wanted, he said, "I'll take it, the table and eight chairs, and I want delivery tomorrow. Is that possible?"

The happy clerk assured Doug that the set was in the warehouse and could be delivered within twenty-four hours. With that news, they went to the business office where Doug turned and asked M&M, "Are you sure you really like this set?"

When she nodded, he handed over his credit card. Before leaving the store, he cancelled the previous order and told the clerk to call about the delivery time. He left the store so quickly that M&M almost had to trot to keep up with him.

"What's the hurry?" she asked.

"We got that done. Thanks. I'm hungry. Let's go eat."

Chapter 32

Brian was so excited to see the furniture truck coming up the drive. He yelled to his father, "It's here! We *really* will have Thanksgiving in our new house."

"Yes, we will, and we'll also be sleeping in our new house. The other furniture is coming later today. We'll have quite a bit of work to do, getting it all put where it belongs."

"Is anybody gonna help us?"

"Sure. I've asked Jean to be in charge of everything in the kitchen. I think you and Jerry, and Jessie and I can manage to move the furniture. I have furniture dollies. The hard part will be deciding exactly where everything belongs." Doug paused, then added, "I almost forgot. Susanna will come over after we get the major stuff done and help with the décor part—you know, where to hang the pictures and put the lamps and all that."

*****

Three mornings later, Jean quietly entered the kitchen in Doug and Brian's new house, turned on the oven and began to stuff the turkey. She was making pies before Brian wandered in from his bedroom.

"Hey, good morning."

"Hope I didn't wake you up."

"No, you didn't. I smelled something, something *good*. I thought it might be cinnamon rolls."

"Sorry. No cinnamon rolls today. You probably smelled the

cinnamon I put in the apple pie. You'll have to get yourself a bowl of cereal today. I'm too busy with our Thanksgiving dinner to cook breakfast."

"Okay."

Doug came in on the end of the conversation and offered to go get doughnuts and sweet rolls.

"Come on, Brian. Ride with me and help pick out the kinds you and Jerry like best."

As they rode to town, Brian reassured his dad, "Don't worry. I won't pick out too many jelly rolls or doughnuts to ruin the meal Jean is cooking.

Doug laughed. "I don't think you boys can ruin your appetites with a few sweet rolls. You're always hungry."

Brian was still careful not to overdo it, and they left with just one box full of pastries. They went directly to Pine Park and saw Jessie at the barn helping M&M. Jerry was on the way out the door when they arrived, and Doug surprised both boys by suggesting they step inside for a moment.

"It was nice of you to bring goodies over," Jerry said. "I was trying to skip breakfast because of the feast Jean is preparing, but I'm hungry."

"Brian picked out a good variety, but I wanted to talk with you for a minute too, before anybody else comes back in."

The boys sat down at the kitchen table and reached for a doughnut as Doug continued, "There's something I wanted to talk to you about, something serious and I want you to be honest with me."

Both put their doughnuts aside and waited. Doug cleared his throat, stammered and began, "I think you may have noticed that Miranda and I have been spending a lot of time together."

Jerry nodded. Brian grinned. "Yeah, Dad, we've noticed."

"Are you okay with that?" When both nodded, he continued, "Well you see, I am very fond of Miranda. That's not exactly what I meant to say. The truth is, I love her, and I want to ask her to marry me, but I won't do it without your approval." He looked from Brian to Jerry and back again to his son's smiling face.

"It's great, Dad. We, Jerry and me, we've been talking about it. We want you to be happy and have somebody, you know, when we leave home."

Doug sighed in relief, then turned to Jerry. "And what about you?"

Jerry got up and hugged Doug. "I think it's great too. You are wonderful to my mom, make her feel special." He paused and sat back down, then added, "And I never had a brother, and don't really remember my dad. I think we'll make a happy family."

Doug beamed at them before adding, "That's if she says *yes*."

"Well, when are you gonna ask her?" Brian wanted to know.

"Tonight, if I can get her to myself after dinner."

Just then they heard Jessie talking to M&M as they came through the door and all three got very busy eating their doughnuts.

"What's going on?" she asked, then saw the pastry box in the middle of the table.

"Breakfast delivery," Doug answered and got up to leave.

He was out the door before another word was said. M&M asked Brian, "Where's he going in such a rush?"

Brian shrugged. Jerry suggested, "He's gone to see how Jean's doing in the new kitchen."

*****

At exactly five p.m., the time Jean had named as dinner time on Thanksgiving, they all gathered around a beautifully set table, covered in a linen tablecloth that Jean had found to fit it nicely. M&M had provided a festive floral centerpiece and the delicious aroma from the adjoining kitchen had everyone in the mood for the celebratory meal.

As they took their seats, Doug suggested, "Let's have a brief prayer now, and maybe during dessert we can talk about *all* the reasons we have to be thankful today."

He bowed his head and began, "*Dear God, Thank you for all you have given us, all we have, all we will have because of your grace. We are grateful to be yours. Bless the food before us and the loving hands that prepared it. May it nourish our bodies to faithful service. Amen.*"

The sweetness in his words put tears in M&M's eyes. "Thank you," she said as she squeezed the hand she was holding.

After a moment of silence, they all began to pass around serving dishes and talking at once. An hour later, they were still sitting around the table, eating desserts and talking about how much they enjoyed the meal. Each person had already thanked Jean at least once and she finally held up her hands and said, "Enough of that. I'm glad you loved the dinner, but let's remember to be most grateful for enough to eat and remember those in this world who are hungry."

"Dad said we were supposed to give thanks today, and I'm thankful to be here, with all of you today." Brian said as he turned to Jerry and added, "Your turn."

"I'm grateful to be here with you all too. I love having Jessie and Jean, Doug and Brian as neighbors. I'm thankful that Mom and I can stay at Pine Park."

When Jessie and Jean added that they were happy to be included in the gathering, M&M said, "It seems we're all saying the same thing. We're glad to be here together."

"Good summation," Doug added.

They arose to clear the table. M&M helped put the leftovers into containers and into the giant refrigerator while the boys carried plates to the sink and rinsed them. Jean loaded the dishwasher and thanked everyone.

In a moment of silence that followed, Jerry mentioned, "We have a whole stack of old Christmas movies at our house. Why don't we go over there and watch one or two?"

M&M protested, "But we just finished eating *Thanksgiving* dinner. It's almost a month 'til Christmas."

"I know, but Mom, you know how we usually start getting out Christmas decorations right after Thanksgiving. It's like a warmup for the Christmas season. Come on!"

She agreed, but as everyone started for the door, Doug stopped her. "Miranda, could you wait a bit, I want to show you something before you go."

Puzzled, she agreed and waved the others out the door.

Doug took her by the hand and led her to the entryway. "What is it? She asked.

He half-smiled. "I wanted to show you around the house, now that we're officially moved in. See what you think of it."

"Okay. Doug, it's a wonderful home. It suits you."

Doug stammered. "I guess I'm not doing this very well. I'm trying to find out how it suits *you*."

"What?"

"Miranda, I am not good at this. I'm trying to ask you to share this house, my life. Will you marry me?"

Stunned speechless, she stood trembling until he pulled her close and kissed her softly.

"Say something," he prompted.

"I don't know what to say. What in the world will your son think? What will my son say?"

He grinned. "They both think it's a great idea. I discussed it with them over doughnuts this morning." He continued, "They think we're a good team. I do too. I wasn't sure I'd ever have passionate feelings again, but I do, for you. I know we'll be good together. Don't you think so?"

When she remained silent, he prompted her again. "Just say yes, Miranda. The correct answer is *yes*."

She kissed him then, *really* kissed him and whispered, "*Yes*."

A few kisses later, they went to Pine Park to find their sons. Brian and Jerry looked up expectantly as they entered the house.

"Well?" Jerry inquired.

"She said *yes*."

Jean and Jessie joined the boys in whooping and hollering their congratulations. The movie was forgotten as they sat talking around the kitchen table.

Doug held her hand as he said, "I'd like for us to get married as soon as possible. I don't care about what kind of ceremony, or where it is. That's a girly thing."

Brian spoke up. "Wait just a minute before you decide to run off and tie the knot. I expect to be there when you say *I do*."

"Me too," added Jerry.

Then Jean announced, "Well, Jessie and I, we want to be there."

Doug looked to M&M and she could only say, "Oh, Wow! When my closest friends and all your Wilson Reality staffers hear, they'll want to be there too. Doug, I really want us to be married, but I don't know about having a big wedding. It takes so much planning."

"Call Susanna. She'll know what to do. So will Tiffany," Doug suggested.

She hesitated. "It's Thanksgiving. She's probably busy with family."

Jerry prodded her. "She's like family to us. She'll want to know about this."

Nodding agreement, M&M punched in the number and

Wildflower Wednesday

made the announcement to Susanna, who squealed with delight, "Oh, that's wonderful news. I just knew he was going to ask you. You're perfect together. So, when's the wedding? Have you set a date yet?"

"We just want to have a simple wedding, sooner the better, but we know so many people that might be offended if they aren't included and—"

"Let me tell you, I *certainly* expect to be there."

Doug took the phone and said, "We're calling on you for help here. *Please*, tell her we can get married soon."

Susanna replied, "Does Tiffany know?" When she heard, "Not yet," she told M&M, "Call her *right now* and tell her you're getting married. I'll go by and get her, and we'll be out at Pine Park within the hour."

Doug was overwhelmed. "I guess I'm not used to your friend taking charge like that."

"Well, you *told* me to call her."

Jean and Jessie started to excuse themselves from the table and the conversation, but M&M put her hand over Jean's and said, "No, you stay."

Turning to Doug, she suggested that the guys go to his house and watch a football game or something. "This will be girl talk," she explained.

All the males were happy to comply and piled into Doug's truck to ride together.

*****

After the guys left, Jean stood up and told M&M, "I feel like I need to leave you alone with your two best friends. You have important plans to make."

M&M told her, "Jean, you are a good friend, and we are about to become family, if not officially, at least in my heart. Stay here, *please,* and help us figure out how Doug and I can have a wedding soon and still let all the people who wish us well be part of it."

Just then, Susanna and Tiffany ran through the door yelling, "Congratulations!" They both hugged M&M, and Tiffany said, "I am *so* happy for you."

Susanna grinned and added, "Now, you know how I felt about wanting to be married soon."

Tiffany interrupted, "Me too. Gary wanted to get married ten minutes after I said *yes*."

As Jean passed around mugs of hot coffee and put a plate of cookies on the table, M&M begged, "Help."

They all laughed, teased her and then Susanna suggested, "Why not do it like John and I did? Just have a small ceremony, go on honeymoon, if that's part of the plan, then come home and have a *big* party—a reception of some kind, and invite *everybody* to come celebrate your life together."

"That sounds good, but how do I go about planning this huge celebration?" Catching her breath, she added, "And what if Doug doesn't want to have a big party?" She paused, "And how and where do we get married?"

An hour later, the four women had a plan in place. They thought the little prayer chapel next to the church would be ideal. It would be just big enough for the wedding couple, their sons, plus Jean, Tiffany, Susanna and their husbands to witness the ceremony. It could probably be arranged within days.

Susanna told the bride-to-be, "Now, you need to consult your future husband, see if he has a honeymoon trip in mind. If you trust me—no us; me and Tiffany and Jean to do it, we can make all the arrangements for the celebration. All you have to do is show up."

M&M got up and hugged Susanna. "Thank you, thank you. It seems like too much to ask of you, but I'm saying yes anyway."

Just then, her cell phone chimed. Doug was checking in. "Have you women got it figured out yet?"

"That depends on you," she answered. "How soon do you want to get married?"

"Would next week be okay?"

"Doug, that really is soon. I don't know. I don't have anything to wear."

Tiffany poked her in the ribs. "I'll take you shopping *tomorrow*."

Doug heard that and added, "Remember, Miranda, the correct answer is *yes*."

She and Tiffany laughed and then she asked, "Are we going on a honeymoon?"

"You bet! Anywhere you want to go, just pick the place."

"But the horses and—"

"These guys here with me, Jessie, Brian and Jerry, have already said they can handle everything about Pine Park while we're gone. And your answer then is?"

"Yes, Doug. *Yes*. I'd love to marry you next week. I want to go on a honeymoon with you. Maybe someplace really warm, near the ocean, with a beach to walk on."

"Okay. I'll start making the arrangements tomorrow." He hesitated before adding, "I guess you women will tell me when and where to show up for the ceremony, and what I am supposed to wear."

"You bet we will," Susanna yelled into the phone.

*****

When M&M finished her breakfast and started for the barn, Jean reminded her, "You have a shopping date with your friend. Jessie and the boys are already out there, said to tell you not to show up around a horse until this afternoon."

M&M laughed and went to change clothes. Tiffany arrived just as she slipped on her shoes.

Timing is everything, she thought as she waved to Jean and went out the door.

"What do you have in mind for a wedding outfit?" Tiffany asked her on the way to the mall.

"I don't have any idea. Certainly not a formal gown, but something special, preferably flattering."

"Okay then. I think we'll go to the big department store and go to the section with special-occasion dresses. We'll find something there, and there's a big sale on *and* Susanna and I are buying. No arguments! She would be along with us, but she's already busy working out plans for that celebration, probably juggling twins on her lap as she scribbles notes."

Two hours later, Tiffany was carrying their selections back to the car and assuring M&M, you are going to look fabulous on your wedding day. It's awesome that you asked about booking a hair and nail session too. Just remember to call back and schedule the appointment."

M&M laughed. "I'll try. I don't know for sure what day we'll have the wedding yet."

*****

As his bride-to-be shopped, Doug was trying to hold up his end of the planning. He checked on the time frame for the marriage license and found that the prayer chapel would be available any time on a week day. Then he called a travel agency friend to quickly secure a suitable package that included travel, hotel reservations, honeymoon suite, the works.

"Call me right back when you have it lined up," he instructed.

The agent laughed and said, "Okay, but you have to tell me where it is you want to go."

It was Doug's turn to laugh, at himself. "I don't really care, but it would be okay to stay within the forty-eight, if possible. It has to be warm and oceanside."

He took leftovers out of the fridge and went to Pine Park for lunch, expecting Jean would want to make turkey sandwiches.

Wildflower Wednesday

As soon as the date was set, he had to let the travel agent know, call his favorite florist to line up a bouquet of wildflowers, and go see John and Susanna about a very special wedding gift for Miranda.

*****

When they gathered around M&M's kitchen table eating sandwiches, Doug reported his findings which helped Miranda decide on a Wednesday wedding. "We can get the license by then, we have a place, you have a dress, and I'm lining up the honeymoon. What else is there?"

She almost nodded, then shrieked, "Oh, no! We don't have a preacher!"

"Couldn't we get a judge to officiate?"

"I guess so," she stammered, "But—"

"But it's not what you want, right?"

Her lip quivered and his smile disappeared before Jerry spoke up. "I know you didn't ask my opinion, but I have an idea. Ross, the youth pastor at the church might do it. I'll go ask him."

Motioning for Brian to join him, they were out the door and on their way before anybody could stop them.

In an hour that seemed like four or five, the boys were back. "Great news!" Brian said as Jerry handed a note to Doug. "Ross just got his license, or credentials, or whatever you call it. He can officiate a wedding and he is *so* excited. He'd love to do yours." Jerry added, "But, you have to go talk to him. It's about having pre-marital counseling. Just give him a call. His number is on that note I just gave you."

Doug breathed a sigh of relief and looked at his bride-to-be. "You okay with all of this?"

When she nodded, he leaned over and kissed her. "Good! Then I'm going home to make a bunch more phone calls."

Back in the privacy of his house, Doug notified the travel agency to relay info on the date, then called the florist, who promised to have a wildflower bouquet ready by noon Wednesday.

He started to call the Hunters, then decided a face-to-face conversation would be better.

Doug had just turned the ignition key in his truck when his cell phone chimed. His travel agent said, "It's all set! I got you on a late-night flight Wednesday out of Shreveport all the way to Key West. You have reservations in a five-star hotel on the beach, honeymoon suite, for ten days. Sound good?"

"Perfect," Doug answered.

A few minutes later, he was explaining his unannounced visit to the Hunters. "I know I'm imposing a lot, especially since you are already involved in planning a reception for us, but I want a really special wedding present for Miranda, and I want to surprise her."

"What do you have in mind? John asked.

"I know the story about how she's struggled, and she and her late husband had plans for breeding some top horses and then she had to sell the mares to keep the place going. I'd like to surprise her with breeding stock so she can continue that dream."

Susanna had tears in her eyes as she hugged him. "Oh, Doug, that is the sweetest and most generous thing ever. Of course, we'll try to help, but what is it, exactly, that you want us to do?"

"I know little about horses, nothing about their pedigrees. I was hoping you could help me find mares that are of the same lineage as those she originally had."

Susanna looked at John and laughed. "The funny thing is, we would usually go to M&M for information about pedigrees, but we'll do our best. John has some experience in tracking down a certain horse or two."

"Thanks. Just let me know how it goes, and remember, this

is a surprise."

Doug whistled happily as he headed back to Pine Park. He could hardly wait to tell his bride-to-be that their plans were all set.

Chapter 32

Late Wednesday afternoon, Susanna and Tiffany helped M&M slide her lacy long beige dress over her head, smooth her hair into place and freshen her lipstick.

"I feel a little silly. Are you sure this glitter she put in my hair isn't too much?"

Tiffany soothed her. "It's just a few sprinkles and it matches the sparkly threads in that gorgeous dress."

"And the sparkle in your eyes," Susanna added. "Now, here is the bouquet I was instructed to give you just before you walk down that aisle."

M&M took the wildflower bouquet and smiled. "I might have known Doug would remember."

Just then Jerry stuck his head in the doorway of the tiny dressing room, "Come on, Mom. Let's get this show on the road."

Susanna and Tiffany hugged her and hurried to their seats. Doug and Brian were already standing at the front of the chapel with Ross. As the recorded music began, the little group stood and watched Jerry walk his mother to the altar. Doug and Brian wore matching smiles that grew brighter as she came closer.

Ross offered an opening prayer, led them as they pledged their vows, then pronounced them husband and wife. He didn't have to tell Doug to kiss his bride. Doug held that kiss until the others applauded and cheered. Then he whispered, "I love you, Miranda Wilson," took her by the hand and led her outside and to the waiting limo.

"What's *this*?" she asked her husband.

He laughed. "I didn't want to depart for our honeymoon in the farm truck. Besides, now I can kiss you all the way to the airport."

They actually alternating laughing and talking and kissing all the way to Shreveport.

"I'm so excited, Doug. I've never been to Key West. However did you think of it?"

"Actually, I didn't. The credit goes to my travel agent friend. I just told him it had to be a warm place on the beach and that's what he found for us. It was kinda short notice, you know."

They exited the limo and Doug checked the time. "We're a little early, but we might as well get through the security thing and then we can get a bite to eat. Okay?"

She nodded and took his hand as they strolled toward the security gates. The line was short, so they walked around the food court until they found a café specializing in seafood. "Let's eat here," she suggested. "It'll get us in the mood for Florida."

After a leisurely meal, they went on to their boarding gate, and they were met with a surprise, but not a good one. The attendant at the desk told Doug, "I'm sorry sir, but that flight has been cancelled."

"You mean delayed?" he asked.

"No. I mean *cancelled*. There's a tropical storm brewing off the Florida Keys and all flights to that area have been cancelled. You will, of course, be able to book a later trip, or if you wish you can choose another destination ."

Disappointment clouded M&M's face. "What now?"

Doug shook his head. "I'm not sure. Do you want to just go home and reschedule this trip when the weather clears?"

"I guess so."

"Okay then, let's go." He took her hand, and they went to

retrieve their luggage. In minutes they were on the curb and Doug was hailing a taxi.

"A taxi?" she asked. Will it take us all the way to Marshall? And won't that be terribly expensive?"

"We aren't going to Marshall—not tonight."

"Then where?"

"To a downtown, five-star hotel that has a nice suite and room service."

A bit puzzled, M&M nodded but said nothing more until they were inside the hotel suite. Then she asked, "Why are we here?"

He grinned and pulled her close for a kiss. "Because, Mrs. Wilson, I didn't wish to spend the first night of our honeymoon under a shared roof with our teenage sons. Okay?"

She blushed, smiled and nodded. "I'm a little nervous."

"Me too."

"Doug, I thought this part of my life was over. A long time ago."

"Well, it's not. You are one sexy woman, Miranda, and I'm so glad you said *yes*."

She snugged against him for a kiss and reminded him, "It was those kisses of yours that got me to say *yes*."

*****

Sunlight brightened the room when she opened her eyes. Startled, she sat up and gasped when she saw the clock.

"It's after nine! I never sleep this late!" Then she looked around but didn't see her new husband.

Just as she reached for her robe, he came in rolling a full serving cart. "Good morning, Mrs. Wilson. Hope you like the idea of breakfast in bed."

"Doug, I never sleep so late. I already feel lazy and now you're encouraging me to stay in this bed and eat breakfast?"

"Absolutely. I'm going to sit right down beside you and see

Wildflower Wednesday

what all we have in these covered dishes. But first, a good morning kiss is in order. Then coffee."

Soon she declared, "The kisses were sweet, the coffee was hot, and the biscuits, ham and eggs were delicious. What a wonderful way to start the day. Thank you."

He grinned. "What do we do now? Go home?"

"I guess so."

"I'm going to call my office manager. Disappointing as this is, I have lots of work to catch up on, so there is *some* good in delaying our honeymoon."

"Well, I can use time at home to get ready for Christmas, get the barn organized for the new year and all that."

He nodded. "But do we call the boys or Jean to let them know ... or just show up and surprise them?"

"Let's surprise them!"

They were on the road towards home within the hour.

"Doug, while we have this time to ourselves, can we talk about what to get the boys for Christmas?"

"Sure thing. Do you have anything in mind?"

Pausing to recall the hints from both teenagers, she remarked that both had hinted about having their own mode of transportation. She added, "Jerry told me Brian wants his own horse. Jerry wants a dog, he's *always* wanted a dog."

"Brian and I talked about getting him a horse. I'm not opposed to that, but I reminded him that he'd be off to college in another year. Then what would I do with his horse? He got my point. So, let's not do a horse for Christmas."

"Okay. No horse. What about transportation? I would love for Jerry to have something to drive besides my farm truck. He would love it even more. I can swing a used economical car for him."

"*We* can afford a new car. I wonder how the *almost brothers* would feel about sharing a car?"

"Good plan, and it will work great, at least for awhile. They'll be going to all the same places."

"How about Jessie and Jean?" he asked. "I don't have a clue. I'm more concerned about where they're gonna live. That motorhome is going to get smaller and smaller to them."

"Do you think they've been comfortable in my house?"

"Yeah, they've seemed quite content there. Of course, we've all liked the closeness, the convenience of living near each other." He paused. "What are you getting at?"

"Doug, is there *any* way I could make my house their house?"

He thought for a long moment before answering, "Maybe. Maybe not. It's a complicated question. Pine Park is yours and they want their own place. I suppose you could sell them just the house and the land it sits on. I'm guessing the market value would put it in their price range."

"I was thinking more of giving it to them."

"What?"

"Giving it to them. You know, a gift. *Why not?* Doug, I have a wonderful, beautiful new home with you. I don't need that house anymore."

"Even so, that's more than generous of you." He paused. "And I'm not sure they would accept such a gift. Pride might get in the way."

She agreed, but hoped, "Maybe we can figure out something."

They were still thinking about that when Doug turned their rental into the drive at Pine Park.

Jerry, Brian and Jessie were all working around the barn and looked up when they saw a strange vehicle parking by the house. Jean walked outside and was the first to recognize the occupants.

She threw up her hands and yelled, "Oh, what happened?"

Wildflower Wednesday

Jessie, Jerry and Brian abandoned their work and hurried to the car as the newlyweds got out.

Doug was laughing when he told them, "Shortest honeymoon in history!"

"Glad you can laugh about it," Jean commented, "But really, what happened?"

He explained about the tropical storm and assured the frowning teens that they would take that trip to Key West later.

"The good news in all this," M&M interjected, "Is that Doug and I both left a lot of loose ends, or unfinished business, so we'll get a chance to get organized before we leave again."

"What kinda things?" Jerry asked. "We're really doing okay with the horses and barn chores."

Jessie and Brian nodded before she explained, "I know Pine Park is in good hands, but there are other things I need to do, like Christmas shopping."

Doug added, "And I need to get busy in both offices, see that profits are good enough for her to do that Christmas shopping." Seeing Brian's worried frown, he continued, "No worries, but I promised my employees a year-end bonus, and I've spent a lot of money on the house so I need to hustle up some listings and generate sales before Christmas."

M&M saw the dismay on Jean's face and asked, "Is something wrong?"

Jean shook her head and chuckled. "Nothing bad, it's just that these boys of yours placed their orders for meals while you were going to be gone. You may not love their menu suggestions."

Doug assured her, "Whatever you've planned will be fine, and since we've returned unexpectedly, we can all go out to eat or get takeout."

M&M added, "Or, I can help Jean with the grocery shopping and meal prep, if she'll let me."

Jean smiled at the offer. She gestured to M&M and suggested, "You guys get back to your work. We will see that you're well fed."

Glancing at his watch, Doug told his wife, "Let's unload our bags, and I'll return the rental car, get a ride to the office and call you for a ride home about five. Okay?"

*****

While all the men were out of the house, M&M took the opportunity to sit down with Jean to plan meals and make a detailed grocery list. Then she asked, "Jean, are you and Jessie comfortable here? I know the kitchen is not up to standard for you, but you've managed to provide fantastic food anyway."

"I thought I'd be doing the cooking for you all over at the new house."

"Oh, you will. Or I hope you will. That's the plan. But, what I am asking is, do you like this house, not just the kitchen?"

"Jessie and me, we've loved being here, and so appreciate you letting us move in. I thought you knew that."

Frustration clouded M&M's features as she tried to get to the point of the conversation. She shrugged and admitted, "I'm not saying this very well. Jean, Doug and I have discussed this, and we wonder if you and Jessie would consider living here. The location is convenient, but maybe the house doesn't suit you, or you don't want to be quite *this* close.

Seeming confused, Jean said, "But this house, it's in the middle of Pine Park. It's yours."

"And I'll always keep Pine Park, or I hope to, but I have a new husband and new life and that beautiful house to share with him."

Before Jean could question her further, she continued, "Doug says there will be some way to deed the house and the land it sits on to you and Jessie, if you are interested."

"I don't know what to say."

Wildflower Wednesday

"Don't say anything right now. Just think about it and talk to Jessie about it. I think ... hope that Doug will discuss it with him too."

Jean nodded, too surprised to say another word.

M&M grabbed the grocery list and headed for the door. "I'll bring back everything on our list. You can start baking those pies the boys wanted, and I'll help you with supper when I get back."

*****

Doug spent a good portion of his office time going over financial reports, gave his sales staff a pep talk, and checked his personal account balance. Then he called home and learned that his bride and Jean were busy in the kitchen, so he asked if Jessie could come pick him up.

His wife met him at the door with a kiss. "You look tired," she said. "Is everything okay?"

"Yep. I just rallied the troops at the office. We'll finish out the year in good shape, with bonuses as I promised, but I won't be buying you a new car for Christmas."

"Doug, I don't need a new car, or any kind of car. I am used to my truck and it's got plenty of miles left on it."

"Love you," he told her.

"I love you too, and if money is tight, we don't have to take that expensive trip to the beach."

He laughed then. "You're not getting out of our honeymoon, *Honey*. It's all set, and actually, all paid for too."

She changed the subject. "I talked to Jean, tried to feel her out, you know, about my house."

"How'd it go?"

She shrugged. "I'm not sure. She seemed too surprised to say much. I asked her to talk it over with Jessie."

"Good idea."

"I was sorta hoping you'd talk to him about it too. You

know, man-to-man."

"Okay, I will. First time we can get off to ourselves, I'll bring it up, see what he's thinking. But now, I am hungry. Do we need to go out, or get takeout tonight?"

"Nope. Jean and I planned the meals for a week. I went to the store, and she's cooking right now. We're eating in the Pine Park kitchen tonight."

*****

After supper, the boys told Jean and M&M to go watch tv, *they* were going to clear the table and load the dishwasher. Since the women picked a romantic comedy, Doug opted to go home and find the landscaping book he'd saved to show Jessie.

M&M suspected it was Doug's way of getting Jessie to himself, and it was.

*****

As soon as they got out of earshot of the others, Doug asked Jessie if Jean had mentioned the idea of staying at Pine Park.

"Yes, she said something about M&M offering us her house."

"Well, what do you think?"

"I don't know what to think. It's feels like charity."

"Well, think about it from another viewpoint. My wife doesn't need the house any longer, but it's a part of Pine Park. She can't just let it sit and get run down. She'd rather you have it than have to rent it out or something."

Jessie nodded. "I hadn't thought about it that way."

"Well, talk to Jean some more. We, Miranda and I, as well as our boys, would really like to have you close by. I guess Miranda would rent you the house if you don't want it permanently."

Jessie agreed and the men went back to Pine Park to their wives. Both couples had things to talk over.

Back in the new house, Doug asked his wife if she'd let

Wildflower Wednesday

their friends know about the change in trip plans.

"No," I hadn't even thought to, and I should let Susanna know right away. She's planning that reception, or party or whatever we should call it, and our timing could be a problem."

"Okay," Doug told her. "Here's our new honeymoon schedule. We'll be leaving here December 12, spending ten days on the beach, and be coming home in time for a Merry Christmas. See if she can work with that."

*****

M&M dreaded calling her best friend and possibly throwing a big kink into the already made party plans. With fingers crossed, she made the call right after breakfast the next morning, explained the situation and heard Susanna's response, "It's *really* okay. Your reception is all set, scheduled for December 11. It just means your celebration will be a send-off instead of a welcome-home party."

Relief flooded through M&M. "I'm *so* glad to hear that. So, tell me all about the plans."

"No way. It's going to be a surprise. I will let you know when and where to show up. It would be neat if you wore your wedding clothes. That's it."

M&M was laughing out loud when the call ended. "What's up?" Doug asked, and she related the conversation she'd just had with Susanna.

"Well, I'm glad that's worked out. Now, you and I have some other stuff to take care of."

"What?"

"We need to negotiate a plan about your house with Jessie and Jean, and we need to shop for that vehicle for our boys, plus I need to spend plenty of time at my office." He chuckled and corrected himself. "I need to spend time at *both* offices. I'll be pretty busy until we leave, but I don't want you to feel neglected."

He kissed her and waited for her to reply.

"Don't be *silly*. I also have work to do. I need to get everything in order at the barn, set up a new schedule for horses coming in for training. *Maybe* I can even get a handle on the therapy program start-up."

He kissed her again. "We'll get it all done and then take off for the Keys," he promised.

When she left for the barn at Pine Park, he started making phone calls and got exact figures for expenses for the pool and barn on his new homesite. Then he checked in with John Hunter.

John told him, "I've had some luck finding mares, but I had failed to ask you how many you wanted and how much you wanted to spend."

Doug assured him that he was still interested, but he needed to cut back his original plan. "To tell the truth, the final construction costs on this house exceeded my expectations, and I have already contracted for a pool and start-up of a barn. So, I am hoping that, for now, I can manage two horses, preferably for a total of no more than ten thousand."

"Then just maybe Susanna and I have found mares that will fit. There is an actual granddaughter of one of the original Pine Park broodmares available. She was injured on the track as a three-year-old and can't run, but she's breeding sound. Since she never proved herself on the track, she won't be too pricey. The other is of similar bloodlines, and is in foal to Restless Ribbon, the sire of our filly. M&M likes the stud. The owner will probably negotiate a price with you because the horse is for M&M. She has quite a following in the horse world, you know."

"I'm beginning to see that. Thanks, John." Doug ended the call and turned to see Brian standing nearby.

"Dad, what's up? I didn't mean to eavesdrop, but I heard what you said about expenses. I thought you planned to put a big barn over here, maybe for the therapy program."

Doug shook his head. "I sorta had that in mind, but I can't afford to do it, not just yet."

Brian sat down and rubbed his forehead. He got up and got himself a glass of juice and a muffin. He sat down again, hesitated before speaking. "Dad, I have an idea."

After Brian explained, Doug Wilson was astonished at his son's suggestion. "Are you *sure*?"

Brian nodded. "Don't you think it's a good idea, and a good way to use the money?"

"I do. Thank you. I'll get the ball rolling, and maybe it can be a Christmas surprise."

*****

M&M was saddling a horse when Jessie joined her in the barn.

"Jean and I have talked it over. We'd love to have the house and are honored that you want us here. But we want to buy it, and an acre of land that it sits on, so we can really feel good about owning our own place. We have a good amount of money saved up, if it's enough to at least make a big down payment."

She turned around and hugged him, surprising them both. "That's wonderful news! I don't know exactly how to proceed, but Doug will. The thing is, Pine Park isn't totally paid for, I still have a mortgage. Now I will need to split the property to give you deed to the house and lot. I think I need to talk to my banker too."

When he frowned, she assured him. "We can make it work."

She called Doug with the news, then called Elliott James at her bank and asked for an appointment as soon as possible.

*****

By the tenth of December, Doug announced to his wife and their boys, "We've got all our ducks in a row, and hopefully they can swim while we're gone."

M&M tried to stifle a yawn as she smiled and agreed. "Now, we can just go celebrate at our party tomorrow and then head for Florida."

"I hope it's not a late-night party," Doug admitted.

"No. Susanna *finally* filled me in on the plans, at least partly. "We are all to wear our wedding clothes, show up at the country club at 5 o'clock, and be prepared for hugs, well-wishes and lots of good food."

"I think I can handle that assignment."

"Wow! The country club and lots of food. It sounds pretty good to me," Jerry added. Brian seconded that. "Nice of your friends to have such a cool party for you."

*****

The newlyweds didn't know quite what to expect when they walked into the country club. They were greeted with cheers and applause from a crowd of friends and co-workers. All of the Wilson Realty employees, most of M&M's clients, Vet Dan Marsh and his wife, Susanna's parents, even Tiffany's SSS girls were there, along with the host couples Susanna and John, Tiffany and Gary Hunter. As the greetings and congratulations were concluding, Tiffany showed Doug and M&M to their special seats, centered where everyone could see them.

A trio of musicians moved closer and began to play.

Overwhelmed, M&M turned to Doug. "This is way more than I expected."

He hugged her. "I'll say it is. That table over there is piled halfway to the ceiling with gifts. I didn't expect *gifts*."

Just then, Susanna stepped up to let them know, "The buffet tables will be ready shortly and you two, of course, will be first to go through the line."

Tiffany came over and added, "After dinner, you can dance, if you want to, before we have wedding cake."

M&M looked to her son, who had remained speechless.

Brian, however, seemed to be taking the festivities in stride. She whispered to Doug, "Brian seems to be totally comfortable with all this, but Jerry is a bit out of his comfort zone."

Doug hugged her again and whispered back, "Brian's mom was involved in the social whirl enough that he got exposure. Jerry will be fine."

Loaded buffet tables proved to be the boys' main interest. They were still eating when Doug walked his wife out on the dance floor and whirled her around a few times then led her to the cake table.

After the cake was cut and served, he looked to her and asked, "What do we do about the gifts? If we open them now, we'll be here all night."

She shrugged, just as Susanna approached to answer his question. "Nobody expects you to open gifts here. John and I will load them up and haul them to your house, you'll have plenty of packages to open for Christmas when you get home from the Keys."

Relieved, Doug smiled. "Thanks."

*****

The next morning, M&M was going over her checklist of barn chores with Jessie and Jerry when Doug tugged her by the hand. "Come on, wife, we've gotta get to the airport."

She hugged Jerry, thanked Jean for looking after the boys, and hurried to the truck.

She sighed as she sank into the passenger seat and admitted, "I'm *so* tired. *Please*, if I fall asleep on the plane, don't let me snore."

He reached for her hand. "Miranda, I will probably fall asleep before you do."

Both of them napped on the flight, and they arrived at their hotel in time to enjoy a light supper and walk on the beach before dark.

*****

Ten days later, they were strolling on the beach again. Hand in hand, they waded until waves lapped at their knees, then backed up onto the sand.

"This has been wonderful," M&M said. "I've never felt so pampered."

He smiled. "That's just what I wanted to hear."

"Doug, it will be good to get home, but I feel like we've already had a big Christmas."

He smiled, thinking of the surprises that awaited his wife at home.

Chapter 36

Jessie, Jean and the boys all wanted to meet them at the airport. Doug tried to talk them out of it. He told Jessie, "I have the truck parked in the airport garage. No need for you all to come to Shreveport."

But they did. Jerry and Brian were holding up a *Welcome-Home* sign and waving balloons as they deplaned. Jessie just shrugged and said, "You were outvoted and outnumbered."

After hugs all around, Doug said, "Since you're all over here, should we go out to eat?"

"No Way," Jean informed him. I've planned your welcome home dinner ever since you left."

"Yeah, and it's gonna be great," Jerry added.

So, Doug collected their luggage, and the group piled into two vehicles and went home to Marshall.

As they ate, Brian reminded them, "Tomorrow is Christmas Eve. When can we start opening presents?"

M&M laughed. "Your Dad and I have that pile of wedding gifts to work through. Why don't you boys help us with them tomorrow, and save the real Christmas gifts for Christmas day?"

Doug chuckled to see that their boys weren't totally enthused. When they finished the meal, Jerry told them to check the family room, where he and Jerry had put up a little Scotch pine tree and decorated it. "We cut the tree ourselves and everything," Brian told them.

Jean laughed when she told everybody about the popcorn

and cranberry ribbons on the tree. "Those boys ate so much popcorn, we had to do three batches to get enough for the tree."

*****

Then the newly blended Wilson family went to their new house and saw another decorated tree, a giant spruce loaded with blinking lights, and silver and gold ornaments.

"I'm guessing you boys didn't do this one," Doug teased.

Jerry grinned. "Nope, we can't take credit for this. Uncle John brought the tree and put it up and then Susanna and Tiffany showed up with a mountain of decorations when they brought all those wedding gifts. Susanna said you had to have a tree to put the presents around."

"Sounds just like her," remarked M&M.

Christmas Eve was an all-day celebration. The boys helped M&M with all the barn chores first thing. Then they gathered around the big tree listening to Christmas carols and Jean kept passing around what she called "party food" that included fancy little sandwiches and chocolate covered strawberries, her much loved fried chicken, and a choice of desserts. Jessie appointed himself the clean-up man, carrying out piles of wrapping paper, ribbon and boxes, as wedding gifts were unwrapped and put away. It was late afternoon when they decided to attend the candlelight Christmas Eve service right after a light supper. When they got home, both Jerry and Brian were wondering about what they called "the real Christmas presents."

Doug laughed. "Santa knows better than to put out presents early. You boys would be into them before it's really Christmas!"

"Guilty!" Jerry agreed.

The adults all said goodnight. Jessie and Jean headed home, and Doug said he was tired and ready to *hit the hay*. When they got to their bedroom, he said, "*Shhh!* We have to be very quiet and maybe those boys will think we're asleep. Then we can sneak the presents out and put them under the tree."

Wildflower Wednesday

    M&M nodded and quietly went about gathering up the gifts she had carefully hidden behind the luggage in their big closet. It was almost midnight before they thought the boys were sleeping and they tiptoed down the hall and placed the gifts, turned the tree lights back on and went to bed.

    It was barely daylight when Brian and Jerry came down the hall yelling, "Merry-Merry Christmas!" and their parents knew the routine well enough to get up and dressed. Doug insisted that they have juice and coffee, and the cinnamon rolls that Jean had sent over before they tore into their packages. He winked at Miranda as both boys ripped into their gifts and found a set of car keys.

    "What's this? Brian shouted, and Doug explained. "You each have a set of keys, but they go to the same vehicle, one car that you will share like brothers."

    Jerry was clearly the most surprised. "You got us a *car*?"

    "Your mother and I bought it together. It's parked next to the Pine Park barn."

    Without another word, they raced outside, almost colliding with Jessie and Jean coming in.

    "Sorry we're interrupting family time," Jessie began, "But we wanted to bring our gifts over to you."

    As they placed two little, bow-trimmed, red envelopes under the tree, Doug said, "You are part of this family. Glad you came on over."

    "And we have gifts for you too." M&M added. She reached under the tree and selected three little boxes, then handed them to Jessie, Jean and Doug.

    Jean loved the gift card for kitchen appliances and Jessie thought his card to select a cart to pull behind his landscape tractor was great. Doug was puzzled when he opened his gift and found a key. "What's the deal?" he asked his wife.

    "Jessie told me you had always wanted a little garden

tractor of your own. It's parked in the barn at Pine Park."

He hugged her tight and said, "Thank you, but you shouldn't have."

"I was so blessed to be able to pay for it and my part of the boys' car with money from the house."

Jean encouraged them to open the little red envelopes and when M&M opened hers, a key fell out. Puzzled, she said, "This seems to be the Christmas of the keys. What does this one go to?"

"It goes to your office," Jessie explained.

"What do you mean?"

"Well, me and Jean, we know you worked in that office and looked out that big window at your barn and horses, and you should still be able to do that. It's *your* barn and horses. So we had carpenters cut a hole in the wall, install a door with a good lock. That key fits it. Then we had the other door covered, repainted the wall, so you have a private office with a great view."

"That's so incredible. I don't even know how to thank you." With happy tears lighting her eyes, she hugged them both.

Jessie motioned to Doug. "You need to open your little envelope too, and your wife will probably like it as much as you do."

She did. It was a landscape drawing of the wildflower patch designed to flow from the yard into the woods.

"I've already ordered the seeds and a few plants, and come spring, you'll have wildflowers." Jessie explained.

"You're right. We both love it," M&M said.

Doug nodded, then handed over a glittery box, "Now, wife, open *your* present."

She shook the box and heard nothing, felt nothing. "It seems to be an empty box."

"It's not."

She carefully pulled back the tissue paper to uncover papers—registration papers for two horses and detailed plans for a barn."

"Doug, how did you do this?"

"I had help, John and Susanna found the mares for me so you can restart the breeding program you had to give up, and Susanna helped me plan the barn design. I think she got input from some PATH director."

As she was hugging him, he said, "Wait, there's something else," and he reached for the box remaining under the tree.

She ripped it open to find an engraved plaque.

"It's to go on the barn," he explained as she read, "*Pine Park PATH Therapy Center serving in memory of Gerald Johnson, Lyndsey and Thomas Wilson.*"

"It's beautiful," she stammered as tears fell.

"I can't take all the credit for that. It was Brian's idea."

"But I *am* the one who wants to make your dreams come true."

She assured him with a kiss. "You already have."

The End

Made in the USA
Columbia, SC
08 September 2021